THE BURNING MAN

THE BURNING MAN

SOLANGE RITCHIE

New York

THE BURNING MAN

This is a work of fiction. Names, characters, businesses, places, events, and incidents are either the products of the author's imagination or used in a fictitious manner. Any resemblance to actual persons, living or dead, or actual events is purely coincidental.

Published in New York, New York, by Morgan James Publishing. Morgan James and The Entrepreneurial Publisher are trademarks of Morgan James, LLC. www.MorganJamesPublishing.com

The Morgan James Speakers Group can bring authors to your live event. For more information or to book an event visit The Morgan James Speakers Group at www.TheMorganJamesSpeakersGroup.com.

A **free** eBook edition is available
with the purchase of this print book.

CLEARLY PRINT YOUR NAME ABOVE IN UPPER CASE

Instructions to claim your free eBook edition:
1. Download the BitLit app for Android or iOS
2. Write your name in **UPPER CASE** on the line
3. Use the BitLit app to submit a photo
4. Download your eBook to any device

ISBN 978-1-63047-519-2 paperback
ISBN 978-1-63047-520-8 eBook
Library of Congress Control Number:
2014921241

Cover Design by:
Rachel Lopez
www.r2cdesign.com

Interior Design by:
Bonnie Bushman
bonnie@caboodlegraphics.com

In an effort to support local communities and raise awareness and funds, Morgan James Publishing donates a percentage of all book sales for the life of each book to Habitat for Humanity Peninsula and Greater Williamsburg.

Get involved today, visit
www.MorganJamesBuilds.com

Habitat
for Humanity®
Peninsula and
Greater Williamsburg
Building Partner

ACKNOWLEDGMENTS

This novel is dedicated to my husband, Steve, as well as my mother, Guylaine, and father, Paul, who taught me to never surrender and never quit. I want to say thank you to W. Terry Whalin, who took the time to listen to my pitch and took a chance on a never published author. And finally, a big thank you to Angie Kiesling at SplitSeed and fiction publisher for Morgan James Publishing, for her great editing work.

Razors pain you;
Rivers are damp;
Acids stain you;
And drugs cause cramps.
Guns are lawful;
Nooses give;
Gas smells awful;
You might as well live.
—**Dorothy Parker**, "Resume" in *Enough Rope*

ONE

Easy is the descent to Avernus, for the door to
the underworld lies open both day and night.
But to retrace your steps and return to the breezes above—
that's the task, that's the toil.
—Virgil, *The Aeneid*

Jesus, what the hell is it?" Pete Langley recoiled.

"It's the damn tooth fairy," Stone Kilroy said, snapping his bubble gum between his back molars.

Pete stumbled forward, then back, his hand glued to his nose, trying to prevent the stench from consuming what little good air there was left in his lungs. One step forward.

"Don't go any farther," Stone grunted, slapping Pete broadside on the back of his head.

"Sorry." Pete shrugged. "I didn't mean to screw things up."

Stone rolled his eyes, wondered if he'd ever teach this rookie how to deal with a crime scene. This was a crime scene. That much was unmistakable. Stone sighed, leaned heavily against the door jamb. Dreading what was inside.

A putrid stench permeated Pete's nostrils as soon as he thrust his body weight against the door—as real and ominous as the blackness inside. It seemed to take on a life of its own, swirling around him, engulfing him. Pete had only smelled stink like this once before, but he remembered it.

And froze in fear.

Stone Kilroy recognized the stench too, although to him it was more familiar. The smell of death. This case would haunt him, like the others had.

Stone shoved Pete. "Get outta the way. If we only had more time," he grumbled under his breath. This was the third one of these he had seen in a month—slender, slashed, mid-twenties. When he'd seen the first one, her eyes were dry, wide open to the heavens.

She too had been shredded. Shredded—it was the only way he knew how to describe what he saw, he decided, after he'd seen the second body.

One step farther. The smell intensified, making Stone's eyes water. That same terrible foreboding. He knew what the smell meant, just didn't want to deal with it. Didn't want to find her like this.

Burnt flesh illuminated under his flashlight.

"Damn."

The Orange County Sheriff's Office had been cooperating with the Irvine Police Department to locate Consuelo Vargas. Now they had. From the looks of it, someone had made Consuelo's death personal. Real personal.

"Jesus…" His words trailed off, eyes adjusting to the fading twilight.

Stone had a report of lights in this abandoned shed near Trabuco Creek a few days ago. At first he'd thought nothing of it; some kids out in the bush, smoking grass.

In the meantime, the Orange County Sheriff's Office covered the area around Irvine's crop fields, where Consuelo worked. Turned up nothing. After repeated efforts canvassing Santa Ana's Fourth Street, nothing. A search effort that fanned out from Anaheim to Oceanside had led to this—a rundown shack on the edge of a near dried-up riverbed.

Stone checked his gut instinct, breathed heavily in the direction of the body now, his flashlight beam dancing off shadows and flesh.

"Don't look real, does it?" Pete questioned from behind, voice shaky, his Alabama drawl more pronounced from nerves. Stone heard the boy's boot meet the wooden floor with a hollow thud.

Stone wheeled round. "Don't" was the only word he could get out between clenched teeth. "This is a crime scene…"

Pete stopped everything, even breathing for a second. Then backed up.

All day long, Stone thought of Consuelo Vargas, wishing he would find her, now reluctant he had. His men had searched for two days, plastering the woman's face all over the county.

"Connie," as she was known to her family and friends, had been a person, with kids and a future. In this August heat, no one seemed to notice or care. Stone wiped sweat from his brow. His search had turned up nothing but more questions, leading to pent-up frustration and explosive nerves. At least now that frustration would be over.

People in this community of million-dollar homes had faith in the system, a false sense of security. Consuelo Vargas would shatter that. People here wouldn't sleep for weeks.

Stone's gut wrenched. He wasn't sure it was a woman.

His flashlight raced across the body, the acrid smell of acid eating at his lungs. It was awful. Stone longed for a blanket of clean air, sunlight, freshness.

Pete continued speechless, backing away from the corpse, as if putting distance between him and the body would make a bit of difference.

Stone knew it wouldn't. Like the two women before. He thought how Consuelo Vargas's face would become a nightly, non-mortal visitor, its dark features constantly shifting, changing. Like all the others, her mouth would open in the dream, but nothing would emerge except the screams of a woman being eaten alive by acid. Just like the others.

Pete and Stone exchanged nervous glances. Stone took another step. His hand instinctively went for his weapon, forefinger twitching there. With each step, he pulled his chest up, stomach tight, as if visibly bracing himself.

Consuelo's body cast strange shadows. Shivers jittered in Stone's belly, gooseflesh threatened to overtake his arms and legs. A deafening buzz clipped his ears. Consuelo's presence, the presence of death, hit him like a dense force. It was not easy to look at her. As he did so, the room seemed to swallow him up; the evil wrenched him to his bones.

An irrational response, he told himself.

He could not say what he saw was a body, much less a woman. Yet twenty-three years on the force told him that it was her. In the darkness, he could make out what seemed to be the back of her head, auburn shoulder-length hair knotted, lying partly on her side, her torso twisted at the waist, her lower extremities spread wide, posed. His stomach turned as he registered the savagery—so hacked and burned that her skin appeared translucent, white on red, veins showing through like a roadmap. Caustic fumes lingered. His senses told him there should be more skin, but about half of her was cut—hundreds of tiny cuts, each a comrade to the other, friends acting together to drain her life. At first Stone Kilroy thought that was the only thing wrong. But when he got down on his knees, looking closer, he understood the stinging fumes. Immediately he drew out his handkerchief, covering his mouth and nose tight. She had not just been cut but burned. Burned all over.

Instinct took over. He felt bile rise in his throat. He swallowed, running the flashlight the full length of her, praying he would find no further indignity. Satisfied there was nothing else, he turned the light back to her head. Stone put one hand on her shoulder, to turn her to him. As he did so, her hair pulled right out of its follicles, a clump of it clenched in his fingers. Yes, it was Consuelo Vargas. Her face altered, spoiled, her body tortured, but it was her. He recognized her almond-shaped eyes, happy eyes, imagined the kind of playful smile that children flocked to.

Suddenly one of her eyes fluttered slightly. She groaned.

"Sweet Jesus, Pete, she's alive," shouted Stone. "Get a goddamned doctor, she's alive!"

* * * * *

He watched from a wooded switchback, reverse throttling his mind to his adventures with Consuelo Vargas. Watching the cops bringing the body out, feeling certain he had power over them. He could take any of them if he wanted. He could do anything with them he wanted. Here in the woods, anywhere, as a matter of fact, he could do as he pleased. Feeling magical, all-powerful.

He was the giver of life. He looked at his hands, awed by their capabilities.

Over the sound of sirens, he dwelled on his dark and powerful presence for some time, remaining invisible. When they brought Consuelo out, he imagined he was there with her, alongside the gurney, calmly giving orders to the EMS paramedics. Commanding the team of lesser men to orchestrate life.

Even from this distance he could still see the desire etched on Consuelo's face.

By now they would have washed her down with copious amounts of water, to dilute the syrupy, colorless sulfuric acid he had used. At an 80 percent concentration, there was little time. The acid had done its work. So far, from what he could see, the EMT team had done fine work, administering an intubation tube, treating for hypovolemic shock, the subclavian line placed. Consuelo was doing fine.

Muscles bunched in his jaw as the EMT team rolled the gurney over the rocky uneven terrain, visibly jostling the woman. He could almost feel the IV needle pulling at her vein. The pain.

"Come on, boys, watch the patient," he whispered, angrily.

One of the techs loaded Consuelo into the back of the ambulance, while the other barked vitals ahead to the hospital.

He could hear the *whump, whump* of the Life Flight chopper blades before he could see it. As the bird dipped over a ridge and moved closer, he made out a handful of locals gathering on the roadside, necks craning, wondering what all the excitement was about.

A mock grin played over his clean-cut jowls. "Yes, yes, come to see my work." He held up his hands, this time in front of his face, marveling at them.

In the distance a flight surgeon leaned out the bubble window as dirt and leaves swirled in a halo, creating a beige veil around the road. He could see twelve figures, uniformed and plainclothes cops most likely, and the mass of onlookers covering their eyes.

He watched with rapt attention as they finished loading his patient, knowing full well they would find her alive, knowing what she would say.

It was unrelenting hell, the waves of nausea and nerves that washed over her. The flight from Quantico, Virginia, to John Wayne International Airport in Orange County had been like a roller coaster ride, complete with ups and downs that played havoc with her stomach.

Catherine Powers's equilibrium seemed to shift violently sideways as the plane veered to the left, its right wing tipping down so she could see the Western seaboard still blanketed in what she guessed was fog and, further inland, smog. She grasped the sides of her seat. Descending at 25,000 feet, couldn't this pilot avoid the air pockets that had plagued the flight?

Still, it was good at least to feel something. Living the life she had been for so long was hell. For the past six years, Catherine's life had been devoid of emotion, or so it seemed to those around her. She wore an external armor that few could penetrate. In her line of work, as the FBI's forensic pathologist working closely with the Behavioral Sciences Unit, it was her duty to remain detached. Catherine, or Cat, as she liked to be called, dealt with the most evil of criminal minds, hunting down not men but animals capable of the most atrocious evil. At present, the Behavioral Sciences Unit had over a hundred active cases, but she had been assigned to this one—the FBI had given it top priority.

Cat had read the case files, watched the reporter's renditions of the killer's MO on the local channel's tapes. Somehow the story appeared unreal. No, it wasn't the story, it was Cat's defense mechanism getting stronger, making her more detached.

Sometimes she wondered if the feeling was inevitable, if that necessary indifference was what drove cops to retire early, to drink and do drugs. Nowadays she felt herself moving in that direction, having one too many glasses of wine. Sometimes, alone in her hotel room, a scotch.

She knew she was walking a fine line. In this case, she could not afford a screw-up.

Thinking back to the news footage, it was foolish that the newscasters characterized killers as evil, irrational. She knew the types she hunted were highly rational in their own minds, many times planning a crime for months down to the smallest detail. Then they waited and watched for the perfect victim, enjoyed watching police fumble, reveling in the chaos that they so masterfully created. Cat resented the misperception that these people were irrational because it demeaned what she did—made it seem easy to put the pieces of the puzzle together. She knew it was not.

Unlike most people, like the press, Cat did not respond with outrage to cases. Instead, she was controlled, objective, learning what she could from fibers, blood, semen.

Only now, she felt that objectivity slipping away.

At Quantico, she built a reputation on being the best of the best. Keen, quick, intelligent; she decided she wasn't going to let that all crumble. Her mind wandered back to Virginia, to Joey; she had to hold up for him—for her six-year-old. She remembered running her fingers through his blond hair as he flashed her a quick smile.

"Take good care of him, Mark," she had said, leaving the child with her ex-husband at his home in Washington. She knelt to Joey, eye-to-eye with him. "Mommy will be back as soon as she can. I'll call you to see how you're doing, okay?"

"I'll miss you, Mommy," Joey whimpered, teary eyed.

"I'll miss you too, but we'll be together again soon."

She had mouthed "I love you" as she stepped into the waiting taxi, Joey holding Mark's hand tight, chin quivering.

She had not looked back in the cab. Could not afford to, because she too was crying. Now she wished she had looked back. Wished she hadn't been assigned to this case.

She laughed to herself, thinking how easy it would have been to refuse this assignment. But she hadn't, couldn't. Maybe because this case would answer questions, not just about the killer, but about herself.

Cat Powers stared out the window, thinking of the string of brutal murders in South Orange County, between Fullerton and Irvine, that had left the local authorities baffled. The killer seemed capable of leaving his victims in such a state that it shook up homicide detectives with twenty years on the force when they got their first sight of the remains. At least that's what she had read in stories pulled from the *LA Times*. At the same time, the killer seemed capable of disappearing, taunting the local cops with his chosen method of death. The only clues he left were gashes, not deep penetrating wounds, but multiple small incisions about an inch into the skin.

And what about the use of acid? Preliminary testing had shown that he used sulfuric acid. Not commercial-grade sulfuric acid that contained 98 percent H_2SO_4, but the fuming sulfuric acid, commonly called Oleum, which was up to 80 percent pure.

The first victim, Nancy Marsh, was an eighteen-year-old freshman at Chapman College, a small private college in the quiet town of Orange, the campus located about a mile from the Orange Circle. Cat had visited the campus once. The university presented itself as moneyed, accepting those who were well connected, with sufficient cash flow. Nancy Marsh had been the ideal student, her father a respected physician practicing with Hoag Memorial Hospital, her mother a woman who viewed high-end malls, like South Coast Plaza, as her second home.

"The Burning Man," as the press was calling him, chose his second victim from a different strata of society. Kim Collins had been a lap dancer at the Flamingo Theater, a seedy joint on Ball Road in Anaheim. From what Cat had read, it was a place that cared so little about the quality of "entertainment" it offered that men were admitted for one dollar with an ad that ran in the back of the local *OC Metro* magazine. Like Nancy, Kim was tortured. Third-degree chemical burns covered 85 percent of her corpse—her arms, legs, back, and torso. Strangely, the only part left unscathed was her face. A disposal truck driver found the corpse near the Bee Canyon Landfill.

Cat pondered the details, searching for a common thread. Other than the method of death, there was nothing similar. No clue to the killer's identity. Cause of death was listed as shock, secondary to massive severe burns and trauma.

"Mrs. Powers," the flight attendant's voice interrupted, "there's a message for you. A third victim, alive. What's that about?"

Cat braced herself. "Thank you," ignoring the improper question.

She blinked and began to breathe hard.

The plane could not land soon enough.

TWO

A word is dead
When it is said,
Some say.
I say it just
Begins to live
That day.
—**Emily Dickinson**, *poem no. 1212*

Flight surgeon John Walker had already called ahead to UCLA's burn unit. He was barking at Stone Kilroy over the roar of the chopper.

"Do you know where she was when the burn occurred?"

"No, just found her in the shed," Stone said, snapping his gum. "Looked to me like she'd been moved. Not a lot of blood, you know."

"The shed, was it a closed space?"

"Yeah, I guess so."

"You have any idea how long she'd been out there, exposed?"

"Naw, can't say for sure. Got a call about a day ago that some kids had seen some activity out here, but that don't mean much."

"All right then," Walker said as he turned his attention back to Consuelo Vargas. Four members of the shock trauma team moved into action, scalpels, forceps, needles, sponges, catheters laid out in easy reach. Intubated, the respiratory therapist ventilated manually, squeezing the Ambu bag, getting much needed oxygen into her lungs.

Thankfully, the paramedics had stopped the burning process, removing what little clothing the woman had and flushing the wounds with water to remove the acid.

"How bad is it?" Stone knew it was a dumb question, but he had to ask.

"She's got third-degree burns, over 70 percent BSA. Cases like this, well the tissue necrosis is severe."

"Give it to me in English, doc."

"It doesn't look good."

"Give me a liter of Ringer's lactate at 360 milliliters per hour. What's the blood pressure?"

"Sixty-five. Pulse 120," a female nurse answered, as another nurse drew blood to determine Hb, Hct, typing, and cross-match. On the off chance that some of the wounds were second degree, Walker started an immediate IV drip of morphine. Even now he could not tell whether all the wounds were third degree, though it appeared from the skin's white translucent tinge and Consuelo's rapid shallow ventilation, they were. The wounds did not ooze and blister as second-degree burns did. Walker knew the chance of this woman making it were slim; the rule of nines told him so.

"Do we have fresh frozen plasma waiting?"

"Yes, we've already called ahead."

"I need a tetanus immune globin, 250 units IM now."

Another team member followed orders, administering the medication intravenously through a large bore needle.

Stone Kilroy leaned back, out of the way, as best he could, popping his gum.

"Asystole," one of the team shouted, as the ECG's monitor flatlined. Immediately Walker's gloved hands were pumping the woman's chest, while the respiratory therapist continued to ventilate.

"Let the hospital know we're bringing her in code blue!" Walker shouted. "Can't you get this damned thing to go any faster?"

The chopper was screaming over Long Beach, passing over the 405 Freeway, which was caught in its customary gridlock traffic.

"We'll be there in a matter of minutes."

"She doesn't have that long," Walker said, grabbing the defibrillator paddles, pressing them up against the woman's chest.

"Clear."

Everyone leaned back as a quick jolt lifted Consuelo's body. The monitor was still flat.

"Nothing," shouted one of the team.

"Again," Walker said, rubbing the paddles together.

"Jesus," Stone mumbled.

Walker slapped the defibrillator paddles down again. Once more, Consuelo Vargas's body bucked and heaved.

"Come on, dammit," Walker coached. He looked up. She was still flatlined.

"Piggyback a bottle of high-dose epinephrine and titrate," Walker cried. "And we need to push another amp of sodium bicarb, now." A team member injected 10 milligrams of epinephrine into a 100 cc bottle, then hung it to run piggyback with the IV. A young man took over cardiac compression.

"One more time," Walker said, paddles bristling each other again. He ordered the team back and blasted electrical current at Consuelo's heart.

Her lips tinged blue.

"We've got something!" he shouted.

An erratic line blipped on the screen, then disappeared to flatness.

"Damn," Walker shouted.

Stone watched as they tried to bring her back two more times. Consuelo's heart refused to beat, succumbing to shock. The forceful chest depressions stopped; the nurse looked at Walker for direction.

The surgeon turned on his penlight and flashed a light beam into each of the woman's pupils. Fixed, unblinking eyes. It had been over ten minutes since they started to respond to code.

"Crack the chest?" the flight nurse asked.

"Pupils are dilated, fixed." Walker sighed. "There's no reason. She's gone."

The plane's roller coaster gave way to a lull in the turbulence before they descended into John Wayne, named for one of Orange County's most famous residents. Cat heard the stories about how his family had jostled for power since his death. One grandson disinherited, a granddaughter divorced from a well-known physician.

Cat was all too familiar with the way the media grabbed hold of anything, twisted and contorted it to their own liking. John Wayne's family was no less susceptible than anyone else's.

A new turbulence wave lurched the plane just before touchdown, leaving Cat to wonder where the vomit bag was, just before the tires hit tarmac.

A soon as the plane began to slow, Cat snapped off her seatbelt and raced to the bathroom. She was going to be sick.

⁂

Disembarking took an eternity. Catherine was anxious to get the hell off the thing. She was anxious to find out about the third victim, the one that was alive.

She gazed out the plane's window for anyone who resembled a detective, cops, Feds. They were easy to spot. This guy was easier than usual. David Binder stood there practically hopping off the ground, arms flailing as if his life depended on getting her immediate attention. She waved at him, wondering if he could see her. Thirties, a tinge of gray hair just appearing at the sideburns, no wrinkles. Not a rookie, she thought, but pretty close. No wonder he had pulled this duty—transporting her from the airport.

After a brief exchange of formalities, David gave her the scoop.

"Here's the deal," he said, not taking an extra breath between words, "we located a third victim just a half hour or so ago. She's en route to UCLA's burn trauma unit. Heavy corrosive burns over a majority of the torso and extremities. Same shallow incisions. If it's not our guy, I'll eat my shorts."

Cat smiled. "I don't think that's necessary. Sounds like our guy. Where is she now?"

"She's in the air." He whirled his finger in the air then glanced at his watch. "Actually, by now they should be touching down."

"We need to get to her," Cat said sharply.

"Already got that in order, doctor," he said, his tie whipping back, leading her to a waiting chopper, its door open, the blades engaged, engine screaming.

Once they were in the air, Cat stared through the thick bubble window to a world that was far removed from Washington, DC. Across the landscape, freeways stretched and intertwined as if living breathing snakes—caught in some primordial dance. At three-thirty in the afternoon, traffic was already backing up. Would California's engineers ever buy into mass transit? The chopper followed the coastline; she could see the beach cities, Dana Point in the distance, and closer, Newport, Huntington, Long Beach—each boasting its own pier jutting out into the ocean. Beyond the cities, the Pacific was disturbed only by the occasional sport fisher. Gathered on buoys, seals basked in the afternoon sun. On the edge of the panorama, San Clemente loomed, the thin, almost invisible lining of its hills twenty miles or so away.

The pilot took one glimpse at the freeway and said in the headphone set, "Welcome to sunny Southern California, land of smog and freeway congestion."

"Looks like it's gotten worse," Cat said, remembering her trip here five years ago.

Bosco, as they called him, replied, "Yeah, just about every year there's more gridlock. Can't say I envy them down there." He flashed her a quick smile beneath chocolate brown hair, which Cat guessed he had been nicknamed for.

"How much longer?" David said into the headphones.

"Not much really. We'll be in Westwood in no time." Bosco could tell his kind was nervous, nervous being around this woman. They hadn't told him who she was, but from the way the kid was squirming in his seat, Bosco could tell she was a big wig.

As the chopper dipped and banked left, Bosco could see the woman's face blanch white.

"You okay?"

"Yeah, sure." She motioned with the wave of her hand. "Just a combination of bad airline food and turbulence."

"Sorry 'bout that, I'll try to be more careful."

"It's all right really. Just get us there."

Bosco saluted and said "Aye, aye, captain" with a wry grin.

Cat forced a smile in his direction, looking out the window, trying to concentrate on the horizon.

"There it is," said Bosco as UCLA's multistory facility came into view. The building had no doubt been built in the sixties when square brick buildings were the norm. Nothing imaginative about the structure. Tall pines provided shade for those sitting in a square courtyard, shrubs neatly trimmed and tended. To the left of the building, a parking structure, cars—black, green, burgundy—reflecting the sun.

Beside Cat, David was anxious to land. Like her, he was not a good flyer, and it showed on his face.

"There's the helipad. We'll be down soon enough," Bosco said, sensing they had both had all they could take of the ride.

From the roof, a man in a long white coat waved at them. Cat pointed to the man. "Any idea who that is?" David stared at his hands, looking like he was trying to keep his mind off his stomach. He shook his head.

As they got closer, she could make out the man's physical features. Tall, broad-shouldered, hair the color of just-poured asphalt. Another man joined him, standing behind, wearing a cop's uniform, beer gut poking out of a too-small belt.

David pulled himself away from his turmoil to look out the window. "The guy in the back is the cop that found her. Orange County Sheriff's Office. Name's Stone, Stone Kilroy." Cat nodded, waiting for the chopper to land.

※ ※ ※ ※ ※

David was the first to disembark the chopper. Rather than lending a hand to Cat, he stumbled through the double doors, no doubt searching for a toilet where he could vomit.

Cat grabbed her medical valise and hopped out onto the concrete, glad to have something solid under her feet for the first time in six hours.

The man in the white lab coat approached, jet-black hair tousled wildly in the wind.

Cat ducked below the whirling rotor blades as Bosco cut the engines. The doctor was instantly before her with a keen smile and a firm shake.

"Dr. Powers, I'm Dr. Walker, head of the surgical trauma team that brought the woman in."

He continued to shake her hand vigorously. "This is Stone Kilroy, Orange County Sheriff's Office. He's the man that found her."

Stone was soundless, as his name implied, eyes averted to the ground.

"Yes, I heard. How's she doing? What's her name?"

As always, Cat had a million questions to ask, each one tumbling out in quick succession. The questions kept her job interesting; the answers usually kept her coming back.

Walker brushed off the question and ushered her inside.

She followed the fat sheriff through the double doors. Entering the facility, it was nothing impressive. Carpeted, walls painted an odd shade of sea green, the place seemed as antiseptic as any hospital. Inside, the light was artificial, casting a greenish-yellow glow over everything. Betadine fumes filled her nostrils.

She tried the question again. "So how's the woman?"

The doctor fell strangely quiet, thrusting his hands in his coat pockets. "Maybe I can show you better than I can tell you."

He led them casually to the elevators, punched the down button.

Cat looked at him, studied him. "Shouldn't we be hurrying?" With burn patients, every second counted. She knew the risk of shock, and subsequent death, was great.

"We don't need to hurry," Walker said quietly.

"What?" Cat grabbed his arm, turning him to face her.

He looked her square in the eye for the first time. "There is no need."

"She didn't make it?"

"She coded in the chopper right before we got here. I tried to resuscitate, but nothing worked."

"I'm chasing a lunatic and you can't keep his one victim alive long enough for me to talk to her. Most surely the woman said something."

"She was intubated," Walker said, as if apologizing.

"Before she was intubated?" She turned to Stone Kilroy. "Did she say anything to you? Anything?"

The cop chomped at his gum like a cow chewing cud. "Yup."

"What?"

"She kept asking for a doctor."

THREE

The belief in a supernatural source of evil is not necessary;
men alone are quite capable of every wickedness.
—**Joseph Conrad**, *Under Western Eyes*

D r. Catherine Powers, this is Irvine Police Chief Robert Richmond." The man held out a firm handshake.

"It's a pleasure to have you here, doctor. I'm the one that requested your help, the FBI's help. I have heard you have excellent instincts, and your intuition is, well, above average. I'd like you to remain here for as long as you can."

Richmond held himself like a man destined for public office. Neat cut hair, gray pin-striped suit. It looked like he had dressed for this meeting. How much thought he had given to calling in the FBI, Cat could read from his sunken eyes. It was clear he had not slept in some time.

"I am here indefinitely, Chief Richmond." Cat sighed a long exasperated breath of air, used to the formalities. "I assure you I am here for as long as it takes. And please call me Cat."

"All right, then." He nodded but seemed somewhat taken aback at her informality.

Behind Richmond another man stepped forward.

"Dr. Powers, this is Dr. Conrad James, Orange County's head medical examiner," Walker said. The doctor, in his demeanor as well as his touch, appeared icy. Mid-fifties, an exacting man, Cat guessed. Not a hair on his head out of place.

"Pleased to meet you," he said, his voice trailing off.

Cat met his gaze. "Likewise."

"We should proceed to the body," he said flatly, turning on his heels.

Cat's high heels clicked behind him as she struggled to keep up with the man. The other men brought up the rear.

"I want you to know right off the bat, I'm not happy with the FBI's involvement in this case."

"That's extremely obvious, I assure you."

"Bunch of bureaucrats worrying about their next election, half of them on the dole anyway," he said. "The only reason you're here is politics, Dr. Powers, plain and simple; although I must say your reputation precedes you."

Cat had encountered this pettiness before. She was used to it, decided to let the words, like drops of water, roll off her back.

"How so, doctor?" She emphasized the word *doctor* with some reverence, buying into the man's ego for now.

"I know of your work on the Saint Croix case, how you brought that criminal in."

A year ago, the Saint Croix case involved a string of mutilation murders of teenaged boys, their bodies dumped, painted, and sodomized. The killing occurred all over the United States. Cat had run tests on the paints, reasoning they were the type used by actors, street musicians, maybe circus performers. Bodies' locations were then cross-matched with major circuses, state fairs, carnivals. Cat believed a circus performer's nomadic existence would provide the perfect cover. This, with a match on trace semen and DNA, led to Rene Saint Croix's arrest, a performer with Cirque du Soleil.

"Thank you, doctor. It appears that case will be far easier to solve than this one."

They walked briskly down a dimly lit corridor, approaching automated double doors that announced the ER.

"At last, we agree on something." He smiled for the first time, her charm apparently winning him over.

"Dr. James, I assure you my presence here, my goal, is the same as yours—to catch the killer that is out there. Neither I, nor the FBI, have any desire to make you or your esteemed office appear inept. The FBI offers its full assistance, all its resources."

"Thank you, but I just don't understand why Richmond believes we can't handle this on our own."

"The FBI has resources which your office doesn't. We have access to the world's foremost behavioral specialist and forensic pathologist who perform tests with the utmost accuracy—"

"I know all that, but it all comes down to scientific deduction, a guessing game, doesn't it, doctor?"

"Yes, and no one is better than the FBI at playing games," Cat responded quickly.

James's outrage had completely dissipated.

Over the body now, which remained just as it looked when Consuelo Vargas flatlined, Cat asked when they would move her.

"A van is on the way. They'll be here any minute. In the meantime, what can you tell us?" Sharpness and sarcasm returned to his tone. Cat knew he was testing his younger colleague, twenty years his junior. She was up for the challenge.

She turned her attention to Consuelo Vargas; the victim's wounds shouted the killer's razor-sharp aggression.

"The injuries tell me this man's one complex sonofabitch. From the look of the incisions, he uses an instrument with a small, very sharp blade." She stopped for moment, thinking. "Uses it with surgical precision, a scalpel, perhaps. The wounds correlate with the other victim's, one half to one and one half inches deep each from the look of it. Probably dealing with above average intelligence, perhaps genius IQ. The killer is most likely male, mid-twenties to late fifties." Searching Conrad James's eyes, Cat asked, "Did she know the other victims?" She knew the answer.

"No connection to each other as far as we can tell."

"The randomness of the kill, then, suggests a smooth, easygoing type. Nonthreatening at first. Probably uses his charms to disarm their defenses, get them where he wants them. He is calculated in his choice of victim; each abduction is carefully orchestrated, probably even practiced beforehand. This woman had no idea she was in a madman's presence until it was too late."

James's thick eagle-eye brows loomed low.

"Incisions here and here"—Cat was careful not to touch the corpse as she pointed to the chest and abdomen—"are precise. He knows exactly how deep to cut, without piercing any vital organs. My guess, he wants to keep the victims alive, he enjoys watching them as he tortures them. That's why none have been disfigured in the face; that way he can see their pain, experience it with them."

"Interesting," James responded, his forefinger and thumb pinching his chin. A moment of silence. "Continue."

"The manner in which he kills these women is much more than his MO. It is his signature—a way for him to shout for attention to the authorities. He wants us to find him, wants us to know he did this. He is proud of it. To him, it is art. As surely as if he had left us a signed confession, each of these wounds, the use of acid, is his calling card. Through it, he validates himself, his life's work. These women can tell us as much or as little as we want." She glanced at James. "All we need to do is observe objectively."

"Very perceptive," Richmond mumbled from behind her.

"Whoa, you're losing me," Dr. James complained.

"At Quantico, I've been trained not only in forensic medicine but in the behavioral sciences. The art of profiling, understanding the nature of the beast, can help predict his behavior and bring him to justice."

As Cat spoke, her voice sounded more detached. He recognized the drone. He too had used mechanical, monotone diatribes when a body was especially gruesome. It was a defense mechanism. He knew it well.

Just then, the van arrived to pick up Consuelo Vargas. Dr. James quickly oversaw the removal, placing bags over the deceased's hands and feet to preserve any hair, skin, or blood evidence that might be present. Within two minutes, Consuelo Vargas was on the move.

"Would you like a lift to my office?" Dr. James asked. "My car's just outside. I presume you gentlemen won't be joining us for the autopsy?"

Stone Kilroy turned white, looked like he would pass out. Richmond feigned an important meeting. Walker flat out declined.

As Cat left the ER with Dr. James, a wave of nostalgia overcame her when she saw what must be Consuelo Vargas's children grieving in the hallway. A small-boned, dark-complexioned boy, not much bigger than her own, was holding to his father's thigh tight, crying. Cat picked up a few Spanish words. "*Morte, mama, aqui.*" Her thoughts drifted back to her Joey—she would phone him tonight to be sure he was all right. Cat longed to hold this woman's child, to comfort him, but it was not her place. She and the woman's husband exchanged knowing glances, his dark eyes stained with tears.

She knew this family would have no solace, even after her work was done.

Quickly, Dr. James and Cat left UCLA. At least Cat believed she had won him over.

The autopsy room gleamed—ten stainless-steel tables. The air was cold. Like death. Icy air forced through a huge vent overhead. Despite Dr. James's concerns, Orange County's autopsy facilities were better than most.

"I presume the appropriate photographs, clothed and nude, have been taken?"

Dr. Conrad James nodded through his surgical mask.

"And X-rays taken?"

He nodded once more.

Cat Powers adjusted the microphone attached to her surgical garb's front, with a latex-gloved hand, and began to dictate. She looked briefly at the camera lens as she continued, having turned the unit on with a handheld remote.

Moving to the bottom of the body, she checked the toe tag, confirming the identity. After rote dictation of the case number, condition of the body, age, sex, race, length, weight, and general condition of the dental work, Cat began sizing up the wounds, her expert eyes roaming.

"Rigor mortis is present in the extremities," she said. As she spoke, it was hard for her not to concentrate on the wounds, the rage that the victims of this burning killer had faced in their last minutes. Whether old or young, the killer displayed an inordinate amount of medical skill, trained no doubt. His savagery was extreme, given the multiple stab wounds and his use of acid to further disfigure. It took no great imagination to understand that this man was deliberate with each cut, enjoying his work. From what she knew of the semen found at the scene, she surmised that throughout the cutting ritual he became sexually excited and that excitement culminated in ejaculation over his prey, either immediately before or after her death. At this point, Cat couldn't tell.

She forced herself to focus on the victim.

What could she tell?

"There is a single scar in the lower right quadrant, well healed, from a previous appendectomy. No moles, tattoos, or other scars are present."

She continued. "The skin texture is abnormal. White ubcutaneous veins are visible over the ventral sternum and abdomen. The third-degree burns appear more pronounced on the ventral buttocks. Third-degree burns cover 70 percent BSA, including all extremities. There is deep tissue damage and extensive necrosis. The face is untouched. There are multiple lacerations to the skin."

Cat picked up a plastic ruler and held it against the largest wound. "There is a one-centimeter incision…"

She reached up and turned off the camera.

"Her throat, did anyone catch this?"

Despite the intubation, Cat noted that tissue near the trachea had bruised so severely that there were discoloration scars on the back and side of the neck. The trachea is a nearly cylindrical tube of cartilage and membranes that extends from the larynx to the fifth thoracic vertebrae. Injury to the eleven-centimeter-long tube could cause difficulty breathing and speaking. It was clear to Cat that the only reason Consuelo Vargas had not said more to her rescuers was because she simply couldn't.

She desperately wished the woman had lived.

"Was this exhibited in any of the other victims?" she asked Dr. James, anger running just below the surface.

He remained silent, then responded, "Not that I recall."

Silently, Cat made a note of the killer's apparently escalating violence. Or perhaps Consuelo Vargas simply refused to go quietly, and he had sickened of her shrieks—his remedy the destruction of her means of communication.

Cat turned the camera back on and described the injury with great care and precision, removing a tissue sample to a sterile surgical tray for further analysis. Proceeding down the length of the body, she continued to document the incisions as best she could, counting the number and the portion of the body where each appeared, estimating the size and depth, using a plastic ruler.

The most pronounced cut warranted special attention. "There is a three-centimeter-long incision to the left anterior abdomen, just deep enough to reach the subcutaneous fatty tissue. Blood vessels below have not been affected. The incision is a straight clean cut; edges of the incision are not serrated in any manner."

Dr. James liked what he heard. "Continue," he said.

"Like the others, this looks like the work of a small, very sharp blade. This wound doesn't penetrate the abdomen's vital organs."

"Semen was collected from her skin?"

"Yes. Already at the lab."

Cat carefully looked under the victim's fingernails. There was no blood, but she managed to scrape what appeared to be skin onto a glass slide.

Satisfied she had covered all the cuts, she briefly examined the chest for rib fractures and moved on. Cat made a Y-incision, midline running down to the pubis. Dr. James fidgeted as if getting bored. If this one was anything like the others, there would be no internal injury other than expected lung damage from the sulfuric acid's vapors being breathed in. Consuelo Vargas was true to form.

Like her predecessors, there was no sign of sexual intercourse or penetration. The head and brain were unremarkable, no evidence of petechia of the conjunctiva, indicating strangulation or hanging.

After dictating the remainder of the findings and sectioning tissue samples of the major organs, Cat felt exhausted.

Snapping off her surgical gloves, she asked if Dr. James would mind taking her back to the hotel.

"Yes, of course," he responded in a casual manner.

Did he think she was coming on to him? She found herself noticing for the first time that he wore no wedding ring. Within minutes, they were in his midnight blue Lincoln Continental, the car accelerating smooth as silk through Santa Ana's streets. After dark, downtown parts of Santa Ana took on a seediness, a callousness for anything and everyone decent. Visited by drug dealers, prostitutes, and lowlifes, what was a major hub of Orange County during the day descended into filth at night. Cat was pleased she was being spirited through the streets with a man at her side. Dr. James seemed impervious to yellow stoplights, as if he felt the same sense of urgency.

"You seem very at home in my autopsy room."

"Guess I'll take that as a compliment. It's better equipped than most."

"Thanks. Our lab's one of the best on the West Coast." He sounded like a proud captain of a ship, boasting the merits of each of his seaworthy mates.

"Yes, from what I hear your turnaround time is about half of downtown Los Angeles's lab."

"And a bit more precise too. You heard about that DNA screw-up they had?"

"Yes. It made every national paper including the *Post*."

Dr. James rolled his eyes skyward.

Enough of the small talk. Cat asked, "What do you make of the damage to the trachea today?"

"Perhaps he wanted nothing more than for her to be quiet."

"I don't believe so." Her pale blue eyes glistened, boring into him. "On the surface, that may be what occurred. But at a deeper level, it indicates accelerating aggression. The other bodies, from the photos I have seen, don't have any outward signs of aggression." Cat had to work from photos because Nancy Marsh and the other girl had been buried, their families given some small semblance of dignity and closure. Exhumations were out of the question and not necessary. The photos and autopsy reports said enough, speaking volumes about the predator.

She continued. "This third corpse, the injury to the neck, shows his hostility is escalating. The earlier cases indicate a meticulous attention to detail, cool, cunning. Deliberate. Nothing was left to chance, from the random choice of unrelated victims to the method of the blood sport."

"A lot to assume from one look at the throat?"

She ignored the question. "With two killings behind him, he feels more confident, sure of himself. Enjoying the police fumbling. Initially, the act of killing appeared to have a ceremonial aspect. But this third one—she's different. This one was not the perfect murder. It did not go as he planned. Perhaps he was startled midway through the ritual, and he injured her to keep her screams at bay."

"What are you saying, doctor?"

"I'm saying this predator was disturbed unexpectedly. Something spooked him. We got too close."

"What do you make of the acid?"

"Less than 9 percent of female deaths in the United States fall into the 'other' category, the majority being gunshot, poisons, hanging. Our madman is definitely imaginative in his method. Sulfuric acids are used in industry and, in more diluted forms, in medicine. I'll do some research on who could get their hands on the stuff easily."

"In your opinion, were they killed before or after the burns?"

"After, I believe. With the Vargas woman, he may have incapacitated her with the injury to the neck, then allowed her to revive, to listen to her pathetic animal cries for help. No doubt he chooses his cuts very carefully. My guess is the smallest ones come first. He allows these to gape open, then pours in the acid, enjoying the sounds of sheer terror. He waits between each infliction, cutting as he goes."

"With what reason? It would seem he would want it over quickly."

"Far from it. His control of the death process is very much a catharsis. By gaining control of her life, he gains control of his own. Perhaps he needs to gain control of this more animal part of himself, and this is the only way he knows how."

"Then he seeks to control death itself?"

"Maybe. I think, more so, he intends to control himself, the cruel inhuman part of himself. Maybe because it is so at odds with the rest of what he projects to society."

"Interesting."

They rode in silence for the remainder of the trip, each replaying the conversation, the autopsy, the possible reasons in their minds.

When she got out and removed her bags, Cat said to him, "Get a good night's sleep, doctor. Tomorrow will be no more pleasant than today." They both understood what she meant as she watched him drive away.

FOUR

Breakwater beckoned him, the open sea beyond. Just out of Huntington Harbor, now under Pacific Coast Highway's overpass, the waves lapped at his fifty-four-foot yacht's stern. To his left, the jetty painted a lovely picture against a mid-afternoon sun's sky. He maneuvered the sailboat past what used to be the navy's Long Beach shipyard. A great loss to the sea, he believed. A mistake.

Mistake.

The word haunted him.

His last one had been a mistake. Consuelo Vargas had been pretty enough, but her social rank was below him. Somehow that night it didn't matter; he had wanted her and he'd taken her. But he was a man of taste, culture. He would have no more migrant farm workers, at least not tonight.

He'd lost his cool; that was a mistake too. Letting himself stroke her the way he did, sliding his fingers slowly along the soft skin of her thighs, under her cotton panties. He blinked and breathed hard, allowing himself to relive it. He stroked her through the cotton at first, till she moaned, her breathing faster. Then, slowly, he moved below, his finger making small slow circles on her. She squirmed to get closer to him, but he would not allow it, would not let any other part of her touch him.

He was careful not to penetrate her, as he touched himself.

She screamed out in delight, breaking the spell. Instantly, he removed his hand, recoiled from her.

"*Te quero, Papi.*" she had told him.

"*Nada.*"

From then on, she had been almost like the others. He had held her round the throat till she lapsed into unconsciousness. That's when the cutting began. The blessed cutting. His release.

Blinking, he regained command of the present. Some distance out over the water now, he intended to head out a mile more, then due south toward Newport. Passing an oil rig, seals barked a warning to him to stay away. Winds were favorable. He made quick work of sailing by the Huntington Beach Pier. It seemed to him a sad testament to today's youth—garish neon-signed multistory complexes replacing the quiet mom-and-pop surf shops and burger stands. Some managed to stay on, but they were fighting the ebb tide of dreaded modernization. Kids didn't realize that it was those small establishments that had seen the great days of surfing, the giant wooden boards, the old school surfers who had made Huntington Beach the home to the Surfer's Hall of Fame. Now the pier was nothing more than a tenuous monstrosity.

An hour and a half later, he neared the mouth of Newport Harbor. A far bigger harbor than its neighbor to the north, Newport was where he felt most at home. Multimillion-dollar homes lined both sides of the breakwater. This was the playground for Southern California's elite. Forty-thousand-dollar vehicles were as passé as mom's station wagon. Even Ferraris barely turned heads. This was his town. He smiled, thinking of his plans. Squinting into the setting sun, he pulled his corduroy baseball cap squarely down over his eyes.

Another half hour at no wake speed till he docked his vessel in a slip he rented from a friend. Nothing here would be purchased or rented under his name. He could not be too careful.

The sun was just beginning to set, casting a golden halo around Catalina. A cool ocean breeze swept up off the marina. He let it wash through him, calming his nerves.

The walk to Lido Island was another half hour, which he didn't mind. It invigorated him, made him ready for the chase.

A two-story nightclub on the tip of Lido Island called The Warehouse beckoned the young and restless. Young women here, some in their twenties, others merely appearing so, were the norm, their bodies tight, not from exercise but plastic surgery, the latest diet drugs, and cocaine. As much as cocaine was considered "the drug of the eighties," its popularity was still alive and well in this crowd.

He paid the cover charge and walked into a sea of strobe lights and cigarette smoke. Patiently he waited. Waited for someone to catch his fancy. Many of the women roamed in packs, apparently out for a quick night's screw with the girls. He did not want one who seemed experienced.

Rather he searched for innocence, a kind of insecurity that told him this girl did not belong here, for she was special. Watching women flirting and swigging back martinis, he found no one who met his needs.

Better try my luck upstairs.

Ascending the dark staircase, he entered the first bar, ordered a vodka tonic, and kept moving. Coming upon what he wanted, he watched her at a distance for some time. From what little he could hear of her voice, she was a tourist, Southern girl, by the drawl. Dressed in black ruffled taffeta, she looked more like a prom date than a serious lay. The girl she was with had been whispering in her ear, pointing at some nerd seated at the bar.

"Go on, go up and talk to him," she'd said, shouting over the booming music.

"How can I? What if he's with someone?"

"He's been sitting there for an hour nursing that Coca-Cola like it's the last drink on earth. You think if he was with someone, she would have showed by now?" The girl did not disguise her sarcasm.

"I guess you're right," her friend said shyly.

"Yeah. How do you expect to have a good time if you don't grow some balls?"

With this statement, she simply blushed, getting off her barstool cautiously.

He took his chance; rescue the damsel from her fate. Exactly what he was looking for.

She took ten steps in his direction across the smoke-filled bar. He got down, walked to her, and took her arm, guiding her away from the object of her intentions.

"Now, you don't really want to be seen with him, do you?" he asked charmingly, eyes dancing over her, delighting in her.

"Not really. My friend's been goading me all night. I guess I'm not exactly date material out here, although in South Carolina…"

He stopped himself from grinning.

"Would you like to have a drink with me? I promise, I'm harmless." He bowed just slightly, his arm making a debonair swirl in the air, as if he were at her command.

Laughing, she gave him the once over and responded, "I guess it's okay."

Attentively, he guided her to a table in the corner, away from the blinding light and blaring music. "There, this is much better, isn't it? We can talk."

He was amazed she even sat like a lady, her hands running along her buttock as she sat to smooth out her dress, ankles crossed demurely. She was, in a word, refreshing.

"Are you here visiting?" He asked the obvious question, figuring it would be an easy way to get the conversation rolling, put her at ease.

"Yes, my daddy's out here on business. He works with Toshiba, you know, the electronics company. Management. Some big seminar they're having."

"That's very nice. And what brings you to a place like this?"

"Well, I got all excited when Dad said Mom and I could come along. Never been to California before." The girl was so excited the words shot off her like bullets. "Already seen Disneyland. Tomorrow we're doing Knott's Berry Farm."

He merely smiled. "Would you like a fresh drink?"

"Oh, yes, please. I've been drinking rum and coke. Adds to the California vacation atmosphere, don't you think?"

"Yes." He motioned to the waitress, then thought the better of it and got the drinks himself, without any fuss. He kept his chin down and eyes averted. As many faces as this bartender saw in one night, he didn't want to give the guy a reason to stand out from the crowd, to be remembered.

"Here you are," he said, returning promptly. "So are you in high school?"

Frowning at the question, she responded, "No, I'm a freshman in community college."

A thin painted smirk remained glued to his face, but he appeared to listen intently. His mind was already far away.

"What do you do?" she asked, a spring in her voice.

"I am in the medical profession."

"A doctor?" She seemed instantly awed.

"Of sorts." He changed the subject quickly. "Do you like the ocean?"

"Yes, that's one of the reasons I was so excited to come out here. To be close to the water and all. It makes me feel, well, it makes me feel alive."

"Then I guess you're in luck."

She questioned him with her eyes.

"I've got a sailboat moored about a half hour from here. Would you like to go for a sail?" He did not need her to answer.

"That would be great." She leapt up, practically giddy with excitement.

"Why don't you freshen up in the bathroom, and I'll meet you…"

She sprang from the chair and was gone before he could finish his sentence. He left a not too generous tip, waited a few minutes, and followed.

Outside, a typical Southern California night. The stars stood as if at attention in the sky, the air not balmy, but cool.

"Take your shoes off," he coaxed her. As she did what he said, he savored his growing command over her.

Black two-inch heels dangling from her hand, he caught a whiff of her spicy perfume. On the way to the yacht, he slipped his fingers into hers, tantalized by her touch. A coolness, yet warmth to it. That lyrical quality in her eyes.

Within the hour they were outside the bay, heading farther south for Dana Point, Carrie Ann Bennett sipping champagne, already downing three quarters of a bottle, almost all by herself. They passed a few boats heading in, all with their red and green night running lights reflecting off the water.

Above, the heavens opened its black cloak studded with diamonds. A peaceful breeze from the north caressed the sails, the water rhythmically lapping the sides of the sailboat. Now skirting the distant lights of Emerald Bay, an exclusive community made famous by two events—the Laguna fires and as the residence of Nicole Brown Simpson's family.

He paused the boat here, contented with the twinkling lights of the coastline on one side, endless blackness on the other, and the stars above. Smoothly, she asked for him to sit next to her. As he went to her, he smiled disarmingly, seeing that one of her ruffled shoulder straps had fallen, revealing a milky white neck, delicate bones.

He took her champagne flute and placed it some distance away, wanting her to have no distractions. Kissing and caressing her, she quivered as his tongue darted in and out of her mouth, a teasing kiss that made her beg for more. Over her now, his hands stroked her body through the taffeta. She could see nothing but the stars and the face of this man who was professing his love for her. From the shining tears in her eyes, he could see that it seemed so incredible, so unbelievable to her.

"There is no reason to be scared," he said in a whisper.

"I'm not. It's just I can't believe this is happening. You're so wonderful," she said, her voice deep and throaty, filled with emotion.

"Can you understand what I see for us, a future?"

"Yes," she replied, thinking he was speaking of love, a home, family, togetherness.

In an instant he was back at her neck, the kisses so tender she could not control herself any longer. She moaned in sheer delight, moving her body closer.

His mouth was at her ear again, nibbling on her lobe, a little pain, enough to further excite her. Slowly, very slowly, he brought his lips to hers and kissed her softly, then harder, the way he wanted to. Tenderly, his fingers slid down her back, the zipper now open. Skin soft, the gentle curve of her spine, as she arched up for him. Hands roamed down, then up, slowly to her thigh. He held his hand there, enjoying the feel of the taffeta and her skin. In his ear, she was breathing hard now, the moans occasional, as she pushed her hips into him.

For a second he looked up. It was magical on the ocean, a canopy of midnight black darkness all around, covering them like a shroud, the stars providing the faintest light. Pavarotti playing from inside the cabin, counterbalanced by the peaceful lapping of the water at the bow, in operatic perfection. *How absolutely flawless this evening is*, he thought.

She commanded his attention, moaning louder now. His hands went to work, moving along her contours, underneath her dress. He watched her. The way her back arched at his touch, the way her mouth hung open.

She pulled away, surprising him. Standing, she allowed her dress to slip away, so he could see her in the milky moonlight. Sensually, she removed the remainder of her clothes till she stood there naked, making herself an offering to him.

He rose, her eyes looking up to him now. Facing her, he was still fully clothed. She knelt in front of him, her hands on him, one groping at his buttocks, the other busy with his zipper. His hands were on her hair, touching it softly.

In an instant, his touch went from tender to brutally rough, grabbing her long chestnut mane. Startled, she glared at him. What she saw in his face shocked her. Wild, crazy eyes.

Yanking her up to him, she screamed. The lapping music off the water drowned out her terror. With the back of his hand, he knocked her across the face, sent her reeling across the bow. He watched as she looked for something to fight back with, frantically trying to open the top sliding storage cabinets. But there was nothing. He had carefully locked away anything she could use as a weapon.

Flashing a wicked grin at her, he laughed.

And approached.

Reaching up, she touched a wet trail on her chin, looked at trembling fingers to see blood. She began pleading with him, her naked body shivering suddenly, even though the air was warm and balmy from the Santa Ana winds.

"Please don't hurt me…" Her words trailed off as she realized the futility of her begging. She began to weep. Closing in on her, the Burning Man took her in his arms again, his tenderness returned. Painted on her face, he could see the relief, feel it wash over her. He held her like this for a moment, her body bleeding, shivering, defenseless. Coughing, hard labored breathing, tears on his shoulder.

Lifting her chin so their eyes met, he told her softly, "It will be all right." With this, he reared his head back and, with his full body weight, rammed his forehead into hers, forcing her to the deck. Slamming his boot up against her cheek, he crushed her bruised face into the deck. Frantically, she grabbed at his ankle. Fright reigned in her face, from what he could see, tears coming hard and fast now, streaming down, into her mouth.

Here, she was his alone.

No one would hear her screams.

Picking up his foot, he brought it back down on her throat. He watched her close her eyes, then open them wide. Above her, he took her entire frame of vision. She realized, no doubt, that the silver-haired man she trusted, looming over her here, would be the last thing she'd see. Her body seemed smaller than before. He smiled again. Eyes wild, staring in her direction, but through her as if she weren't even there.

"Look at me." In his voice, there was something diabolical. His pupils seemed to fill his eyes.

"Please don't kill me. I want to live…" Her pleas came quickly, but without much hope.

"What you want is not important now," he told her in a smooth statement.

"I'll do anything you want. Just don't kill me."

"I will do what is right with you. Nothing more. Nothing less."

With that, as quickly as he had snared her, he let her go. She scrambled to her knees, gasping for breath, coughing and retching, rubbing at her throat. Wide-eyed, frightened, certain that he would kill her, she asked her first intelligent question of the night. "Why?" she whimpered, her voice barely audible above the lapping sea.

He did not answer.

Moving in on her, he knocked her into submission. This time she was too weak to offer any resistance. This time she would not awaken.

He stood, mesmerized. Despite what he believed earlier, she really was an ugly creature. Too much baby fat lodged in the wrong places, her face splotched, bloody. More so than the way she looked now, he found her actions repulsive. Like the others, a whore, nothing less.

He listened to the water for some time, as if in a trance. Reaching up to touch his forehead, above his right eye, it was tender, slightly painful. With a little disinfectant and maybe a butterfly stitch or two, it would be fine.

He could not say the same for Carrie Ann Bennett.

Disappearing below, he brought back the tools of his trade. A scalpel, surgical gloves, sulfuric acid in an antiqued glass bottle with a rounded cut-glass stopper. A six-foot length of sheet metal he had picked up at the local hardware store, nine eyehooks welded into each of the corners and the midsection. Thick black nylon rope.

His fantasy was progressing, developing with each kill.

Tonight he would write a new chapter.

He sat beside the crumpled mass. Dipping her fingers into her blood, he tasted it. Warm, metallic. The elixir of life, just as he was the giver of life.

It was time. He snapped on the latex surgical gloves, squeezing and closing his palms, making sure they were a good fit. Although he was not a big man, he easily moved the girl's limp weight onto the sheet metal. "Maybe the adrenaline rush," he spoke to her, as if she could hear.

"Now, my dear, you will return from whence you came." Reciting the Hippocratic oath, he tied her down to the steel frame, looping the rope tight around her neck, then her forehead, working his way eventually to each arm and ankle, wrapping the rope securely as he went. He posed her like he had the last one, her legs spread apart, arms straight out to the side.

"...Do no harm..." That phrase struck him as ironic. The world had done him harm, the odds against him from the very beginning, and yet he had made a success of himself. In the face of the adversity, he was a giver of life.

He continued to bind her. Picking up electrical tape, he considered taping her mouth. No, that would be no fun, being able to see the eyes alone. Who was it that said the eyes were the windows to the soul? He could not remember. It would be far more exhilarating to hear her screams. Her voice, after all, had that pleasant Southern drawl to it, the drawn-out r's, the rounding out of words ending in g. It would be good to listen to her.

Satisfied, he stood back, examining his handiwork.

Pulling down a cushion from one of the seats, he placed it below him as he sat. He touched her hair as tenderly as a father would his newborn child. Picking up the scalpel, the blade reflected moonlight, glistening as if it had a life of its own. Kneeling over her, he began to cut, pouring the acid in each wound as he went.

Shrill animal screams filled the night.

By the time he fulfilled his perverse sexual needs over her, there was only silence.

FIVE

Pleasure is the only thing to live for.
Nothing ages like happiness.
—Oscar Wilde, *An Ideal Husband*

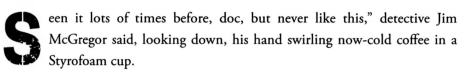een it lots of times before, doc, but never like this," detective Jim
McGregor said, looking down, his hand swirling now-cold coffee in a
Styrofoam cup.

"So you took the photos at the scene of the first girl?" Cat asked.

"Yeah, Stevenson over there—" His big Irish alcoholic nose pointed in the
direction of a man across the room. "He was busy that day. So I took them.
Photography's sort of a hobby on my days off. Helps me relax, ya know?"

Cat nodded. "Mind if I have a seat?"

"Help yourself; it's a free country ain't it?" Jim "the Coach" McGregor
responded. The press had tagged him "the Coach" when he had helped some kids
from Rancho Santa Margarita make it to the Little League World Series semifinals.
He didn't really like the name, didn't dislike it either. Just kind of stuck. None of
his colleagues used the nick name. He told them not to. He hated it. He went by
McGregor now.

"I've seen your work, very impressive."

"Thanks." He seemed genuinely not to care, far more impressed with swirling dregs.

"When you took the pictures, was anything moved?"

"Nope, everything was by the book. I swear on St. Anthony." He put his right hand up in a mock gesture.

"There's no need for that."

"Hey, when the Feds come in, better make sure you dot your i's and cross your t's, know what I mean?"

Cat merely nodded. This man did not fit the Irvine Police Department's newly modernized image. Other cops walked around in polished-looking yet casual denim shirts and Dockers. This guy sat in front of her with one shirt tail hanging out, circles under his eyes, a definitive double chin. She wondered what his cholesterol level was.

"The first one, what was the location like where you found her?"

"Nothing unusual really, for a homicide, if you know what I mean."

Cat looked at him puzzled. From what she had heard, the man spoke from fifteen years of experience as a cop, the last ten years homicide exclusively. He had seen a lot. In a way, she understood the quiet, deliberate distance he maintained. It was born of the need to isolate the soul from the horrors he investigated, day in and day out.

He took his eyes off his coffee dregs, met her quizzical stare, and returned to them.

"We found her dumped on the southern edge of Caspers Regional Park, off Ortega Highway, about a half mile from the 3,300-foot elevation. By the time we got to her, raccoons and possums had made good work on her fingers."

"When you got to the scene, was she positioned in any particular way?"

"Yeah. A modified cross, I guess you'd call it. Arms straight out to the sides, legs flared out as well."

"Head facing any particular direction?"

"Her head was facing due east, toward Newport Beach."

"Nothing was touched? Moved?"

"Like I said, we got a fixed point of reference after snapping on the gloves. Man, that was tough. You ever tried to get a point of reference in California's back country with nothing to look at but native weeds and cactus for miles around?" He muttered something under his breath that she couldn't make out. Closing his eyes, he could see the victim, a young girl…could be his daughter for all he knew, same age, height. Slim, delicate build, wrists the size of sparrows.

They'd found her after a hiker spotted something up in the hills, he said to Cat. Daring not to get any closer, the hiker had doubled back his tracks and called the Irvine Police Department from his Woodbridge home. Neither McGregor nor his partner, Darrell Stevenson, had much relished the thought of climbing up in the woods to see what was back there. But, as much out of their jurisdiction as it was, it was their job. Unbelievably, McGregor got to her first. Maybe he hadn't lost all the athleticism from his days as a Mater Dei star football linebacker, he told Cat.

They'd found animal droppings, although the mountain lions hadn't got to her. "Maybe the acid stink scared them away," he reasoned. "Anyway, she'd been placed under a sycamore bush; the only part of her immediately visible was her left hand. Only thing I disturbed was a purse we found about ten steps away from her, one of them Chanel, Gucci types. Had to check inside for her ID. Find out who she was."

He bowed his head, as if in reverence for the dead.

"At the time, Orange County Sheriff's Office was glad to turn the case over to us, although it was way out of our geographic jurisdiction. They had their plates full with other stuff."

"I understand," Cat said, not just patronizing him. She did understand how finding a body so mutilated and disfigured could do dire harm to the psyche. Even after years on the force, Jim McGregor was no less immune to that.

The man rubbed at his temples. "You gotta understand, she was all torn up. Her skin, it didn't look like skin. Maggots were already working away at her insides, like a cesspool, just doing their thing. She'd been made to suffer like an animal. Then left out there for dead. It ain't no way to go. Alone and naked like that."

He raised his face to her. There were pools in his eyes. Visibly, he pulled himself together, straightened up in the chair. "Anyways that's how we got the first case. Didn't really think nothing much of it at the time. Figured the girl had been beat up by a boyfriend. She had a boyfriend who worked in Chapman's bio-lab, had access to that weird chemical shit. We just figured a fight and the thing escalated. Got out of hand. That's why we didn't call you guys in sooner."

"There's no need to apologize, really," Cat said. "There's no way you could have known what you were looking at, at that time. You did all the right things, bagged her hands right off the bat, preserved any trace evidence at the scene."

She wanted to reach for his hand but knew it would be inappropriate. "By photographing the body, exactly where it lay, exactly in the condition you found it, you provided me an invaluable tool, for which I am grateful."

He continued to stare at the dregs, his voice quivering. "She was my kid's age. It was real tough telling her dad. The mom remained stoic, couldn't think that something like that could happen to her little girl. Mrs. Marsh, well, she was better at, you know, dealing with reality. But Dr. Marsh…the guy, he just crumbled right there in front of me when I gave him the news. Started sobbing and hitting things. Couldn't take it. Mrs. Marsh, she clammed up, wouldn't say a word, wouldn't look at anyone. It took them a while to get over it."

He fell silent.

"Naw, you know what? I'll take that back. They're still getting over it."

"From the looks of it, you are too."

"I guess. Cops ain't supposed to be affected by these things. Tough guy and all that stuff, like that show on TV, *NYPD Blues*. Those guys always running round shooting stuff up, never affects them. Never shed a tear."

Cat understood the demand. Loneliness, isolation, depression all went with the territory. How could a detective or an FBI field agent expect the normal nine-to-fiver to understand? They simply couldn't. It was impossible. The job demands weren't the same. In one you deal with paperwork, the other life and death.

Feeling like she had established trust with the cop, she pulled out the grisly crime scene photos—the carnage that was Nancy Marsh laid out in front of them in black and white, skin butchered, the body bloated from the expanding gases within the corpse. Flesh on her fingers up to the knuckles had been eaten away. Arms out to the side, legs splayed open as if the killer wanted to embarrass or discredit the girl by placing her in this revealing position. Posing the victims was part and parcel of this type of killing, Cat knew.

Many killers lined their victims up just so, displaying them in a line, like trophies stacked up on a shelf. John List, who had been on the FBI's most-wanted list for eighteen years, had been such a killer, murdering five members of his family, then lining them up on sleeping bags, like trophies, before he made his escape.

Many of the gashes gaped open, the gas below causing the skin to warp and stretch. Nancy Marsh's face was untouched, her fine features distorted by death's ravages, hair laid to one side purposefully by the madman. Even beyond the death mask, Cat could tell she had been a pretty girl, hair the color of a Southern California beach, eyes blue and big, freckles lining the bridge of her nose.

McGregor sucked in a long breath, seeing the photos again.

"We've tested what Dr. James pulled from under her fingertips."

"Anything?"

"No. No hairs, no fibers. The skin was her own. Probably scraped it trying to get the acid off."

"Tell me something, McGregor." She called him by the name he preferred. "From what I can see here, no defensive wounds. None noted on the autopsy report either. Is that right?" Cat was looking for the defensive wounds—cuts to the dorsal side of the arms and palms of the hands that occur as a victim tries to defend herself.

"Didn't find none. Nope."

"So she either knew her assailant and the stabbing was so quick that she didn't have time to react, or she may have been unconscious at the time the stabbing began."

McGregor nodded.

"No knife found at the scene?"

"Nope, we combed the place pretty thoroughly. Couldn't find nothing."

"From the autopsy report, no sexual penetration. Semen found on the naked body. Anything else you saw that might suggest a sexual motive to the killing?"

"Nope. Some of the semen had dried up on her chest. It was right in the middle of her chest, right here"—he put his hand square in the middle of his burly chest— "but other than that, she wasn't raped or nothing."

"Any signs of injury to the neck, was her head at an odd angle, anything like that?"

"Nope. Why you asking me all these questions anyway?"

"The third victim, the one we autopsied yesterday, her larynx was severely injured, not crushed exactly, but injured badly enough that it would have been difficult for her to speak."

McGregor listened, then sat silent for a moment.

"Wasn't nothing like that on Nancy Marsh, I can assure you."

"Can you take me to the place where you found the body?"

"Sure, not right away though. I got some paperwork to finish up. I swear they're gonna turn me into a regular desk jockey. The damned standardized report paperwork just keeps getting longer and longer."

Cat's lips curved up in a grin. At least he was thinking of something other than Nancy Marsh.

"What time then?" he said, rising from the chair, heading to a beat-up metal file cabinet the color of cooked okra.

"I'll be at the FBI office."

"I'll pick you up at 1:30."

"Fine," Cat said, satisfied she had gotten some answers.

SIX

I was angry with my friend;
I told my wrath, my wrath did end.
I was angry with my foe:
I told it not, my wrath did grow.
—**William Blake**, *"A Poison Tree"*

Cat checked in at the office, found David Binder on the telephone. Seeing her, his eyebrows shot up. She could hear him hurry to get off of what was, from the sound of it, a personal call.

"Yeah, I'll pick up something for dinner on the way home."

He said nothing, listening to a response.

"You don't have to cook. I'll grab some takeout Chinese."

Silence for a short while again.

"How does Pick Up Stix sound? All right then. It's settled. I'll be home around seven." He blushed, glancing Cat's way. "I love you too," he whispered into the receiver and hung up. "Sorry about that, recently married. You know how that goes. Can't stand it when I'm gone, can't wait for me to get back. Calls the office five times a day. All the guys do around here is give me sh—" David caught himself. "Uh, I mean, grief about it. They call me the newlywed, how do you like that?"

40

"It's all right. My life was once like that." Saying it, Cat realized it had been like this for her a long time ago. It had been a long time since she let anyone get inside her head, much less her heart.

Now the only object of her affection was Joey. As tired as she had been last night, she called him. He had been half asleep, with the three-hour time difference, almost midnight his time, but he had still managed to relay an interesting story about a lizard he had caught, named Charlie. Cat told him that she would love to meet Charlie when she returned home, though at this point she didn't know when that might be. With the lack of physical evidence, a shortage of fingerprints, bodies turning up, it was likely she would be here for a long time. Nevertheless, she assured Joey that Mom would be home soon.

"Oh, I'm sorry," she apologized, only now realizing she'd been staring into space. "Have we checked to see if there's a pattern to these cases? Do they correlate with anything from any other offices? Maybe this guy is more than what he seems… more than just after mutilating pretty girls with acid, in a city full of them."

"Huh?" David gave her a blank stare. Maybe he was a rookie.

"Maybe this guy's done this elsewhere. The most recent victim shows evidence of an escalation of his violence. Maybe there were others before Nancy Marsh, just not in Orange County. Perhaps there's more to his MO than there appears."

"You sure are obsessing over this, aren't you?"

Cat could hardly control herself, feeling the blood rush to her head. She got down in the young agent's face. "What I am doing is not obsessing. We have three unsolved murders here, all horrible, none of them giving us much of an answer. Certainly not giving us anything remotely concrete that could narrow the killer down from, let's say, half the population of the United States," she said, breathing hard, "and nothing so far that would make the FBI look good under the circumstances."

"I'm sorry."

"The police here have called us in to help them out. FBI's got the best crime lab backed up by the best behavioral specialist in the world. We've got nothing to go on right now. You hear me? Nothing. How do you think it will look if we can't stop this guy? You think it'll be good for you? For me? Hell, if we can't bring this guy in we might as well…we might as well apply for a job at the takeout Chinese place you were just jabbering about."

"Shit." David's eyes were wide; he shook his head.

"Now why don't you get up off your ass and make some calls. I want calls into the San Francisco, New York, Boston, Chicago, and Miami field offices. Find out if they've got anything similar to our case, any multiple slashing or stabbing of young women along the same lines. Also check if they have any cases involving acid, anything homicide or not. Then check on sulfuric acid in particular. Go back twenty years if you have to."

He had picked up a pen and was scribbling the instructions on a pad.

"Check the same with Euronet and Interpol. Anything fitting this guy's MO. Twenty years again."

He took a long, aggravated breath, still scribbling.

"One other thing. I want a rundown of all the uses of sulfuric acid. I know you can get hold of it in medicine, but where else. Where could someone get it, and in what concentrations?"

His note-taking continued.

"You got that?"

"Yeah, I got it."

"And while you're at it, why don't you pick up some lunch. I saw a decent looking Italian place across the street. Any good?"

"Yeah, but it ain't cheap."

Cat handed him forty bucks. "Don't worry about it. I'm paying."

His frown warmed up just a bit as he walked out.

SEVEN

A lie is an abomination unto the Lord
and an ever-present help in time of need.
—**John A. Tyler Morgan**, *Comment to the US Senate*

It was a foggy morning when Joey sprang awake, wondering what his mom was doing. His second thought was how Charlie was doing. Thankfully, when he looked at the lizard in the now empty ten-gallon aquarium, it was chomping away on a lettuce leaf Joey had left the night before. The lettuce looked gross and slimly, but to Charlie it appeared a good meal.

"How you doing there, buddy?" he asked the lizard.

It bobbed its head up and down, the way lizards sometimes do, as if understanding his question.

"Guess things in the new home aren't too bad?"

The lizard continued its agitated movements.

Joey lay back in his Ferrari race car bed, putting his hands in the air on a make-believe steering wheel. "*Vroom, vroom,*" he said, eyes staring at the ceiling, now transformed magically into the Indianapolis speedway. Picturing Dale Searnhardt, Jr., as he called him, on his bumper, Joey turned a quick left, cutting him off. "You can't get me. I'm going to win this race." In his head, a checkered flag appeared and he took it by ten car lengths, sticking out his tongue to Dale in mockery.

"Hey," Dad interrupted the vision. "Hey sport, I thought I heard a race going on in here."

"Oh, Dad. Don't stand there. You 'barass me."

"Sorry. Just wondering what you wanted to do today." It was Saturday, Joey's favorite day, when he could do whatever he wanted.

The boy rolled out from his bed and jumped. "Chuck E. Cheese, Chuck E. Cheese!"

Mark Powers folded his arms, shifted his weight to one foot. "Again?"

"Chuck E. Cheese, Chuck E. Cheese," came the answer.

"Can't we do something different, sport? It's the third time this month we've been there."

"I know, but it's my favorite." Joey put on his puppy-dog eyes, complete with pout. "Come on, Dad, pleeease."

"All right, you win. But next weekend, if your mom's back, she is not taking you to Chuck E. Cheese's. I'll make sure of it and—"

Before Mark could finish, Joey let out a holler, jumping up and down, hands in the air. "Yay, yay, Chuck E. Cheese, Chuck E. Cheese!"

Suddenly he stopped jumping and was strangely quiet. "Dad?"

"Yes, Joey," Mark said, his hand on the doorknob.

"Where's Mom?"

Mark stopped and sat on the bed, taking the boy on his lap. "Now, Joey, remember we had this talk before. Mommy has a very important job. She works with the police, like we see on TV…"

The child had a faraway look. "And like my cars?"

Mark nodded. "Yes, son, like your police cars. Except she works for the police of the whole United States."

"Uh-huh," Joey said, remembering.

"And sometimes, because her job is so important, she has to go on trips away to make sure everything is all right where other people live. She makes sure other little boys and their dads are safe too."

"And she has to go for a long time sometimes, doesn't she?"

Mark nodded again. "Yes, sometimes she has to go for a long time."

"Will this be one of those times, Dad?"

"I don't know, son, I don't know." Mark tousled Joey's hair into an even bigger mess. "Now Sport, how about I see you downstairs for some Cap'n Crunch cereal."

"Okay." Joey started to lift his pajama top over his head but stopped midstream. "Dad, is Mom safe?"

"I don't know for sure, son, but I think so."

⸺ ⸺ ⸺ ⸺ ⸺

Everything hit the fan on August 27, as far as Craig Gray was concerned. Slamming a fist down on the desk, he shouted at FBI Director Carlos Sanchez, "How in the hell did she pull this assignment?"

"Look, I don't know. When they needed FBI, they went straight through Washington. She was assigned from Quantico. One of their best from what I hear."

"I don't give a damn if she's Gandhi," Gray seethed. "She is in our backyard, assigned to the biggest case to hit this area this year, and we weren't informed?"

"That appears to be it." Sanchez wasn't going to buy into Gray's ire. He knew the man liked to blow things out of proportion, just to get his opinion heard. This was no different. "What do you want me to do?" Sanchez turned to face the window, staring out at the federal courthouse across the street. All around downtown LA, skyscrapers seemed to cloak the human life that lived in the city. People, looking like ants, scurried in and out of towering monstrosities, moving at a blinding pace, never stopping to look at one another, interact, communicate. Sanchez wondered why he had taken this position. He liked Boston's streets much better, the hominess, the cleanness of that city. This was a living cesspool.

"Are you listening to me?" Gray demanded.

"Yeah." Sanchez waved his hand in the air, dispelling the man's concerns.

Gray would not shut up. "Here's the deal. The case is being handled by some small-time Irish homicide detective. I hear the guy's into booze, or at least used to be. Schmuck can hardly keep a step away from the whiskey."

"So what do you want me to do about it?"

"And she's a woman. A woman, head of the Behavioral Sciences Unit. How is that for woman's lib? Jesus, maybe I should start doing nails for a living, open a damned nail salon. What's with all this role reversal crap? I don't get it."

"Look, she ain't no desk jockey," Sanchez said. "She's a forensic pathologist. Got her master's at Yale. Then on to Harvard Medical School. Graduated cum laude. She's trained with the best. Hell, she's trained the best. She's very capable from what I hear."

"Hello, is anybody in there?" Gray shouted, his knuckles rapping on Sanchez's head. "Don't you get it? She waltzes in here, backed by the FBI's crime lab, nabs the killer. All's well that ends well. Quantico gets another feather in its proverbial hat. 'Put away the next friggin' Jeffrey Dahmer.' I can just see the headlines now. That's our glory, Sanchez. Don't you see, man? They should've called us."

"Fact of the matter is they didn't, and at this point we can't get involved."

Gray continued to rant. "And what about that Irish cop. Guy's five years from retirement. If they solve this, he's gonna get one hell of a career boost. He don't need it; he's due to retire."

"So that's your thunder they're stealing is it?"

"Yeah, it's my damned thunder. It should be anyway."

"Ain't right now. You ever thought of it this way…" Sanchez stopped, lit a cigar, and kept talking. "…Let's just suppose they don't solve it. They have killing after killing after killing of these nice young girls. Then who do you think's gonna have egg on their face, and who do you think's gonna come out smelling like a rose? You thought of that?"

"No, not really." Sanchez knew that Gray was a hothead, wondered how the FBI had ever accepted him as an agent.

"Well, why don't you squish it through that one brain cell you got up there for a minute and let me know when the light bulb comes on."

"Come on, man. I'm just thinking about our welfare."

"Wrong again, Gray." Sanchez raised a thick black eyebrow. "The only well-being you ever think of is your own. You don't give a shit about me or this department. You've always been a hotrod, always will be."

"Don't give me that psychobabble crap," Gray said. "you gotta keep on it – make sure and monitor it. Whatever glory there's gonna be dolled out, I want a piece of it."

Sanchez nodded, "I'm on it."

Gray ran his fingers through his wiry hair, beamed approval, and slammed the door behind him as he left.

One-thirty came and went. McGregor didn't show. No phone call. Nothing. Cat sat in the lobby, flipping through the pages of a six-month-old *National Geographic*, her finger drumming against the wooden armrest.

"Damn, where is he?" She glanced at her watch for the third time in as many minutes. One of her pet peeves was chronic lateness. Something about it didn't sit right with her. Maybe her military upbringing had instilled it. A respect for one's word. When you said you'd be somewhere, you were there. In Cat's case, you were there a few minutes early. *I don't have time for this sitting around.* Right then and there, she decided she'd arrange for a rental car as soon as she got back to the hotel.

People watched as Jim McGregor's 1992 red Toyota Corolla rolled around, coughing an acrid gray smoke from the muffler. She checked her watch again: 1:54. Then walked out to the car.

"Hop in." McGregor's smile was doing automatic pilot.

"I thought our agreement was one-thirty." She stared for a moment at the gung-ho cop, knowing that he wanted to be able to brush off the fact he was almost twenty-five minutes late. "Look here, McGregor, I don't know how you boys do it down here, but where I'm from one-thirty means one-thirty. My time is valuable. I've been sitting here waiting…" Cat got in the car.

"Look, before you get your panties all in a—" He remembered who he was speaking to. "Before you give yourself a fit, the reason I'm *late* is because we've got another young girl disappeared two nights ago." They zipped down the freeway toward the Ortega Highway.

Cat felt foolish and tried to recoup her words, like spilt milk.

"Call came into Missing Persons yesterday morning. Marlin Bennett, executive in Toshiba's middle management, out here for some seminar on the new computers they're going to be bringing out, called in all upset like. Says his daughter, Carrie Ann, disappeared the night before. She's only seventeen. Bright kid, finished high school ahead of her classmates. Anyways, last place anyone saw her was at a bar in Newport Beach, down Lido Island way."

"What was she doing there?" Cat answered her own question. "Out for a night on the town?" Cat drew the obvious conclusions from the questions. Another messed up kid, growing up too fast, into sex, drugs, rock and roll, and anything else she could get her hands on. She let the warm Santa Ana winds tousle her hair as they clipped along through Mission Viejo.

"Yeah, well, sorta." McGregor shook his head. "She hooked up with another manager's daughter, who convinced her to go out. Then the friend left her to hook up with some other girls. Left her in the bar. Told her to get a taxi home." He considered his words for a moment. He could see what Cat was thinking—party girl.

"She's not that type of kid," McGregor said.

"So what do we have right now?"

"Stevenson's down there checking out the bar. Trying to get ahold of the staff by phone. They don't get in till four or five o'clock. See if anyone remembers the girl, you know."

Cat did know. She knew that in all likelihood no one would remember seeing the girl. With a thousand faces in a bar in one night, people learned to tune out faces, names. The nightclub scene in Newport, although more pricey, was the same as any other when it came to the common denominators—money and flesh. Cat felt certain no one would remember anything. Even if they did, they wouldn't be helping out the cops with it.

"I doubt that'll do any good."

"I know, but we've got to be thorough."

"I agree."

McGregor and Cat sat silent the rest of the way. Cat watched as the car slipped past Irvine's fastidiously groomed houses and high-rises. Heading south, they entered Irvine Valley, named for the famous Irvine family, the area still one of Southern California's major crop-producing areas. Surrounded on all sides by low rolling mountains, the soil here was rich and black, the climate tepid but cool in the mornings. Crops in abundance included tomatoes, beans, cabbage, corn, peas, berries of all types. Mission Viejo gave way to the more casual mission architecture of San Juan Capistrano.

"Is that the famous mission?"

"Yes, one of the oldest buildings in Southern California. They finished renovating it a few years back as a matter of fact. Swallows still come back, year after year, although they are not always on cue for the news media."

"Speaking of the news media, have we kept this latest missing person quiet?"

"Yeah. Nothing's been said. It's all under wraps as far as I know."

"Hope that wrap doesn't spring a leak."

"I know what you mean."

As they turned off the freeway, heading inland, Cat could immediately tell the difference in scenery. Gone were gas stations, McDonald's restaurants, convenience stores. Smog seemed nonexistent. In their place were rolling hillsides, horses, residences secluded back from the road so far you just barely caught a glimpse of them. Manicured acreage gave way to less formal pastures. Cows grazed. Cat could smell the greenery.

"Reminds me of home," she said.

"You lived on a farm."

"Not exactly. My dad was a military man, real strict. We were moved all over, Guam, Georgia, West Virginia. At the base in Guam, when I was fourteen, we started a vegetable co-op. Staked out a little patch of earth as our own. Planted every kind of seed I could get my hands on—peppers, citrus, even pumpkin. Base thought it was a good idea, kept the kids out of trouble. We started taking care of goats, pigs. Then on Christmas, my dad brought home a near lame mare he had bought from a local farmer for a few bucks. In his way, it was a gift of encouragement, but he told me to take care of the horse or else the farmer would come back and shoot it. Anyway, I nursed that mare back to health, called her Toto. I'm boring you with this, aren't I?"

"No, not at all."

"At first I thought I wanted to go into veterinary school. You know what? I couldn't stand to see animals hurt. It tore my insides out. So I switched to medicine. If Dad had his way, I would have joined the military like he did, made a career of it. But I wasn't up to it. I knew it. He did too."

"Your dad still alive?"

Cat looked afar off, mesmerized by dancing native yellow wildflowers that seemed to catch the slightest breeze.

"No, he passed a few years ago."

"Cat?" He paused. "He didn't understand you, did he?"

Cat was surprised by the question then guessed it was partly the reason why McGregor had been a homicide detective for so long. Intuition. The ability to read someone without them saying so much as a word. "No, never did. He felt

I had simply thrown my life away by going into medicine. Hell, most people would be proud to see their daughters accepted to one of the most prestigious medical schools in the country. Not my dad." Bitterness tolled through each word. "Nope, he always seemed absolutely incapable of understanding the choices that I made for myself. Maybe it wasn't the choices themselves; maybe he just never understood the fact that I could make my own choices. The man never understood the skill required to be in the medical profession. To him, I was always a military man's kid, tough—an athletic, lanky string bean. Had to be tough, we moved around so much."

"Yeah, you told me."

"Medicine was probably the last profession in the world he would have chosen for me. For starters, when I got into medical school, there were only two other women in my class. He couldn't understand the allure of going into an all-male field. And, most importantly, he couldn't understand how I didn't want to be just like him. My medical profession was a constant reminder to him that I didn't want to be just like him. That, well, that was an ego blow. The disappointment haunted our relationship to the day he died. It was as if, with time, we grew more distant, further away from each other, rather than closer. Every time he heard me referred to as doctor, he practically cringed."

"It's hard when a parent doesn't accept you."

Cat nodded. "It was like a stream of despondency that grew into a river, then a sea. In the end, we couldn't stop the ebb flow, even if we wanted to."

The car passed the 2,000-foot marker.

"How about your mom?"

"She died when I was five. I don't really have too many memories of her. Just flashes here and there."

"Car accident?"

"No, she committed suicide. I came home from school one day and found her with a gun. She had shot herself in the mouth."

"Jesus. That must have been awful."

"Can't hardly remember any of it. Shrinks said I blacked it out. Made it disappear. Only memories I have of her are good ones, I assure you." Cat looked at him flatly wondering if she should be sharing such personal details, but she decided in favor of it. McGregor had a comfortable way about him. It was good to talk about these things after so many years.

As if sensing her thoughts, he asked, "Not getting too personal am I?"

"No. Don't worry about it. As long as you don't sell the story to the *National Enquirer*."

He laughed out loud. "I can just see it now. Headlines. 'FBI Chief Pathologist Haunted by Mystery of Mother's Horrific Death, story on page 3.'"

They both laughed. "After that, I don't think anyone would take my profiling capabilities seriously again," Cat said.

"Speaking of that, we're here." McGregor pulled off the road some distance above the 3,000-foot elevation. "I hope you brought some comfortable shoes." He glanced down at her heels.

She reached into her black shoulder tote and pulled out a pair of running shoes and white socks. "Were these what you had in mind?"

"Those will do nicely up here."

Cat busied herself putting on the shoes then stood up and looked out over the expanse. "Now where exactly did you locate the corpse?"

McGregor pointed. "See that big clump of prickly pear cactus off to the left? She was just over that ridge there, behind it."

"Let's go." Cat had already started off in the direction.

Within a half hour they had hiked the distance to the ridge.

Cat began speaking to McGregor once they reached closer to the site where the body had been found. The skin on the back of her neck prickled.

"Sometimes seeing the scene where a body is found tells me about the killer. Sometimes I get lucky and find things others don't see." She looked across the ground. "Now where exactly did you find her?"

McGregor pointed. There was a clear demarcation where the body had lain, staining the grass a darker shade of brown than what was around it. Some of the sycamore bush's branches had been cut away to make the spot easier to see.

Cat started taking notes about everything he told her, where the body had been found, time of day. As best she could, she sketched the scene from what he was relaying to her.

"Okay, I know what you just said, but here goes the second stupid question of the day."

"I already told you…"

His voiced joined in, drowning out her own, mimicking her. "The only question that's stupid is the one that's never asked." He stood silent. "What are you doing?"

"Just taking notes."

"But you've already got my notes, the forensic reports, autopsy…"

"Yes, but they cannot possibly tell me everything about a crime scene, about the crime itself."

"Christ, maybe I understood where you were coming from in the car, but I sure as hell don't understand this."

"No one asked you to," Cat said, shaking her ballpoint wildly. "Blasted thing, great place for it to run out of ink." She fumbled, dropping the pen on the ground.

As she stooped to pick it up, something out of the ordinary caught her eye. A tiny black plastic point was sticking out of the clay-like California dirt. "What do we have here?" she asked herself as she rummaged through the bottom of her tote to find tweezers. She removed them from a clear plastic casing and picked up the black object, placing it in a plastic Ziploc bag she also produced from her tote.

"You always this prepared?" he said cynically.

"In forensic medicine, you consider every eventuality, detective, you should know that."

"What the hell is it?"

Sealing the plastic bag, she said, "Appears to be a panel of some sort, maybe the back of a cell phone, pager perhaps. I can't really tell. I'll have to get it back to the lab."

"You think it might be important?"

"With the little we have to go on right now, everything is important."

McGregor simply rolled his eyes.

Another half hour of photographing, drawing, and retracing steps and they were done. The lab was waiting.

EIGHT

He that will learn to pray, let him go to sea.
—**George Herbert**, *Jacula Prudentum*

At first no one noticed the seagulls pecking at something far out at sea. Riptides in California played havoc with swimmers, but even those who braved the deepest water paid no attention. Doheny State Beach was filled with the laughter, shouts, and fun of an idyllic summer. Cool sand, bright sun, hot bodies. Eleven-year-old boys' mouths fell open at the sight of well-endowed girls in bikinis strolling by.

"Wow, check out the boobs on her, will ya?" one beefy carrot-top kid said, elbowing his scrawny buddy, Matt. Matt seemed not to care, his eyes glued to that thing out in the water. It had been there for a long time, slowly being pushed in by set upon set of waves, seagulls busy pecking at it, squawking as they made their nosedive descents.

"What do you think that is?" He elbowed Leroy back, with equal force.

"Who cares? How can you even stare at the ocean when there's so much to stare at here?" Leroy gawked at another set of hooters bouncing by. "My dad says when I get married to find a girl with a 36C chest. Dad says that's the perfect size. Just big enough to lull ya to sleep at night, not big enough to sag…"

"Is that all you ever think about?"

"Look, just 'cause you haven't reached your sexual peek yet doesn't mean I have to turn my hormones off."

"I just get so sick of hearing you. That's all you ever talk about."

"So you got a problem with that, fart face?" Leroy picked up a handful of sand and rubbed it into Matt's hair. "Fart face, fart face."

Matt jumped up, shaking the sand out of his hair like a wild man. "Shit. Look what you did!" His hands were frantic, batting against his forehead back and forth. "I'm gonna have to go wash off."

"Go ahead, I'll be waiting with more sand when you get back," Leroy said mockingly. He was the heavier of them; he used his size like a weapon. Realizing the other kids didn't like his zits or his hair color, he had tried to be the class clown but hadn't been all that funny. Now he simply resorted to a combination of bully tactics and pranks to accomplish his means. Matt was his best friend. His only friend.

Matt wrenched his boogie board out of the wet sand and started paddling out. *Thanks, buddy*, he thought, *now I've got a reason to go check that thing out.*

"I'll be back in twenty minutes," he shouted over his shoulder.

The surf was no rougher than usual, the waves cresting just over a foot. The Pacific was deep and blue and cold, but Matt liked it. He'd seen *Jaws* twenty-three times, but the thought of a shark never frightened him. Rather, the prospect of sharing the water with a creature that had lived for millions of years fascinated him. A shark was a living dinosaur, his teacher, Mrs. Higgins, had said, and he believed her.

Gulls continued to nosedive the object, their shrill cries filling the ocean air. Looking back to shore, he could see Leroy sitting there, not much bigger than a pin dot. He waved back to the shore, wondering if his buddy could see him. A toothpick arm waving back was his response. *Never been out this far before*, Matt thought. *Now Leroy won't give me any crap the rest of the day. Wonder what it could be. Dead seal maybe? Dolphin that got tangled in a fisherman's met?*

As Matt got closer to the body, a strange sense of peril washed over him. Stomach tightened in a vise grip, horrible thoughts tore through his mind. He felt like running but knew there was nowhere to go. Carefully, he tucked his left leg up on the board, then his right, careful not to cause a ripple in the water. Laughing at himself, he still couldn't shake the feeling.

It was as if he knew he should not be here.

In this place.

Alone.

Still, the mystery of what was floating beckoned him. Yanking up his surfer shorts, he gulped down saliva caught in his throat, regaining his courage.

Within twenty feet of it now, his arms ached from paddling, his muscles feeling like they were filled with acid. "Damned seagulls, get away." He waved his arms, thinking the birds might poop on him. He was on the object now; couldn't tell what it was. All bloated, torn up, mangled. Guts floating on top of the water, bleached white by the ocean's tide. Whatever it was had been ripped apart a bit further by the seagulls.

Inhaling a deep breath, he reached over and put one hand on the mass. Reacting to his touch, the bulbous mass rolled over on itself.

A piercing scream escaped from Matt Bender's lungs, the carnage now evident. Eyes missing from a cavity in the face, mouth gaping open. It hadn't been a seal floating.

It was a girl.

And she was dead.

*   *   *   *   *

"How's the Aromatic Shrimp?" McGregor asked, his face glued to the menu. "Very good, sir. House special. Crispy shrimp in special hot sauce flavored with ginger, garlic, and cooked with chopped green onion."

"That sounds good. I'll have that." He folded his menu and gave it to the diminutive woman.

"And I'll have the Shanghai Duck," Cat said, doing the same.

"Anything to drink?"

"Two iced teas." McGregor looked at Cat for approval, which she gave.

The food arrived within ten minutes. Cat's entree was delicious, duck smothered with a dark sauce and shredded green onions. On the side came a plate of Chinese pancakes, which she eagerly dug into.

"Hey, I thought with the way you looked you'd have a salad."

"I didn't see any salads on the menu, did you?" she asked rhetorically. "And, besides, Chinese food is my favorite."

Cat watched as McGregor's big burly hands busied themselves with the chopsticks. She could see he was no expert, but he was gainfully making an effort with them, perhaps for her. The more she got to know McGregor, the more she liked him. He had been weathered by the job, but somehow that made him more personable, honest. They ate in silence.

"How is it?" Cat asked.

"Great," McGregor said, shoving another bright pink shrimp into his mouth. "And yours?"

"Can't say I've had better."

The moment was interrupted by a whirring, then chirping sound. McGregor's cell phone. Quickly putting down the chopsticks, he checked his text messages. "Office."

In one fluid motion he was up from the table. "I'll be back. I've got to call them."

She watched him disappear toward the back of the restaurant, then reappear a minute later, already in a jog.

"Come on, we gotta go," he shouted her way.

"What is it?"

"We got another body. They think it's our boy."

Cat was up as quickly as she could be, left thirty bucks on the table. "Where?"

"Doheny State Beach."

"Is it the Bennett girl?"

McGregor shook his head. "Don't know." His eyes flashed a steely light.

Two minutes later, McGregor and Cat were on the freeway, a dome light flashing. McGregor was replaying the telephone conversation in his head, upset and agitated.

"God," Cat said, "another one."

"Second one in two weeks. No doubt, if it's our guy, he's getting angrier."

"Or bolder."

"Or both," McGregor surmised.

"They found her buried on the beach?" Cat was sure before this day was over, she'd have more questions than answers. This was only the first.

"Naw, she washed up." McGregor reconsidered his words. "Well, some little kid found her floating, then she washed up."

The car soared along doing eighty-five down the 405 Freeway, then on to Interstate 5. It was the second time today they had come in this direction, though at this speed Cat barely recognized anything. Immediately in front of them some little old lady stomped on the brakes. McGregor laid on the horn, swerving the car to the left in one nonstop motion, just in time to miss the other car's back fender by inches. Cat sucked in hard and felt her body brace for impact. It never came.

"Freakin' Seizure World drivers," McGregor hollered back, referring to the blue-haired elderly drivers—residents of Leisure World—that made driving hell in this town.

"Jesus Christ, can't you slow down a little?" Cat cringed at the thought of what could have just happened.

McGregor just kept driving.

"It's not like the body is going anywhere."

"Look, you don't get it do you. Craig's down there, his eyes all over my case."

Cat looked at him like he was crazy. "Who in the hell is that?"

"Los Angeles FBI punk named Craig Gray. Had the pleasure of meeting the little prick once. He's so slimy he made me want to vomit on myself, just so I could get the taste of him outta my mouth."

"That's nice." Cat tried not to pay attention to the road.

"Let's just say the guy is oozing so much slime that he drinks motor oil for breakfast."

"What's he doing involved in the case?"

"Someone had to have called him in."

"Who?"

"Hell if I know, but I damned well aim to find out."

Cat let the rest of the conversation ride, seeing McGregor appeared more provoked as they got closer to the beach. Off the freeway now, they swung a right on Crown Valley Parkway, headed up a hill, then right on Niguel Road.

McGregor glanced over, caught a glimmer of excitement in Cat's eyes. Her right hand was rubbing the black valise that never seemed to be far from her side.

"How much farther?"

"Just a few minutes more." They were on Pacific Coast Highway, commonly called PCH, careening toward Dana Point Harbor, then a quick left and they were at the beach.

McGregor almost plowed through the parking gate, stopping with a screech.

"Dammit, police business!" he shouted, flashing his ID at the parking attendant, who quickly raised the gate, calling a "sorry" as they sped through.

As Cat looked around, people were leaving the beach in droves, packing coolers, beach chairs, umbrellas in the back of minivans, trucks, cars. Cat got out and started toward the beach. A muumuu-clad woman grabbed her arm. "I wouldn't go down there, miss. They found"—she gulped hard—"a body."

"I know, we're here on police business," Cat said matter-of-factly. The woman gave a curious look, cocking her head to the left, then frowned.

"Hope you didn't eat lunch before you came, 'cause if you did you're gonna lose it." The woman walked away, ushering her bawling young children ahead of her in a protective gesture.

As expected, the beach was deserted but for one area, which was swarming with cops. McGregor was ten paces ahead, moving in a much too deliberate jog. Cat knew he was determined not to let any LA agent steal this case.

After four difficult strides in the sand, which felt like quicksand, Cat swept her shoes off in one quick, effortless motion. Recognizing Richmond, she walked over to where he stood. The chief wore a navy suit, dress shoes, a tie—clearly out of place at the beach. He was sweating profusely, beads pouring down his forehead, rolling to a stop at his too-tight collar.

Beside him, dressed in beige baggy chinos, a white oxford shirt with blue ink stains on one pocket, and white canvas sneakers, stood a slim, pretentious man she did not recognize. He appeared as if he had just gotten out of the shower, shirt clinging to his long, lanky limbs, long hair greased straight back in a ponytail. Behind round silver-framed glasses, the man watched Cat with startling green eyes, set off by long black lashes and arched bushy brows. Speaking in a resonant baritone, he leaned forward and presented his hand. "Dr. Catherine Powers, I presume?"

"Yes, and who might you be?"

Chief Richmond interjected. "Cat, this is Craig Gray, field agent FBI, Los Angeles."

Cat shook his hand, noting the man's apparent charm, which came without trying. He appeared to be genuinely taken with her. "I am very pleased to meet you. I've read some of your published work in the *Journal of American Medicine*." Eleven months ago Cat had written a piece on the aberration of criminal violent behavior and CAT scan abnormalities in the cerebral cortex. Much of the work, the theory even, was experimental, but it raised the eyes and ears of many experts to the possibility of an organic correlation to violence.

"Thank you," she said, appearing polite. Shaking this guy's hands gave her the creeps. Outward appearances could be deceiving, Cat concluded.

"I see you've met Mr. Gray," McGregor said, cynicism in each syllable. Agent Gray merely nodded in McGregor's direction, wearing a pasted frozen smile. Cat thought of McGregor belting this slime bucket in the face. It made her smile inside. It was not her intent to dance around another forensic pathologist from the FBI's LA office. She did not want to bow and scrape to the local boys or become involved in some local feud between warring FBI factions. Gray's loss was her gain; she had been given carte blanche on this case, and she wasn't about to have the local boys interfere.

Sensing the hostile undercurrent between Gray and McGregor, Chief Richmond interrupted. "The body is over here." Instinctively, he pulled a handkerchief out of his pocket, dabbed a big swab of Vicks under his nostrils, and covered his mouth and nose. Cat did the same.

A photographer hovered, snapping off photos of the body at every angle. On a landing about 150 feet away, a crowd of curious onlookers stood, pointing, some of them snapping pictures of their own. It never amazed Cat, the depths of some people's morbid curiosity.

A Channel 2 mobile news van pulled into the parking lot; Cat could see the van's live feed antenna above the cars. She glanced at her watch: 3:30. *Perfect*, she thought with a groan. *Just time enough to make the four o'clock news.*

She shouted at the plainclothes officers in the area. "Get those people out of here. And keep the media back. I want them out of my way." Officers in blue corralled the crowd back. They halted the media team emerging from the Channel 2 van. They set up a media and crowd area 100 feet back from the body.

Gray leaned over and whispered in Cat's ear as she knelt beside the body, the stench far worse than that of a normal decaying body. "You got a public relations problem with this case? The media has a right to know."

"The media doesn't have a right to anything until I see it first, and as far as my having a public relations problem with this case, I don't. I just have work to do, and I can't do it very well with people like you gawking over my shoulder." She was honestly used to having people working close by, but something about Gray unnerved her.

Tall and straight, built like a freight train, a man dipped under the yellow crime scene tape and approached rapidly. He took her hand and pumped it hard, his succotash-shaped mustache bobbing up and down as he spoke. "Mrs. Powers, oh, pardon me, Dr. Powers, I am Dana Point Mayor Lewis Needleman." He sounded out of breath. "I can assure you, we've never had anything in this city like this before." He raised his arms high above his shoulders, as if Cat hadn't taken in the scenic seaside town. "But let me tell you, if you need anything—anything at all," he said with an obvious sexual connotation, "you just let me know."

He leaned over and gave her his card. Taking one glance at the body, it was plain he couldn't accept the fact that what he was looking at was once a human being. The sight was jarring. Ever the politician, he wheeled around on his heels, avoiding the horrific sight. Raising his head, he waved at the onlookers, making sure they could see that he, Mayor Lewis Needleman, had everything under control.

Cat put the card in her pocket and disregarded the remainder of the grandstanding. "Has anyone touched the body?"

Richardson responded. "Lifeguards helped bring it in, but no one's touched it since it hit the beach."

"Good, would you gentlemen mind stepping back? I have work to do."

The men did as she asked.

This girl, who had no name except Jane Doe right now, had been in the water for some time. Adiponecrosis, the body's mechanism for breaking down fatty tissues, had started. The result of this process, a waxy yellowish substance, filled the girl's abdomen. Adipocere had started to replace the muscles. Her face showed telltale decay signs from being in the water. Grotesque, irregular features made up the bulk of it. Cat consciously reminded herself that this girl once had a face.

She felt the afternoon sun beat down, the humidity burdensome at 80 percent. Removing her navy blue jacket, she tied it around her waist, swatting at flies. Out of her valise she pulled tweezers, scalpel, vials, and some other instruments of her trade. Cat worked quickly over the victim, trying not to look at the girl's face, or what was left of it. No doubt, whoever this was, or had once been, she had been pretty. The water-bloated body still revealed slender fingers, delicate hands, small wrists.

Cat's anger grew seeing this brutalization. Whatever mindless, satanic creature had done this, she meant to find him. The wounds he had inflicted were somewhat the same as before. The girl's sternum had been ripped with vertical slashes, some of them two, three inches long. The body had long since stopped bleeding. Instead, the wounds splayed open to the hot sun, baking. To the face, the damage was severe; the girl's teeth, gums, and bones around the mouth were exposed. Seawater had collected where her eyes should have been. From the nose, a tar-like slick. Cat was angry. This was someone's daughter, someone's baby.

"Sweet Jesus," she said to herself.

Looking over her shoulder from a kneeling position, Cat saw news trucks gathering, the crowd growing, appearing now like vultures. By now the word was out on the street, the story making the four o'clock news. She could almost hear the Channel 2 anchor's drone: "*Authorities have located yet another young woman's body, an apparent victim of the Burning Man. This is the fourth victim in as many weeks, the first in Dana Point. Facts are sketchy, but lifeguards on the scene tell us that a young boy paddled out in the surf and found the woman floating facedown. Her identity remains a mystery. This victim displays the same mutilations as the others, multiple stab wounds, the use of acid. As with the others, the killer has gotten away scot-free, and authorities don't have a clue to his identity. One thing is certain. The women of Orange County are under siege. This coldhearted killer will kill again and again until he himself is killed.*"

Fact of the matter was California had never been at a loss for serial killers. Charles Manson, Ed Kemper, Herbert Mullin had all had their particular brand of madness hatched in this state.

The heat was oppressive. Cat's sweat-drenched hair hung in her face, clung to her forehead.

McGregor approached after questioning the kid. "We got a friggin' circus up there," he said, seeing what she saw. "It's a damned zoo." He looked at the body closely. "Looks like more damage than the others?"

"Yes. Ligature tears in the skin, here and here." Cat pointed to the swollen corpse's wrists and heels. Dark discolorations surrounded the areas.

"Here too?" McGregor pointed to a dark circle surrounding the neck, which was mostly hidden by the victim's damp hair.

"Yes." Cat nodded. "It appears that, as well as escalating the number of attacks, he is escalating their violence."

"Any idea of her age?"

"It's really hard to tell. She's been in the water for some time," Cat replied, scraping out what was under the nails into a glass vial. She frowned. "Whatever there was under here, the ocean's already eaten up and spit out."

"It's our guy, huh?"

"Appears to be, unless we have a copycat. But I don't think so; the lacerations are almost identically placed. That information has not been released to the press. There is no way a copycat could know."

Cat looked at McGregor's eyes. They appeared competent and in charge, but worried. "What is it?"

"This isn't Carrie Ann Bennett. Not unless she had a dye job."

"What?" Cat stopped what she was doing.

McGregor stood up, turned, and squinted at the sinking sun. "Carrie Ann Bennett was a brunette."

"And this body's been floating way too long."

NINE

From a distance, he watched and waited. Part of the ebbing sameness of bodies, he was one of them and yet not.

Cat Powers had arrived. She was tending to the girl, to his patient. He appreciated her assistance. It was nice to have someone competent around.

Men overdressed for the beach, obviously law enforcement, backed off from the body as her stench blew upwind.

Focusing his attention back on Powers, he noticed she was indeed a fine specimen of a woman. Even kneeling, he could tell her legs were long and lean, auburn hair pulled up. She tucked a stray wisp over her left ear.

How alluring.

This woman coming all this way for me.

He stared harder at her, etching every nuance of her into his mind, her movements, her coloring.

Closing his eyes, he even caught a whisper of her voice, yes, just a bit. Sweet, melodic…he had to stop himself from smiling.

From the way she tended to his patient, he could tell she was a compassionate woman. Graceful. Beautiful. Even more so than the black-and-white newsprint photos dared portray.

He was sure now.

She was worthy.

TEN

Our deeds determine us,
As much as we determine our deeds.
—**George Eliot**, *Adam Bede*

The autopsies were becoming routine. That scared Cat. It meant the killer was getting better at his work. It meant she was numbing to it.

This time the recording camera's whirl was joined by lights that beckoned from an overhead viewing area. Standing in front of four rows of seats were Chief Richmond, agents McGregor and Gray, Director Sanchez, and, for some reason, Mayor Needleman. Inside two hours of retrieving evidence from the body, Cat was standing over a stainless-steel table. To her left, a gleaming stainless-steel scale; above her important men waited for the autopsy to begin.

"We meet again, Dr. Powers," Conrad said smoothly as he entered the room. His eyes roamed hers, then her torso, down to her feet, and back up to her eyes. "I see our guests have arrived." He looked up to the viewing gallery, his lips curled in an odd grin.

"You invited them?" Cat tried not to sound angry, but it was difficult.

"Yes, I did." He glared at her, then the smile returned. It was immediately evident that the man felt at home here. "Shall we begin?"

Cat nodded, holding her gloved hands up, and let her anger go, reciting the standard jargon. Time of day, tag number, age, height, weight, sex, the victim's name, which at the moment was Jane Doe. Like the others the cuts were clean, not jagged, made with an extremely sharp knife of some kind, the blade perhaps an inch or so long. The cuts ran in a vertical pattern over the anterior portion of the body, bare horizontal rents sometimes intersecting like some bizarre crossword puzzle. The wounds were not hacks, nor placed randomly. Each one was precise, often repeating itself on both the left and right sides, as if the killer had slashed one side, held the body to a mirror, and the identical wounds had magically appeared on the corpse's other side. After close scrutiny of the wounds, Cat could tell sulfuric acid had been used; the tissue deep in each wound had been eaten away. Occasionally, however, there was a laceration that appeared to be only that, just a laceration, as if the killer had been torn between using the acid and a slow painful death due to blood loss.

Each of Cat's findings was recorded, the camera zooming in and out as needed. Again, the largest wound appeared to be a ventral wound to the abdomen. Cat looked closely at this area and determined the wound was placed like the others, just above the haustra of the ascending colon, not deep enough to penetrate, although the fish had chewed their way through.

From above, Cat could hear the occasional gasps as she examined, dictating her findings. The agents had seen their share of autopsies, but it was clear Needleman had not. "Bend at the knees if you start to go," she could faintly hear McGregor coaching the politician, who was visibly sweating through a tasteless blue and white striped seersucker suit.

There were no scars, tattoos, moles, or other obvious identifying scars on the victim. A detailed external examination of the genitals revealed no rape or sexual assault. Fluids were withdrawn, swabs taken and sent off to toxicology.

The victim's breasts were speckled with freckles in a star array, much like the Big Dipper. This provided little, if any, help in finding out who Jane Doe was. But it was the only thing Cat had to work with. Maybe it would be enough to help her identify this Jane Doe.

Cat took her time, trying not to feel rushed, despite six pairs of eyes watching her. In a Jane Doe autopsy, missing just one detail could mean the difference between a victim being identified, with a proper burial, and a pauper's funeral. This girl deserved a proper resting place, given the sheer terror in which she died.

Carefully, Cat drew a scalpel down the center of Jane Doe's blue-white breasts. The skin parted, revealing the pink muscle of the pectoralis major. Cat cut a Y-shaped incision, as she had a thousand times before, down the midsection. Drawing the flaps back, she cut through the ribs, lifting out the breast plate onto the stainless-steel table to her right. Then she put her hands into the body, working below the sternum, as she continued to whisper into the microphone.

The internal organs, first from the chest cavity, then the lower abdomen, finally the pelvic area, Cat meticulously removed and weighed. She removed a thin tissue from each after taking its weight. Like the external examination, the internal prodding revealed no evidence of voluntary sex or sexual assault.

Coming upon the stomach, she carefully analyzed the contents for excessive fluids, a sign the girl drowned. As she expected, Jane Doe had not drowned.

Blood, semen, and hair were collected and sent to the FBI's labs of DNA typing. The bladder was removed and sent to toxicology. It would reveal if the killer had pumped Jane Doe full of drugs, such as barbiturates or street drugs, prior to her untimely death. From the postmortem bruises to the wrists, ankles, and neck, Cat suspected they would find no drugs in this girl. The Burning Man had wanted her very much awake.

Cat moved the young woman's head. Leaning over the girl's lifeless eye sockets, she found petechiae in her conjunctiva. The tiny red and purple spots to the mucous membrane that lined the inside of the lids revealed that Jane Doe had been strangled or choked during the final minutes of her life. This went hand-in-hand with the deep, penetrating discoloration to the neck, Cat thought. Probably tied her down to something.

Cat's fingers probed the waxy pale body's scalp, her eyes just inches away. "I've got something here. Take a look." She parted the hair.

Dr. Conrad James leaned closer. "What is it?"

"You tell me."

"Appears to be a letter carved into her head."

They both looked down at the letter "I."

"He's sending us a message."

"How do you get that from just one carving? He might not even have intended to make a letter, just came out that way."

"Come on, McGregor. Most serial killers either take something or leave something. This guy's not a trophy collector, at least not as far as I can see. So what's the next best thing? He leaves us something. Can't you see it? He wants us to know him. He wants recognition for his actions. He wants the media attention. He likes the media circus."

From the courses she had taught in Applied Criminal Psychology, Cat could tell there was step-by-step escalation to this killer's fantasy. She wondered if this case was typical, if those escalations were fueled by childhood physical abuse from a person in a position of trust, usually a parent, relative, coach, or teacher. She sensed the fantasy was not driven by pornography or macabre experimentation on animals. No, from the looks of it, this man had no need to experiment on animals; he was cutting people for a living every day. In all this, the need for recognition was dominant and overriding. He'd gotten the nerve to face what he really wanted to do: to send a message to the FBI. To her.

"Don't you see, if you break down the components of this latest crime…" She hesitated, choosing her words carefully. "If you break it down, pre- and post-offensive behavior, the vast majority of the mutilation is premortem, before death. He watches them cry out while they are alive; his motive is to inflict pain. Their screams are like a symphony to him, and he is the maestro. He wants us to share his work, wants us to know."

"Come on, Cat, we won't know till we get another body."

"I'm telling you, I've dealt with this type before. If you want to understand the craftsman, take a look at his work. This latest body is a refinement of his style, the ligature bruises."

She padded up and down the floor. "Equally significant is the way he disposes of the bodies. The first three were dumped out in the middle of nowhere for the animals to get them. This latest one was dumped in the sea. All the corpses have been left out in the open. This is another signal to us, that he wants us to know him. He makes no effort to bury them. He treats the bodies with no respect. He is taunting us."

"You're getting too tied up in this." McGregor rolled his eyes and went to get coffee. Once this woman had her mind set on something, he knew there was no turning back.

"No. I'm not. I'm telling you. He is sharing a piece of himself with us, with me."

The words left a bad taste in her mouth.

"And he is watching."

ELEVEN

Skepticism is the first step toward truth.
—**Denis Diderot**, *Pensées Philosophiques*

Chief Richmond stood in front of the 40-foot-deep room, the camera bulbs blinding his vision. A barrage of questions came at him like machinegun fire. God, he hated the media, hated the way their concerns, questions, became paramount, at least in their own minds. Hated the fact that clips from this briefing would likely appear on *Extra* or one of those sleazy tabloid shows his wife couldn't get enough of.

From what he had seen of the four o'clock newsreels, speculation was already running rampant about who the girl was, that there was a copycat killer who had changed the MO just slightly. One reporter even stated that the killer's media tag should be changed to reflect the escalation in violence, "the once a week killer." As promised, the department delivered on its guarantee of an eight o'clock briefing.

Raising his hand, Richmond stated that questions should be held till the end of the briefing. He introduced McGregor and Stevenson and briefly outlined the case for the media.

An overly ambitious reporter jumped up, hair and makeup primed for the spotlights. "What can you tell us about this victim?"

"I'll turn that question over to Dr. Powers," he said, stepping off the podium.

Cat stepped up to the plate, watching the room now, bodies silhouetted against harsh lights. Her auburn highlights were set off by the glow, yet the gold-rimmed glasses could not hide her exhaustion. Still, she appeared proficient, masterful, in her description of the investigation. Purposefully, she made no mention of the ligature bruises. She also did not disclose the lacerations' exact placement.

Cat was careful.

She listed the evidence, keeping the reporter focused on the Burning Man investigation while two plainclothes officers surveyed the room. From Cat's estimation, the killer would be here. The officers scanned the faces. None looked out of place; none squirmed or looked away as Cat spoke. She squinted, trying to get a read on whether the plainclothes guys had anything. Liston shrugged his shoulders.

Yet she knew he was here.

"Dr. Powers, Dr. Powers," an older man called out as he stood up, the end of his pen pressing against his lower lip. He looked like someone out of a Norman Rockwell painting. Snow-white hair, ruddy checks. His chest was rising and falling, as if he had run a marathon. "Do we know anything about the killer yet?"

"Not much. We believe he is a white male in his late twenties to early fifties, likely employed in some capacity in the medical profession. A fit man, though not overly large. He takes good care of himself. He is a control fre—" Cat chose her words conscientiously, mindful that the wrong word could set him off. "He is domineering. He is a man of power, of position."

"What can you tell us of the latest victim?"

"Right now we don't have a name. Jane Doe appears to be slim, attractive, early twenties. We are asking anyone who might have a friend or relative missing that fits that description to contact us right away. The number should be on your screen. I know it's not much but that's all I have."

As Cat talked, she scrutinized the faces in the crowd, looking for someone who fit the killer's description. It was impossible. Hell, the reporter who fired the last question at her fit it. They all did. When the conference was over, she stationed herself to the side of the room, close to the back door, watching men as they funneled out. The plainclothes guys mixed with the crowd but looked as befuddled as she felt. She was pissed.

They didn't have anything concrete on this guy.

Not anything.

As a man moved through the crowd to the door, his eyes would not meet her gaze. He fit the profile, mid-forties, fit, white, wearing expensive Italian shoes. He was wearing a Yankees baseball cap, pulled down over his face. As he turned to go, she glimpsed just a bit of his hair showing from under the cap. At that instant Cat's instincts screamed *it's him!* She lurched across the room, drawing her firearm from its holster in one seamless motion. Her mind was spinning at the possibility of the guy bolting.

As she grabbed his arm, he gasped. The plainclothes guys were walking over chairs as if they were water, crashing through the furniture.

"What?" The man jerked his arm.

She held on. "You knew them."

He turned away from her now, looking over her shoulder, eyes fixated on the door. "I what?"

"You knew them."

"I've got to go."

The plainclothes cops worked their way through the crowd. Two people stopped at the door, turned at the commotion.

The man gathered himself up, preparing to speak.

For the first time, he looked at her. A steely stare. He looked through her eyes, not at them. It gave her the creeps. His eyes were a strange shade of hazel that seemed out of place with the rest of his coloring, his hair dark—almost black. This too did not fit with his pale skin.

"I am an admirer of your work," he said coolly. "Nothing more."

She pulled him off to the side.

"You know who I am?"

"Doesn't everyone who is here?" he mocked. "You are the matchless Dr. Catherine Powers." He used her name for the first time. "You are the FBI's chief forensic pathologist, I believe with the Behavioral Sciences Unit, out of Quantico, Virginia." Neither cocky nor arrogant, each word was controlled, delivered in a deep baritone. This man was cool and well-spoken.

He didn't seem to hear them, two plainclothes surging up on him from behind.

"What is it?" one of them said, out of breath.

She did not reply. Rather, she concentrated on the man.

The first thing that struck her was how ordinary he appeared. Below the baseball cap, trimmed dark hair, clean shaven, oxford shirt. Yet he was strange. The way he looked at her, studied her. The color of his eyes.

"We were just having a conversation," she said to the agents, her gaze never leaving his. They backed off.

She cocked her head to one side. He did the same. He had the weirdest smirk, not quite a smile, not a frown, but something in between as he looked at her as if she were a specimen butterfly he had just pegged to a corkboard.

Touching him, she was suddenly aware of a strange intimacy. He held her in it, as he wanted to. "You are quite beautiful."

She did not speak.

"I know of you by reputation. Reputation as the best."

"You knew them."

"Knew who?" He remained in control, though clearly he was becoming impatient with her questioning. "To whom are you referring?"

"The girls."

"I have absolutely no idea what you are talking about." He gestured toward the door. "Now, I would like to stay to chat, but I have an appointment." He glanced at his watch, breaking eye contact with her for the first time.

Cat felt like she had been in a trance, her head fogged over, her thoughts not right.

As he tried to pull away, she could feel his bicep flex. Hard, rigid, yet smooth, like the man himself.

She looked around at McGregor, who was talking to one of the plainclothes guys, then turned back to this man. She felt herself smile at him. He smiled back.

"I have every intention of finding him," she said.

His arm twitched.

"I am sure you do." His words were confident, monotone.

He paused. "Do you have any theories about why they were killed?"

"Why don't you tell me?" she challenged him at his own charade.

"I have no idea what you are talking about."

"Tell me about Nancy Marsh. Was she some girl you picked out in the crowd, or did you know her?"

"This is ridiculous," he said, his anger growing. He tried to pull away. Then, as quickly as the anger came, it dissipated, replaced again by the country gentleman. "I know I can trust you, doctor. I have seen your work."

She shivered, watching his transformation.

He stared at her lips, mouth. "Perhaps we will meet again." He gave her an intense, sincere look. Began to move away.

"I'm sorry, I didn't get your name."

"My name is not important," he said over his shoulder as he walked away.

It was as if she were caught in a nightmare with not a lick of peace. Cat was drained by the day's events, yet as she ambled into her hotel lobby, a reporter was on her.

"Doctor, doctor, what is the connection between the victims? Did they know each other? Has the FBI turned up any leads on the assailant?"

Assailant, that was a nice word for a madman, she thought.

The questions persisted, this man in his mid-fifties lapping at her feet like a puppy.

"You know, I've had a very long day. I have no intention of giving an interview." She tucked her black valise close to her chest, her heels clicking faster on the beige marble floor.

The man would not take no for an answer.

She tried to be pleasant, offer the idiot an alternative. "Perhaps if you leave your card with the front desk, I can call you in the morning."

Still not good enough. Typically reporters with any heart let her be after a day like today. She had been going nonstop since seven, with barely a break to use the bathroom.

She got a good look at him as he squared off in front of her like a high school quarterback waiting for a delayed hit. Tall and rangy, a modest build, disproportionately enormous hands. She recognized him from the press conference.

"*OC Metro* magazine, isn't it?"

"Very observant." He seemed fascinated by her observation, or perhaps that he was the object of that observation. Either way, she had no intention of answering his questions.

She stopped in her tracks. "As you can see," she glanced at his press pass, dangling like a dog tag, "Cooper, is it? I am very tired. When I'm tired, I turn real bitchy, you get my drift? So unless you'd like your press credentials suspended for any future press conferences I hold on this case, I suggest you get out of my way."

"Come on, doc. Not everything's so black-and-white. The public's got a right to know. You up for dinner?" He spoke to her as if they had known each other all their lives; she was taken aback by it.

"What?"

"You do look beat, worse than my kid sister when we used to use her for defensive football practice. She made for a great battering ram and all." He grinned in her direction, trying to provoke a smile. There was something disarming in his demeanor, but she couldn't put her finger on it.

"What in God's green earth are you talking about?"

"Come on, sis. I'm harmless. A big puppy dog. And you look like hell warmed over. Haven't eaten a decent thing all day, have you?"

He was reading her mind, though she didn't want him to know it.

"I have work to do." She tried to step around him, but he rolled left, sensing her direction.

"Very good, and do you play tackle too?"

"Let me take you to dinner, doc."

"Absolutely not. I have a number of rules I live by." She stopped, remembering his name. "Cooper, first, I don't buddy up to reporters, no matter how charming or 'harmless' they are. Second, I don't have dinner with strange men I hardly know. And third," she patted her firearm, holstered beneath her shoulder, "if you don't get the hell out of my way, you're going to meet Clarence here. Do I make myself clear?"

The man stepped to the side, scratching his head. "Jesus, just trying to be friendly and all."

She ignored him and walked toward the elevator. In the aftermath of the encounter, Cat thought *what an odd man*. Did he honestly believe she would grant him an interview in the middle of this investigation? She was stunned by his audacity, his informality. Learning more and more about the Burning Man, she felt herself disengaging from any intimate contact with men. It had always been this way.

At this point, relationships seemed neither important nor particularly fulfilling.

Her life was systematized. Get the call, a plane flight to Anywhere USA, then the analysis, the inevitable body trail. Although she wished it were not so, she was married to her work. There had to be a release for her at some point. Right now, she did not know what that might be.

Inside, her emotions felt all twisted up.

When she got inside Room 428, she didn't turn on the lights, didn't check her messages, didn't turn down the bed.

Instead, in the semidarkness, she walked through the room, poured a glass of merlot from the wet bar, and sat down in a wing chair facing a big window. The curtains were open. The window loomed in front of her—a big unfamiliar black void, a few stars from apartments and high-rises here and there.

Kicking off her shoes, she curled her feet up under her, leaning back, letting the wine fall down her throat. Hoping it would ease her nerves. Wincing, she could feel the throbbing over her left temple, pain down toward her jaw. She tried to draw a breath. See if it would help. It didn't.

Close your eyes.

When she opened them, she knew tonight would be no different than before. As she expected, the need to know more rose up in her. Sometimes this came early in a case, sometimes not at all. She didn't know. She only knew it would last till sunlight, as it had done fifteen years ago—when she had her first date with a serial killer.

<hr />

Placing a manila folder on the immaculate hotel desk, she opened her laptop. No death certificates here, just death faces—fanned out across the laminated desktop. Rubbing her eyes, she took a sip of wine, wishing the fluid would wash away her tension. The girls' faces, her headache. She was tormented by these girls' looks, but more so because they were all someone's daughter.

"I'm a professional," she said, trying to convince herself. "What am I missing?"

She read her notes, wanting something to develop. Nothing came but flashes of waxy lifeless bodies.

Then a new image.

A silhouette of a well-tailored dark-suited man. Standing straight. Looming over something. *Can't make out the details.* A flash of light washed over him just as she glimpsed a gentle, loving, maddening mouth…a smile.

Memories stirred. Cat stifled a gasp. She had seen that smile before. But where? She closed her eyes again and the vision returned. Through gritted teeth, a clenched jaw, she wanted to remember. "Come on, dammit, focus," she said out loud, surprised at the sound of her own voice. In her mind, the vision came closer—closer on the mouth. His lips moving, tongue licking them. He was speaking to her but there was no sound. A message she could not decipher.

Hot confusion, like the waking panic of a nightmare. It was always like this. Fluttering in her belly, nerves like insect wings. The mouth was moving, speaking, but no voice. Cat opened her eyes. A chill of panic flooded her, the panic of not knowing what is real and what isn't.

Cat pushed back from the table, massaged her closed eyelids with her thumb and index finger. When she opened her eyes, they felt red, her body numb. She sat heavily for a while, staring out the window. She had learned to live with the episodes, as she called them, learning that they did not mean she was any less of a woman, but perhaps more of one. She used her sixth sense sparingly. Always in private, never revealing it to anyone else. It always came at times like this, when she was so exhausted she could hardly think. Cat typed what she remembered of the vision into her laptop notes.

She stretched her legs and yawned. Lying out on the bed, she stared at the ceiling. "Time to get some sleep," she said to herself as if she were a child, as if she were Joey. It was too late to call him tonight. In spite of her discipline and steady resolve, Cat knew there would be no sleep tonight. The illusion of control had a crack, and it all might come crashing down.

TWELVE

Know how sublime a thing it is
To suffer and be strong.
—**Henry Wadsworth Longfellow**, *"The Light of the Stars"*

Running would be good for her she decided, despite the kink in her back. It was a bright, glorious day, the sun making her eyes squint. She had gotten just two hours' sleep, but she would not let it slow her down. Not today. There was too much to do.

Cat donned a bright red sweatshirt and sweatpants one size too big, the way she liked them. Lacing up her running shoes, she was on Main Street in Irvine, heading south, within five minutes.

She was right. Running felt good. Exhilarating. By the time she had done a mile, she had put a few things together. For the first time, she was able to correlate a possible connection between the first victim and the killer.

Four weeks ago, Nancy Marsh had been killed. Her father was a respected, prominent doctor. Cat firmly believed that the killer had medical training. There was no way the average layperson would know enough about anatomy, physiology, to make the kind of cuts Burning Man did masterfully without killing someone. Maybe Dr. Marsh had an enemy that he wasn't disclosing? It was the only link she could find at the moment. She would pay the good doctor an informal visit.

For the run's remainder, she thought about Jane Doe. She believed there had to be someone out there who knew who the girl was, had to be a photograph that fit the girl's face. So far the crime had been publicized mostly on a statewide level. The brutal details had not been splashed nationwide. As far as the rest of the country was concerned, this was a Southern California case. Other states had their own criminals to worry about. The fact that no parent had come forward to claim the body yet worried Cat. Did it mean that the killer was a far more serious threat than they imagined, able to traverse large distances, to go out of state for victims? Or did it simply mean that Jane Doe was a transient? Cat knew in investigations that the simpler answer was usually the right one.

Criminals, especially serial killers, get away with what they do by being right under your nose, being the quiet guy next door, the pleasant neighbor. How many cases had she cracked only to later speak to neighbors who professed an utter lack of knowledge that anything was wrong? It wasn't that these people were stupid. Far from it. It was the fact that serial killers knew how to blend in. To make it appear to the reasonably intelligent observer that everything was just fine. That was one of the major reasons why people like Gacy went on killing for so long. No one suspected anything. She shuddered.

Reaching the four-mile mark, Cat checked her pulse and turned around, only to hear a car horn behind her. It made her jump. Glancing over, she was ready to give the idiot a piece of her mind. Cooper, the reporter, smiled at her, his angular body crammed into a Toyota Prius, huge hands wrapped around a little leather-bound steering wheel. She hated the way these electric cars made no sound.

"Hey, doc. How's it going? I thought that was you."

She wanted to reach in and strangle him but smirked instead.

He seemed not to notice or, if he did, simply disregarded it.

"Can I give you a lift back to the hotel? Don't suppose you'd be interested in a meal by any chance?" His eyes scanned her up and down. "God knows, looks like you don't eat much."

She felt utterly infuriated by this man, yet there was an easy charm to him.

"Okay, I'm up for breakfast, but only if it's good."

"You've got a deal." He was already leaning over opening the passenger side door. "Hop in."

Behind him, cars were honking and swerving around, but he did not care. She liked that.

"I didn't get your full name from last night."

"Steven Reginald Cooper. At your service, ma'am." He nodded his head in respect. If he hadn't been sitting, she was sure he would have bowed at the waist, like a chivalrous knight. "But everyone just calls me Cooper."

"It's a pleasure."

"I can assure you the pleasure is mine."

"One rule though," Cat said, watching the words bring an immediate frown to his face. "I can't tell you anything about the case that hasn't been fully disclosed so far, understood?"

The corners of his mouth drooped more.

"Not even a little something?" He was teasing her, his voice like Joey's when he wanted something really badly.

"Nope. And I don't want another word about it." She put on her authoritative "mom" voice, playing along.

"Okay. Scout's honor." He held up his fingers in a salute. "Want some pancakes? You look like a pancake sort."

"That would be great. But what does the pancake sort look like?" Cat heard the rumbling in her stomach, thinking the last real food she ate was three bites of Chinese at lunch yesterday. Had it really been that long?

"Kind a like you," he said.

Cat rolled her eyes at him.

Again heading south on the freeway, they passed the exclusive horse community of Nellie Gail Ranch, huge homes like giants, perched on hilltops. "Beautiful homes," Cat commented, making small talk.

"Yes, one of the nicer areas of Orange County. All horse country. Lots of people with stallions and thoroughbreds, money. Matter of fact, I've got some friends who live up there. Want to go riding sometime?"

He had a forward manner but seemed oblivious to it. She wasn't sure what to make of it. "Well, as you know, I'm just in town to conduct the investigation."

"Come on, doc"—Cat believed that was now his favorite phrase—"you gotta take a break from all that death and murder stuff for a while. The horses would do you good. Get out in the open."

Cat had to admit the jog today had done her good. Cleared away some cobwebs. "Maybe if I have time. But I need those pancakes now, kappish? "

Cooper gave her a slight punch in the bicep. "That's the spirit, doc." Turning off the freeway, they drove up toward the homes. Although it was called Nellie Gail Ranch, these weren't ranch-style homes at all. Rather there was a combination of Spanish Mediterranean, English Tudor, and Cape Cod styles, each property separated by horse trails, stables, and plenty of land.

"It's lovely up here. Feel like you're in the country."

Cooper peered out the window and scrunched up his nose. "I guess that's what having a little money can do. You can create a fantasy, whatever fantasy you want."

She said nothing, thinking how true his words were. At some point she'd like to own a place like this, maybe retire with horses and land and trees. Somewhere with wide open spaces. At this point, that fantasy was a long way off.

"So tell me about our boy?"

"Who?"

"You know. The Burning Man."

"We said we wouldn't discuss it, remember?"

Cooper made the sound of a buzzer and said loudly, "Wrong, doc. We said you wouldn't discuss anything you haven't discussed with the media. We can discuss the basics; that much has been disclosed."

The reasons why Cat had her rule not to be seen with the press all came flooding back, like water after a dam breaking. You trust them and they take advantage. Prey upon prey. She was angry but hid it well.

"Only the basics," he said once more, apparently sensing her misgivings.

"All right then. The Burning Man fits the profile of a serial killer, but he is well trained in medicine and meticulous in his craft. He appears normal, probably extremely well groomed." Cat stared out the window as she spoke. "Age, late twenties to fifties. I believe he is in shape, takes care of himself. Extremely intelligent. Probably genius IQ. He fits into society easily; he could be your pharmacist, your teacher, your neighbor."

"Like Ted Bundy?"

"Yeah, probably a lot like Bundy. A real charmer. Comes across smooth, soft-spoken, analytical. There is no disputing he is an attractive man to women; that is how he is able to lure them. He seems harmless." Cat's face looked sad. "What's ironic is that people consider him a sensitive, caring person, and in one sense he is. But something in his past drives him to kill…women."

"Why do you think he does it?"

She at least appreciated this man's directness. "There is no doubt that his parents abused him as a child. Parents probably didn't get along, may have beat him. Or the exact opposite may be true. He may have had a father and mother who paid no attention. There are many kinds of abuse." Cat spoke from personal experience.

"As a child, he was likely far more intelligent than either parent, and that may have threatened them. Yet that intelligence would not have fit a pattern of behavior almost always associated with this type of murderer. The 'homicidal triad' as it is called consists of bedwetting, a fascination with childhood cruelty to animals, and fire starting. The first of these must have alarmed his parents and possibly, even more, distanced them."

Cat rolled through her own memories, her father's distance from her. In the end, she could do nothing physically to ease his pain, nothing except be there. Perhaps that was what had been the hardest—being a doctor, taking an oath to heal, and not being able to heal one's own. Only now did she realize he had needed her much more emotionally, needed her love more than her medicine. Tears gathered in her eyes. She looked away from Cooper, thankful he did not notice them.

"So our guy fits a profile."

"Well, sort of. He does and he doesn't. Superior IQ is going to make him hard to catch. He's either going to make a mistake, or he will want to be caught. From what I've seen so far, I doubt we will bring him in based on the evidence."

"Why is that?"

"We weren't going to talk about this."

"Come on, doc."

His favorite phrase, Cat thought.

"It's a simple question."

She sighed. "Because we don't have anything concrete. Nothing that's going to ID him out of four million other men. He could be you for all I know." Cat laughed.

"Come on."

Cat waited for the "doc" but it didn't come. "Do I look meticulous to you?" He lifted the rumpled collar—a day-old white oxford shirt.

"Actually, no."

They chuckled some more, pulling into the Original Pancake House off of Moulton Parkway. Inside, the pancakes were hot and good. Cat and Cooper spoke no more about the case. She needed to eat and get away from it for a while.

———

"I want him off the case!" McGregor was shouting at Richmond at nine in the morning.

It's too damned early for this shit, Richmond thought.

McGregor could see it in his eyes. "Was it your idea?"

"I think you know we need all the help we can get on this."

"What? Whose idea was this?"

Richmond bit his lip. "I'm not a hundred percent certain who suggested it. After the autopsy yesterday, it came up, and frankly, I think it's a good idea." He could tell this wasn't going to be easy.

"What about Stevenson?"

"I'll reassign him temporarily to another case. Obviously he doesn't like the idea any more than you do. In fact, he left the room abruptly when I mentioned it. Initially I wasn't too keen on it either, but come to think of it, if this guy's mobile, which we think he is, it's entirely possible LA needs to be involved. This creep could live in their jurisdiction."

"Screw the damned jurisdiction."

"Look, what the hell do you expect me to do? I got the mayors in Dana Point and Irvine breathing down my back for an arrest of this perp. We got squat in evidence, and you're out there like some lone cowboy on a mission."

"Wait just a minute, chief! I'm doing my job. You got a problem with that?"

"When I don't see any results, yes, I do have a problem with that."

"Why did Gray come looking for this case? It's not his area. None of the women have been killed in his jurisdiction. Just who the hell does he think he is?" McGregor was leaning into Richmond across a desk that was buried by paperwork. "Look, here's the deal, pull anyone else off the task force you want. I'll work with anybody, hell, even that rookie, what's his name, Cramer? I'll work with that wet-behind-the-ears punk before I'll work with Gray."

"I don't recall giving you a choice."

"Good God, I mean, what the hell do I have to do around here? I've been twenty years on the force, and you can't at least consider someone else?" His body language backed down. "You're a cop, a reasonable man, Bob. But give me a break. I'm telling you the only reason that Gray is down here is because he wants the publicity. Always been a sonofabitch publicity hound, even when he was in the academy. Oh, what the hell does it matter? I can tell I'm talking to a brick wall."

Richmond said nothing.

"Jesus God," McGregor moaned. "Look, I don't need another partner."

Richmond just glared.

McGregor tensed again, the veins in his neck visibly throbbing. "What the hell does Gray want with me? That fat-ass mayor put you up to this? What's his name… Needlemayer, something? He's the one that put you up to this? Damned politics. When am I ever gonna learn."

"Look, McGregor. Needleman didn't put me up to this. He's a politician, but he doesn't run this department, and he sure as hell doesn't make any choices for me. I got a call from Sanchez last night, after the press conference, offering to help. That's the plain and simple of it. He said Gray came back to LA and told him the condition of the body. Said it was the worst mutilation murder he'd seen in a long time. And right now, in case you haven't noticed, we got jack shit on this guy. We got nothin' solid on this perp, on *your* investigation." Richmond threw the blame in McGregor's lap. "So if you want the responsibility of an investigation that so far is going nowhere, then that's fine with me. But I suggest you put your huge ego aside and let another agency help out, got me?"

"I don't mind the agency helping out, if it's not Gray."

"I get it, you two aren't the greatest friends. Hell, anyone could tell that. But do me this favor, will you? He's one of the best and brightest in LA. They have offered his assistance. Take it."

McGregor considered this in silence, sitting down on a standard-issue vinyl-back office chair.

"Really. So I guess you got a legitimate complaint about how I'm handling the investigation. I've been busting my ass, working the phones, interviewing witnesses. I've got half the black-and-whites combing Irvine for anyone that fits our guy's look. Show of force to the community and all that."

"That don't mean jack."

"Chief, you telling me that ain't good enough?"

"Ain't good enough till we get our man."

"What if we don't"

Richmond didn't answer, didn't even want to consider the possibility.

"Then we keep chasing bodies? And invisible perps?"

"Take the help, McGregor. You need it."

"Okay. I'll take it. But if Gray messes up this case, so help me God, I'll come back here and set you straight."

"You and I both know that's bullshit," Richmond said with a quick hint of a grin. "You've never been able to kick my ass, not since high school."

Neither one wanted to admit it, but they both were right.

THIRTEEN

The constant assertion of belief is an indication of fear.
—**Krishnamurti**, *The Second Penguin Krishnamurti Reader*

nstinct told Cat they weren't going to catch this guy through normal investigative channels. Toxicology had come up with nothing in the girl's systems. No drugs, no barbiturates, no poisons. What was this guy into?

Sitting at a Medline terminal in the UCI Science Library, Cat learned what she could about sulfuric acid.

Housed in an impressive modern structure, the science library held millions of volumes on a wide variety of subject areas in sciences, medicine, and technology. Everything from genetic engineering to environmental impact on California's wetlands could be researched at minimal costs.

Peering over tortoiseshell glasses, Cat waited for the screen to prompt her for a search. She typed in sulfuric acid, then the words "carcinogen" and "human." It was early, eight o'clock. At this hour, the library felt big—empty and cold. Her fingers clicked across the keyboard at a fast clip, the keys the only sound in the library other than a reference librarian who seemed half asleep, sipping a morning coffee that Cat guessed she had snuck in.

The blue screen disappeared, replaced with a gray one. The first few articles she found were not what she wanted. Frustrated, she changed her query to include the word "sources."

Initially, the computer search found much the same. However, the fourth article was interesting. She scanned the abstract, pulled up the full article.

Scrolling through, she realized it was what she needed. Quickly she typed in the commands to print and inserted a card into the slot that would automatically deduct the costs of copies. Cat spent most of the morning doing similar searches on a variety of databases, including Toxline, Cancerline, Toxlit, and Medica. She also searched RTECS, ETIBACK, and BIOSIS. A number of the studies provided relevant information on the mechanisms that might provide an insight into where this madman was getting his stuff.

Cat used her cell phone to get a main line for the people at DuPont Labs. After a short conversation with their engineers, she was assured that they would send an update summary of the scientific literature on sulfuric acid to her, via Federal Express next day air. It was too much to send via email.

By this time tomorrow, she'd have a wealth of information on sulfuric acid, its carcinogenic effects, sources, and production throughout the United States.

Leaning back, she put down her cell phone. Above, the sun peered out from behind silver gray clouds that hung on the horizon. Robins darted from a giant elm, its branches so laden down they almost touched the ground.

For the first time in a long time, Cat felt good about this investigation.

* * * * *

For the time being, with so little to go on, a voice inside her told Cat someone must have seen something. A struggle, maybe one of the girls with him.

Something.

Did people just keep their mouths closed? Someone had to have had their eyes open, seeing Jane Doe with someone. Still, as far as clues, they had nothing despite putting out where she had last been seen alive. Calls came in. Everything was being checked out, but most of it seemed from crackpots and wannabees.

No letters claiming responsibility. No phone calls to the cops. Nothing.

It was time to shake up the investigation, time for a statewide task force.

Time to take this thing national.

To some extent, the local politicians had been calling the shots, orchestrating the investigation from behind the scenes. Cat would change pecking order today.

From here on in, she was calling all the shots.

At noon, Cat sat at a conference table in the mayor's office, watching men file in, all looking very stern and serious. McGregor sat next to her, then Richmond. Needleman seemed to have swapped the seersucker for a more serious looking gray double-breasted number. Craig Gray sat, all smiling and politeness. She wondered if she'd ever have the nerve to tell him to wipe it off his face.

Sanchez plopped down at the far end of the table, a dark, striking, handsome man who seemed to have demons of his own.

Cat had also invited Mack Holston, San Diego Police Department's head honcho, and similar men from San Francisco, Riverside, San Bernardino, Santa Mateo counties, and Santa Barbara.

After the men were seated and the coffee poured, Cat stood. She did not smile but came straight to the point.

"Gentlemen, I'm glad you could all make it here today. What I'm about to say makes common sense in the wake of these senseless killings. What we have out there," she glanced toward the window, "is a savage killer, a machine set on autopilot. Right now we have nothing to go on. No way of stopping him. And he knows it."

She met each of their eyes with a serious and deliberate stare.

"Consequently, gentlemen, we are placed at a distinct disadvantage. He knows that too. And I believe he is enjoying his little game even more, escalating the killings because he knows he can." She paused. "Because we have nothing. Because he has given us nothing."

The man from Riverside County spoke up. "What about the DNA, tissue cultures?"

"Mr.," Cat glanced at her notes, "Norris, is it?"

"Yes ma'am." He tipped his cowboy hat slightly to her. He was the guy from the Inland Empire—San Bernardino and Riverside.

"In the first three cases, the burning was so severe that the epidermal layer of skin is pretty much gone. The first two girls, the only thing under their nails was their own tissue. This last one we pulled up, well, there was nothing left of her. The only thing we have is a star-shaped group of freckles. The ocean took care of her. She'd been floating two, maybe three days."

"So you got nothing?"

"Well, let's just say the tissue samples, blood, and DNA we've sent in hasn't been the most favorable evidence."

"What about this guy's MO?" San Diego's chief, Norman Harley, asked. He was a big man, though well proportioned. He sported the type of tanned good looks that made Cat believe he was a fisherman, an outdoorsman of some type.

"That worries me. His MO is developing, as I believe his killing fantasy is."

"How so?" Harley said.

"Initially the girls were beaten into unconsciousness, mutilated, burned, and left for dead in the middle of bush country. At some time during the killing ritual, I think it was likely each one woke up, but by then he had already started cutting. Shock sets in as the body loses blood. There was little they could do. You all know that?"

The men nodded.

"The first two, if they are the first two…" Cat believed there were more bodies in the California hills waiting to be discovered… "were killed over a long period of time. I think this guy enjoys watching them suffer. He may inflict the cutting over hours, even days, slowly weakening the victim. This is the reason the cuts are so precise. If he goes too deep, he kills them too quickly and his fun is over."

"Bastard," the detective from San Bernardino muttered under his breath.

Harley's ice-blue eyes glittered with anger. "So this guy's a control freak, is that what you're telling us?"

"Very much so. At least initially that's what appears to be the case. He likes to be in control. My belief is that the first two killings were very controlled and that he had been planning out the mechanics of the attack, if not the identity of the victims, for a very long time, months perhaps."

"You keep talking about the first two girls like they're in a class by themselves. Why is that?"

"Because they very much are." Cat had an assistant dim the lights and flip on the overhead projector. "The third girl is quite different." A photo slide of Jane Doe's corpse, shot from overhead, loomed large on a screen in front of them. Some of the men seemed alarmed, but Cat knew she had to get their attention. This was the way to do it.

"Gentlemen, meet Jane Doe. This is our guy's latest victim, this young woman washed up in Dana Point. The reason I called you all here is to inform you that no one who knows this girl has come forward. We got nada."

Cat's eyes focused on the screen. "As a result, I believe it is important at this point to coordinate a statewide task force. I also believe a national press conference is in order. My motives are threefold. Number one, this girl needs to be identified. If we ID her, we might find someone who saw something suspicious. We also need to give her a decent burial. Right now she is being held in refrigeration in the OC coroner's offices. Number two, no one has come forward to claim her. This leads me to believe she is from out of state. That worries me. If our guy is mobile, well, the resources that will need to be devoted to this case increase twentyfold. It's also a reason to go national."

Cat's forehead wrinkled. "Third, and probably most disconcerting, is the fact that this body"—Cat used a laser pointer circling the mass of bloody pulp on the screen—"is entirely different from the other two."

"We got a copycat?"

"No. I don't think so, although I've considered that possibility. In all three cases, the lacerations are almost identical, with the largest wound to the abdomen. There is no way a copycat could know that. We haven't released that kind of detail to the media. And the skill needed to make abdominal cuts like this, without piercing vital organs, is extraordinary."

"What else concerns you about this Jane Doe?"

"Notice the ligature burns to the neck here." She circled the laser's red pinpoint. "And to the midsection, ankles, wrists. Distinctive circular marks. This girl was tied down, unlike the others. I believe standard nylon rope was used. None of the marks appears fresher than the others. She was tied down to something as he began to cut."

Harley was scratching his head. "What's the significance?"

Cat stood in front of the screen, the ghastly image projected on her white linen suit.

"He is escalating, his violence intensifying. As the fantasy develops, fleshes out in his mind, it is becoming more violent. He is losing control of himself, little by little over time, and the result is a more vicious attack. All three girls so far have not been touched in the face."

"Why is that?" San Bernardino's chief homicide detective spoke up this time, apparently taking the words out of Harley's mouth.

"He likes to watch their faces. This sonofabitch, this man, deliberately leaves their faces alone. At our most basic, we are all animals, hunters. Evolution has shown nothing less. Rather than subduing that urge, this guy encourages it, and in doing so their faces are like his trophies. Watching their repeated struggling, watching them bleed, the slow process of shock, then the acid. He enjoys the pain etched on their faces for hours, maybe days."

Secretly, Cat believed he videotaped each one of the murders. Or photographed them. So far she had nothing to prove it, so she kept it to herself.

"What a freak." Harley shook his head.

"You see, by killing them in this manner, he is in control. Able to cheat death as it comes knocking for them, or at least slow its advance. What could be more exhilarating? The control of life and death."

She stepped aside, allowing the men to focus on Jane Doe once more. "One other thing, we found evidence of manual strangulation as well. Notice the wider laceration and bruising about the neck."

"So he hung them and strangled them?" San Bernardino's guy was confused.

"No, the third girl only. Looks like he choked her with his hands first, probably into unconsciousness. Looking closely, you can see that with the rope marks, that thinner bruising is deeper and fresher than the wider bruising to the neck. What this tells us is that he choked first, then tied her down."

"Okay."

Cat continued. "And this was not a hanging. There is no inverted V-shaped bruise to the neck. The bruising line here is inverted in the opposite direction, downward. She was most likely tied to something, an eyehook or something, down below her waist. He dragged the rope down to her waist then used a slipknot to tighten it even further. See the star-shaped bruising to the back of the neck?" Cat circled the bruises as they came up on the slideshow, her voice keeping perfect time with each slide. "He used more force than was needed."

"Tied her down like a hog," Harley observed, shaking his head back and forth.

"And he likes to use his hands," the homicide detective from Santa Barbara said, speaking up for the first time, his voice deep.

"Yes, at least on the last one. Not on the others. In the first two killings, he was very meticulous. Not this last one; he went to town on her. Rope, hands-on. That's what concerns me. With each day, he is more dangerous."

Cat looked down, gathered her thoughts, then lifted her head again.

"And one more thing. We can't verify it based on this last victim, but my guess is that the sexual component of his fantasy will escalate also."

"You mean he's gonna start raping them?"

"No. Right now he gets off after the killings. We found semen on the first two girls. The last one we can't tell. No penetration. My guess is it is his culmination of the killing fantasy, the ultimate feeling of power. Perhaps it is his way of sharing his victim's voyage between life and death. Maybe in that split second of death, he feels the ultimate sexual…" She hesitated, searching for the proper word out of respect for the dead. "Gratification."

Harley spoke softly now. "So start looking for a rapist?"

"No, I don't think so. He does not rape, and we have no reason to believe he will now. I believe, without killing like this, he is impotent. However, he may attempt digital penetration." Cat stopped speaking, deciding how to answer. "He may reason that if he is inside of them, with his hands, or some other object that he is touching at the moment of death, the bond between himself and the victim—between death and life—becomes even more real, more intoxicating."

"But he is not going to rape them?"

"No, as crazy as this sounds, I don't think he is able to out of respect for them."

"Huh?" Even Gray seemed stumped by that one.

"As much as he brutalizes them physically, he does so because of a tortured relationship in his past. Someone he loved and trusted brutalized him. Out of that love and respect, as much as he mutilates their bodies, he is unable to, well, unable to have sex with them."

"So the guy's been pussy-whipped," the detective from Riverside blurted out, then bit his lip, remembering who he was speaking to.

"In a manner of speaking." Cat would not justify the comment with anything more.

She amplified her voice. "So, gentlemen, that is why I have brought you all here today. The FBI has been authorized to create a statewide task force. In a matter of hours, we will be going national with what we have now, with some details left out of course, to prevent copycats."

Sanchez nodded, already knowing this was coming down the pike. Cat's work with the FBI's Behavioral Sciences Unit in profiling, and correlating that information with what she had learned from a PhD in criminal psychology, made for a potent combination. The addition to her advanced knowledge in forensic medicine meant this bastard better watch out. This triad combination had not failed Catherine Powers yet.

Gathering all the FBI resources, with a backbone of statewide and national informants, meant Cat could put together a picture of murder from the victims' and the killer's perspectives. Everything from each victim's character, physical traits, age, sexual preference, habits, and personality would be reexamined. From this, a correlative match with the killer's likely characteristics would arise. Where the two pictures overlapped is where they would find their man.

"What I want each of you to take away from this meeting is the fact that this guy's killing mechanism is changing. I want all of you aware of that. Consequently, if any of you come upon a young female body that fits either of these MOs, especially a floater, I want the information relayed to me immediately. Understood?"

The men nodded.

"And get the word out to other agencies. We will of course be sending out FBI notices via email to all agencies across the state today. That's pretty much it. Any questions?"

There were none. As the men got up to leave, Cat remembered one more thing. "Hold on a minute. If any of you finds a body, floater or not, I don't want it touched. Don't drag it up on the beach. Just leave it. And call me right away."

They nodded and filed out of the room.

Chief Richmond stayed behind. "That was very impressive, Catherine."

"You can call me Cat, like everyone else," she said casually.

"I like Catherine better—far more refined."

"Whatever." She was busy packing away the projector and slides. He held her forearm, stopped her movement. When she looked up, his deep-set, penetrating eyes were fixed on her with the most sincere look. "Do you really think we will catch him?"

"I don't know, chief. I sure hope so."

Her answer seemed to dispel some of his concern. "Would it be too forward to ask you to have dinner with me tonight?"

She stopped moving, taken aback by his frankness.

He wore no wedding ring, she noticed. "I don't really think that would be..."

"Catherine, for once don't think. I just want to have dinner. Nothing covert, no hidden agenda. I figured you'd be getting tired of room service by now. And you're wound tight as hell. I could take you out, show you around a little."

"I'm sorry. It's just..." She was flustered, not knowing what to say.

He spoke as though he had rehearsed what he was saying in front of a full-length mirror, each word and pause measured and precise.

"I know. It's been a long time for me too. Ever since Emily passed away a year ago, well, let's just say I've been out of commission." Hearing his words, his inflection, Cat was sure he had rehearsed them in front of a mirror a thousand times before. The man was heartbroken.

Sincerity returned to his tone. "I know you're the head of this investigation. I think since we are turning a new leaf in it, it would be best if we talk informally, off the record."

Cat didn't understand what he was getting at, but her natural curiosity was piqued. "All right then, what time?"

"I'll pick you up at seven-thirty."

FOURTEEN

But who will guard the guardians themselves?
—Juvenal, *The Satires*

The days had stretched into a week for Joey Powers. He lay on his stomach, just three feet from the TV, his head propped up on his elbows, his body fully encased in pajamas.

"Dad, when is Mom coming on TV?"

"Joey, I don't think this is a good idea."

"Come on, I never get to see Mom on TV. You never let me. I'm old enough. I'm six going on seven."

"I don't care what age you are. You're not staying up to watch your mom."

"Why?"

"Your mom deals with very bad people, very bad men. Criminals like we talked about. You remember?"

"Yessth." Joey's occasional lisp was showing through. He had lost a tooth in a baseball game, and they hadn't made it to the dentist yet.

"And you know that sometimes those criminals do really bad things, really bad."

"Yessth." He stopped, thinking. "Like the cops and robbers on TV."

"Yes, except cops and robbers on TV aren't real. They don't bleed real blood, they don't really die."

Joey rolled his eyes. "I know that."

"The people your mom is going to talk about tonight on TV, they are real people. Like you and me. The people who were killed, they had a real family, a mom and dad, like you do."

"So?"

"I don't think you should see it, son. Your mom might have to talk about some pretty awful stuff. It might upset you."

Joey stood up, put his hands on his hips, and sighed. "But, Dad, I'm six," he said, pleading his case. "It's not like when you were six. All you ever watched was *Leave It to Beaver*, dumb stuff like that."

"So?" Mark felt foolish defending his childhood innocence.

"Kids today are more grown-up. We've got the Internet. I can handle it." Joey stood, feet shoulder-width apart. "And I haven't seen Mom in a week."

Mark thought about what his child said. It did seem that kids today grew up much faster, could handle more and had seen more than when he was a kid. Joey was just a boy, but he understood what violence was, watched the nightly news, knew all too well the violence that surrounded him. Police officers had visited his first grade class to discuss the danger of drugs and child molesters. And he was only six! Joey was right, he was growing up a lot faster. The thought made Mark shudder.

"All right, you can watch. But no nightmares."

"Cool. What time is she coming on?"

"She'll be on in a few minutes."

Cat had called a national news conference for eight that evening. The big three networks were carrying live feeds from their Orange County affiliates. The national anchors were already hyping the killer as a combination of Ted Bundy and Jeffrey Dahmer. A gentleman killer and mutilator all rolled into one.

Joey sat spellbound through the national anchors' introductions, then the minute-long story segue into the conference. The reporter's voice droned, detailing the number of killings, the sheer brutality of the murders, the little the FBI had.

The footage cut away to a police conference room.

"There's Mom!" Joey cried, pointing at the brief glimpse of a woman dressed in a cobalt blue suit, her hair shining against the television lights. The men standing with her looked solemn.

Mark had second thoughts, wondering if this was a good idea. "You sure you want to watch, pal?"

"I'm sure."

A man stepped to the microphone, adjusted his tie, and spoke. "Good evening, everyone, and thank you for coming." His eyes scanned the room quickly. "We have gathered you here today to announce the creation of a statewide task force focused on the killer the media has dubbed the Burning Man. From the Oregon border to San Diego, a statewide network of agencies will be working together on this case, all with the same intent: to catch him."

"Dad, when do I get to see Mom?"

"In a minute, Joey." Instinct told Mark maybe this wasn't a good idea.

Reporters fired off questions as soon as Richmond took a breath. "What has changed in the case to necessitate a statewide dragnet?" a young reporter asked, her hand in the air, pencil in hand.

"For further questioning, I will turn you over to Dr. Catherine Powers, chief forensic psychologist of the FBI's Behavioral Unit out of Quantico, Virginia. Dr. Powers will be heading the manhunt." The man turned, stepped down, and Cat walked onto the screen.

"There she is!" Joey said. "There's Mom."

Mark had forgotten how lovely his ex-wife was. The color of her suit seemed to highlight her aquamarine eyes, the auburn streaks in her hair. She was beautiful but looked thin and tired. "Jesus, Cat. What are you doing to yourself?" he murmured.

"Thank you all for coming." She looked up from her notes and flashed one of those million-dollar smiles. Mark wondered if she was smiling from nerves. "The reason we have called you all here tonight, as my colleague informed you, is to announce the expansion of the effort to bring the Burning Man to justice."

"Dad, she looks tired, huh?" Joey looked back over his shoulder.

"Yes, son. She does."

They listened as Cat continued. "As you know, two days ago we pulled a body out of the water off Dana Point. We have reason to believe that that woman, Jane Doe for now, is a victim of the Burning Man. The girl at this point remains unidentified, although we have circulated her photo to police departments in Los Angeles, Orange, and other Southern California counties. For this reason, we have reason to believe she may be a transient to the area, could even have come across state lines with the killer. Obviously, that possibility puts a new spin on the case. We could be dealing with a killer that is not just a California problem but a national one."

Cat felt the flashbulbs hot on her face.

She caught a glimpse of Cooper off to the side in the back of the room.

The same young reporter was up again, seeming to have a monopoly on the questions. "What has changed in the case?"

"Well, a number of things have. The newest victim does not match the killer's modus operandi, not entirely at least. Although she exhibits the same lacerations, she is the first one that has been strangled and the first to exhibit ligature bruises to the neck, torso, ankles, and wrists."

"Dad, what's a ligature?"

Mark thought of making something up but answered the boy honestly. "Mom's talking about a kind of bruise that you get when you're tied up real tight, son."

"Like when Jason and I play in the yard?"

"Yes. Something like that."

Joey and Mark turned their attention back to the television. Cat was explaining the similarities and dissimilarities of the three victims that had been found. She did not mince words, nor did she take her attention off her audience.

The fire in her eyes told Mark that she was fully into it now. Obsessed, he had called it, with her cases. That obsession for justice had cost them their marriage. It had killed the young, naive girl he had fallen in love with, and in her place had put a woman so driven to find truth that she destroyed and alienated everything dear to her in life.

Except Joey.

Cat said sternly that she believed there were more women's bodies out there.

"What can the press do to help?"

"You can get the word out to every person in this country that Jane Doe is dead." Cat turned to the same girl's photograph she had used before, this time projected onto a five-foot screen behind her. "This is someone's daughter, someone's sister."

She waited for the photo to sink in.

"As much as he brutalized her, she needs justice. We need to find out who she is. If we can, we will have made one more step toward finding and catching the Burning Man."

"Dr. Powers, how is the investigation going?"

"Will he be stopped?"

"Have you narrowed down the suspects?"

"How can we be sure it's even a man?"

The questions came like rapid-fire bullets.

"The investigation at this point is going as well as can be expected. The FBI is running DNA testing, toxicology." Cat knew she wasn't telling them anything concrete, but it sounded like something. It was a skill she had picked up over the years and learned well. "We have a photo analysis team flying in from Washington tonight."

"Wow, cool," Joey said, impressed by what his mother was saying, though Mark was sure he didn't understand it.

"As far as suspects, we have some ideas but no concrete leads at the moment. In that area, the investigation is continuing, progressing nicely."

If he was watching, Cat wanted the Burning Man to believe they were getting close, even if they weren't. Sometimes a psychological game of cat-and-mouse could be best played out before millions to see.

"Are they gonna catch him, Dad?"

"I don't know. But you know what, with your mom on the case, I would bet pretty sure odds they're going to."

"Cool."

"How can you be sure it's even a man," a woman reporter asked again.

"On the most recent victim, we have evidence of damage to the neck, along with other use of force that suggests the killer is probably a man."

"What else can you tell us about him?"

"He is well educated, articulate, probably soft-spoken, knows how to blend in, but is also wound pretty tight, full of fears and phobias when it comes down to it." More cat-and-mouse, Mark thought.

"And he is medically trained."

"How do you know that?" Cooper shouted, even before Cat could answer.

"I cannot discuss that detail of the case, other than to say the precise nature of the lacerations to the bodies indicates a man who has had medical training."

"Like a doctor?" Joey asked his dad.

"Yeah, maybe. Let's listen, okay?"

Joey nodded and turned back around, his head propped on his hands again.

A male reporter finally got in a word edgewise.

"How about the acid? Did he use it on the last one?"

"Yes, he did. He used it on Jane Doe. Let's find her a name, shall we, ladies and gentlemen?" Cat bowed her head, Mark suspected to hide tears. "She deserves better."

The questions, lights, flashes kept coming. Cooper kept trying to ask questions. Cat would have none of it. She simply smiled and said, "That is all we have for now. As the case progresses, we will be holding additional briefings." She stepped down off the podium.

Joey turned, his brow stitched together in concern. "Dad, you think Mom's doing okay?"

"Joey, I think your mom can handle herself just fine."

"You sure?"

"Yes, I'm sure. Now it's off to bed for you, trooper." Mark tried to sound upbeat.

Joey was already in his face, lips puckered with a kiss. "Night, Dad. I love you." A big hug followed.

"I love you too." Mark returned the kiss and popped him on the butt as he scooted off.

Mark was always surprised by Joey's innocence and intelligence, and his love for his mom. His smile faded as he thought about how bad Cat looked.

FIFTEEN

Here's the smell of blood still.
All the perfumes of Arabia will not sweeten this little hand.
—**Shakespeare**, *Macbeth*

The next day, the Burning Man investigation broke wide open.

By eight o'clock, Cat had her answer. Jane Doe was no longer Jane Doe but Melanie Garrett, a seventeen-year-old runaway from Flagstaff, Arizona. Even on the swollen corpse, the girl's parents recognized the star-shaped freckles on their daughter's chest.

Cat flew them in from Arizona. She figured word would get around soon enough who they were, and she wanted to spare them the agony that additional media attention would bring. "Bring them in quietly," she told McGregor. "I don't want them rattled by the press first."

"Will do." McGregor seemed rejuvenated, as if the new leads were like fresh blood pumping through his veins. Even Craig Gray's tagging along couldn't bring him down.

Before long, Melanie Garrett's parents were at FBI command headquarters in Irvine. McGregor escorted the man and woman, both in their late forties, inside.

"Glad to meet you, Mrs., uh, I mean Dr. Powers," the man said, pumping her hand aggressively.

"There is no need for that," Cat reassured him. "You can call me Cat; everyone else around here does." Melanie Garrett's father seemed genuinely awed by the scene. To Cat's right, a team of detectives worked the phones—calls coming in from all over, from people who thought their friend, neighbor, relative could be the Burning Man. In another room, to Cat's left, an expert team was poring over the crime scene photos. On the first two cases, the team had to work from photos. Exhumations of both bodies at this point would cause far more problems than it was worth, angering both girls' families and possibly alienating the media support they had.

Cat simply didn't have any proof thus far that the first two girls had been poisoned. Although she suspected it.

Lidocaine administered in lethal doses, over time, could easily have been missed by medical examiner Dr. Conrad James. Administered via IV, given the brutal nature of the killings, there was every indication that the needle pricks could have been missed. And the girls would have gone quietly to sleep, only to wake to the sound and smell of acid eating their own flesh.

There was no doubt these killings were bizarre. But they pointed to something other than poisoning. Given the situation, Cat may well have missed the finding herself. But she had suspicions.

Mrs. Garrett was teary eyed, red faced. "Thank you for finding our little girl. Melanie's been gone awhile. I never thought I'd find her. Then sometimes I knew we would, but I never thought it would be like this." She wept openly.

"I know it's hard, Mrs. Garrett." Cat took her hand, squeezing it. "It's always difficult at a time like this. But even in death, Melanie is a brave girl. She is showing us things we would not have known. She is a guide to her killer, a roadmap…"

"I hope you find the sonofabitch and he fries," Mr. Garrett said, his anger pouring out.

"If we catch him, you can be damn sure he will," Cat reassured him with her eyes as much as her words, then turned her attention back to his wife. "Melanie's showed us how brave she can be." She squeezed the woman's hand again. "Now, I need something from both of you. I need for you to be strong for Melanie, for me." Cat implored them with her eyes, and they understood.

"I'll take you then." Cat led them down to the morgue where Melanie Garrett waited to say goodbye to her parents. McGregor followed just in case the sight was too much for either of them. "Melanie did not die a pretty death." It was a stupid thing to say, but Cat couldn't think of anything else more appropriate as she led them down a dark cold hallway. Entering a brightly lit room, she walked to a row of stainless steel doors, each door holding death's minion. The Garretts knew what they were going to see. McGregor positioned himself behind the couple, square in between them, in case either should fall.

Cat opened the vault and pulled the stainless-steel slab out.

"Oh, sweet baby Jesus," Carlton Garrett said. He started to swoon but then locked his knees and held himself firm. For Mrs. Garrett, the horror was far less perceptible. She simply stood. After a few minutes, the Garretts moved closer to their daughter's body. Mrs. Garrett touched her girl's hair tenderly, as if she were still alive. "My baby," she muttered over and over.

Melanie's dad took a closer look at the sternum. "It's her," he said, walking away in disgust. He couldn't bear the sight any longer.

"Dammit, can't they give us more?" McGregor cried, a vein popping out of his forehead.

"They haven't seen her in over nine months. She's a runaway. Don't you get it," Gray said angrily. "They don't know where she's been and they don't know who with."

McGregor whirled on his heels, crushing a cigarette into the floor. "They must know something! Sonofabitch, how come he gets away so clean?"

"He's smart and cunning. Stays far away from anyone who can possibly ID him. To those he knows he appears normal. And if you see the other side of him…"

"What?" McGregor shouted.

"Then you're already dead."

"Christ. They got to know something. Maybe there's something they overlooked. A doctor, pastor maybe, that took a special liking to the girl."

Gray shoved McGregor into a chair. "What the hell are you talking about?" He tried to remain calm, although he was getting steamed.

"There's got to be some aspect we're missing. A boyfriend, something…"

"Get it through your thick skull. This is another random killing. Random victim number three," Gray shouted.

McGregor was in Gray's face suddenly. "She's not number three, she's their kid." He looked at the Garretts, visible through glass in another room. "She's not a toe tag number, not a Jane Doe, not a runaway. She's Melanie Garrett, seventeen years old, senior at Grover High School, home of the Indians…" McGregor felt hot tears on his cheeks. "Someone from her community. A man, maybe took a liking to her…" He realized how pathetic he sounded but would not back down.

Gray was suddenly angrier. "So what's the angle you want me to take? You want me to sit her parents down and interrogate them? And what should I ask? Was your daughter a whore? Was she a slut? Did she screw around with older men in town? She doing drugs? Maybe a little prostitution on the side? Is that what you want me to ask them?"

"I do."

"Think about it, make real sure. What else should I ask them? Any incest in the household? Dad, you ever get your rocks off watching Melanie undress?" Gray spoke from years of experience investigating these types of crime. He knew runaways were abused, usually in more ways than one. "You want me to ask, 'Mom, you been negligent all these years pretending nothing was going on?'" He looked across the room. "What do you want me to ask them, McGregor?"

McGregor's head was in his hands.

"You want me to ask Pop if he ever screwed her? You want me to get details? How many times? You sodomize her too?"

McGregor exploded off the chair, fists swinging.

"Shut up, Gray. Shut up." Words came through tears.

Gray grabbed the bull of a man and held him for a second. McGregor pulled away.

"Don't ask them nothin', man. Just let it go."

Arrangements were made for Melanie Garrett to receive a decent burial that day. Her corpse had been out of the water now for three days. Her family wanted to put the whole thing behind them as soon as possible. Take time to rebuild their lives. Move on with things. Cat knew in her soul that they never would.

No family ever "recovered" from something like this.

SIXTEEN

Open not thine heart to every man,
Lest he requite thee with a shrewd turn.
—Ecclesiastes 8:9 (KJV)

Fifty miles to the south, in a hospital cafeteria at Hoag Hospital in Newport Beach, he stood waiting for a bacon omelet and toast. What was offered to him was overcooked, the toast burnt on one side. He took it, sipping steaming coffee as he paid.

At eight-thirty in the morning, remnants of the overnight shift were done, going home, a fresh batch of faces coming on. He was one of those going.

He surveyed the tables, choosing an empty one in the corner.

A dark-haired young man wearing a white lab coat stood nearby studying the specials. Their eyes met and the young man walked in his direction, sat down at the table.

He kept eating, never picking up his knife.

"Look, I'm sorry. I didn't mean to give you a problem back there."

"It's quite all right," he said.

The young man smoothed his hair, leaned closer. "Look, it's just that I thought it was a bad judgment call, that's all."

"You and I both know she was dead when she came in."

"What the hell are you talking about? She was doped up, but we could have saved her."

"Are you questioning my judgment?" He clenched his napkin in one hand below the table.

"You were pursuing her treatment aggressively, then you…didn't."

"That's when I realized she was gone," he said, matter-of-factly.

The young intern would hear nothing of it. "You should have kept on though. When you got there, she had a respiration rate of six."

"And pinpoint pupils. We checked the arms and legs for needle tracks."

"I know that," the intern snapped.

"I've had cases like hers before. The respiration rate didn't mean anything. Her vitals were erratic. All over the place." He kept eating, wondering why he was explaining himself to this boy. "Look, I started an IV, ordered a thousand cc's DELR, 150 cc's an hour."

He glanced up. The intern's face was redder. "Yes, but you didn't order Narcan. You did nothing to counteract the morphine. Shit, you wanted me on your team… and now I'm standing by as you're killing people."

Putting down his fork, he stood, walked around, and sat on the other side of the table next to the young man. He tried to put his arm around the intern, wanting him to understand. He spoke in a whisper. "She'd had such a massive dose, there was little…"

"Don't give me that bullshit!" the intern snapped, pushing away, standing over him. "You didn't follow protocol."

"Will you sit down with me?" He patted the bench. "I have something to tell you."

"What?" the intern said, exasperated.

"Come on now, sit down for a minute. There's something I should tell you."

The young man looked around and realized people were staring. He sat, straddling the bench. "What?"

"I'm sorry about her death. She should have had more time, you know. But I wasn't stupid; I did what I could. I didn't mean for her to die." He whispered, "She would have gone anyway. The amount of morphine in her system would bring down an elephant."

"But..."

"Let me ask you something, son." He looked straight into the young man's eyes, his face showing no emotion.

"Go ahead."

"How long have you been in residency?"

The young man considered the question for some time. "This is my first year."

"And how long have I been practicing medicine?" he said coolly.

"I don't know." The intern glanced at the doctor, sizing up his age. "Fifteen, twenty years maybe."

"Twenty-two years." His voice did not waver. He kept the same monotone diatribe he used when speaking at medical symposiums. "And how many morphine deaths have you witnessed over your one year of residency?"

"Well, we don't get many in Newport. About three, I'd say."

"Now let me ask you another question," he whispered. "How many do you think I've seen in twenty-two years?" He let the words float with their own authority, adding none to his voice.

Normal color began to return to the intern's face. The glare in his eyes was gone. "Mmm-hmm." He seemed to consider the words. "You really think she wouldn't have made it?"

"Yes. With all that trauma, she wouldn't have lived longer than another ten minutes," he said, his voice calming, palm supporting his chin.

"But with oxygen and one amp of Narcan, we could have saved her."

"We?"

"Yeah, we. I should have taken over. Jesus, why didn't you let me?"

He caught a quick breath. "You are an intern, my boy. What makes you think her outcome would have been any different?"

"I don't know," the young man said, his voice muffled, one hand over his mouth. "The medical texts say..."

"What?" His voice rose for the first time.

"The texts say..."

"I don't really care what they say. I've seen ones like her before. She wouldn't have made it. Real-life medicine and what you read in books are two different things. Trust me."

The intern started to relax, the grimace on his face giving way to a look of sheer exhaustion.

He lowered his voice again. "I know sometimes these things upset us. I know. I can tell you're upset. Why didn't you do something more for her? I know the feeling." He raised his head and stared at the young man. "Let it go."

"Huh?"

"Like I have. I simply let it go."

The intern seemed to understand what he was saying. Sometimes the line between life and death got blurred. Sometimes people died for all the wrong reasons. Rising, the young man barely brushed his forearm. The touch registered. "Thanks, I'm glad we talked."

"I am too, Craig."

He watched the young doctor walk away.

He got to the club at about eleven o'clock. The Irvine Sports Cub provided his sole daily interaction with people outside of the hospital. It stood at the end of a paved road that ran though the high-rises south of Costa Mesa. The club's owners took care of it. Gleaming heavyweights waited for the willing. Now, in late August, mustiness from sweating bodies hung in the weight room. There weren't many people here in the daytime.

He made an inspection tour of his muscles as soon as he sat on the ab machine, floor-to-ceiling mirrors reflecting his veins pumping. There was no wedding ring on his left hand. Any one of these girls would know he lived alone. His eyes met a long-legged beauty on the Stairmaster. Breasts firm and high, certainly a boob job, it was easy to tell. She'd watched him for some time but was too obvious. The beauty of the game had long since evaporated.

Satisfied he had done enough stomach crunches, he moved to the lockers. Changing clothes, he put on gray cotton sweats that felt comforting. He grabbed his racquet and walked down a narrow stairway to the courts.

As he descended, he made an inspection tour of the courts; it was useful to see who would be watching. With a hand towel, he wiped sweat remnants off his grip, looking around.

He liked the bare floors. Dead air. His footsteps echoed.

In this place, people were encased under white bright lights, as if for exhibition. It was a show of strength, perseverance, as much as anything else that made him come here week after week. Being able to display a glimpse of himself, the power, raw courage. What could be better? He needed an audience.

There was a difference between him and Higgins. Higgins came to win, he came to show himself.

Yet any layperson would not know him for what he was.

He saw Higgins twenty yards before he reached him. Higgins was standing alone, waiting on court five, raising a hand through the plexiglass. Even though Higgins weighed over two hundred pounds, clothes hung off the man's frame, his hair unbrushed.

He smiled at him. He would cut him to pieces today.

The excitement was there, then evaporated.

They had been doing this for two years.

"How you doing, my friend?" Higgins asked, his frame bending at the knees, stretching his leg muscles.

"Fine, you ready?" He just smiled, small teeth barely showing.

Higgins smirked. "Oh, I don't know. I'm gonna beat you this week."

"I hope to God not. I've got a chance to kick your ass, and you can be damned sure I'm going to take it, as always," he said, making haste to his favorite starting point, three feet in from the back line. "Just like last Thursday."

Higgins said nothing, concentrating on his serve, which came with a blast.

He returned the hard ball with a thumping backhand. The screeching of white-top rubber soles on polished wood and the thump of the rebounding ball filled the small space.

Higgins began talking between quick breaths as he always did. "You heard about this Burning Man killer thing?"

"No, not really," he lied, as he did to Higgins often. Planting his feet, he let go a loaded forearm shot that scored the first point.

Higgins groaned and wiped sweat off his balding head.

He handed over the ball, and a second service followed.

"How come you haven't heard of him?"

"I've been extremely busy. I've got a chance to show my stuff right now, you know, for the director's position."

Higgins's words came in short blasts, between heavy breaths. "Yeah, right. Like they're going to consider you. How do you know you're being considered?"

"They haven't asked me. It's an open position. I don't think they have many choices. Board won't start seriously looking for, I don't know, another month, till Griswold leaves. Four weeks to show my stuff. You still working with Bristol Medical?"

"Yeah, it's a genuine showplace," Higgins said sarcastically. "I wish I was this Burning Man chump, getting all the attention."

"You think he likes it?"

Clapping against the far wall, the ball whizzed by Higgins's head. He couldn't manage a return. He wiped the sweat off his brow, wrung his hand in his shirt, crouched, and said, "You want to put money on the game?"

"Sure."

"Forty bucks says I make a comeback."

"You're on."

Once the ball was in air, they resumed the conversation.

"How do you see the Burning Man?"

Higgins replied, "I don't know. Might be some kind of a pervert, you know, gets his rocks off. Maybe he's got a normal girlfriend, a misses, though I don't think so. I think he can't make it any other way."

Higgins kept talking. "Got strange taste in women, that's for sure."

"How so?"

Higgins said, "Geez. If you're gonna be doing that, why not go for upper-class chicks.

A flat cold feeling. "I thought he did."

"Yeah, I guess two of them were, but I heard he slashed a whore and some farm worker."

Going inside himself, he missed a shot.

"Gotcha," Higgins taunted.

"So you think less of him because he killed those two?"

"Yeah. I guess. Don't make much sense, you know."

"Mmm-hmm," he said, straightening. He could feel the fire rising up in him.

"You know with AIDS and stuff, how careful can the guy be? If it was me, I'd be making it with…" Higgins wiped sweat from his brow and returned a vicious hit. "Newport Beach types."

He slammed the ball as it came at him. It rocketed to the wall in front, just above the painted line, and flew past Higgins.

"Shoulda brought a bat," Higgins joked.

"Or more likely a tank," he said. "So you think he knows them?"

"Huh?"

"You think he knows them? You know, the girls."

"Well, that could be difficult. What if there were witnesses?" Higgins replied.

"You think he's dumb enough to leave witnesses?"

"I don't rightly know. Haven't been any to come forward. It'd be difficult."

"Why?"

Crashing against the walls, ceiling, floor, the small blue rubber ball continued to give them a workout.

Higgins grunted, taking a shot. "They're rich. The first one is that surgeon Marsh's daughter. You don't think someone saw them?"

"What if no one got a lead on it? What if he doesn't draw attention?"

There was a moment of silence.

"Jesus Christ. You might as well give up on that idea." Higgins slapped at the ball and scored a point. He grinned and looked back. "Take that, you sonofabitch."

He felt his blood pressure rising, felt his face flush. Nobody saw it.

"How do you think he could do it without drawing attention to himself?" Higgins questioned, sweat soaking through his sweats.

He served. "Maybe our guy's a gentleman caller. Maybe he doesn't stand out in a crowd. What do you think?"

"Pisses me off, that's what I think."

"Huh?"

"If he's such a gentleman caller, what's he doing carving up pretty girls?"

"You wouldn't understand," he said, his voice muffled by the ball's ricochet against polished wood.

Game point. Match.

Higgins was pissed because he was wet and his opponent was dry and smug. "Dammit if you don't always end up kicking my butt. You want the forty now?" Higgins said, looking at him.

He was used to Higgins showboating, used to his inability to deliver on the goods when the time came. "Don't worry about it. Next week, it's double or nothing."

He got home about 3 p.m. to La Blanca, the house he had built for himself. It stood obscured from view of the Pacific Coast Highway, at the end of a gravel driveway that ran past cactus, succulants, and stone. He fancied the landscaping but did not know why. The starkness of it perhaps, against the blue ocean. Now, in late July, the prickly pear was in bloom. Its yellow-red flower casting no scent, yet magnificent against the sky. The house itself blended seamlessly into the costal chaparral. That is what made it so wonderful. In one instant it was there. In the next it was not.

Turning off the silent alarm, he nevertheless made an inspection tour of the house. There had been an aborted robbery attempt just last year. He flicked on the lights in each room and looked around. A visitor would not think he lived alone. He kept a full line of dresses in a guest bedroom closet. Maria did not question it when he mentioned they belonged to his girlfriend.

"*Sí.*" She had simply nodded and kept on cleaning.

He made sure the collection of clothing changed periodically to reflect the particular style of the season. Keeping two toothbrushes by the sink furthered the illusion. Regardless, Maria understood. He was not like other men. He did not like questions. But he paid her well, and she kept her comments to herself.

Satisfied he was alone in the house, he went upstairs, took a long shower, washed his hair. Dressed in a light blue cotton bathrobe that felt heavy on his tired muscles, he stood looking out over the Pacific and the gardens. Like the house's front, no demarcation line separated the wild country from the garden below. The two landscapes blended seamlessly. That is what he wanted. The site, a triangular chaparral that plunged to the sea, first attracted him for its ruggedness, its connection to nature. He wanted an innocuous garden, a garden that celebrated the surrounding natural beauty.

He remembered his grandmother and her carefully pruned roses. Each one a mere token of what it could be if allowed to grow wild. Instead she had pruned each plant, clipped and directed the limbs to the point they looked cajoled, contrived.

It was much the way he felt around her.

Instead of that, here he had hired a landscape designer who understood the beauty of low-maintenance California natives, such as artemisia and toyon. The melding of his garden and native plants and costal scrub provided him a oneness with nature, as this house did with the ocean. Below him, the slate patio's arched surface seemed to vanish, especially when viewed from the second-story window where he stood.

His human imprint below was slight.

It was as if nature could regain the upper hand at any moment, if it only wanted to. It was as if the sea was lapping at his floor.

This was the view he woke to each morning and savored each evening.

Towel drying his hair, he sat in the red chair and switched the automatic floor-to-ceiling blinds so they covered the windows. Light turned to pitch blackness with a mechanical whir.

He felt excited. Behind him, he turned on a metal reading lamp that cast a halo around him. With another button, a five-foot screen descended out of the ceiling. He turned on the projection television and the DVD. Sitting back comfortably in the red chair, he felt the air conditioning cool and dry his hair. He threw the towel on the floor. Stretching out further, he turned out the light behind him.

Darkness enveloped him. Lying back in it, he could have been anywhere. The video tape images cast a bluish, then red shadow over him. He closed his eyes, imagining he was with the first one. Nancy Marsh. The one he had waited for.

He opened his eyes and she was there on the screen. Closing them again, he let her sheer image wash over him. He could hear her laughing.

Cut to an image of her father's house. A chocolate Labrador name Hershey jumped at her, ears flopping, a playful bark. He closed his eyes, cementing the image in his eyes, his mind. There was no up or down now. No left or right, no backwards, forwards.

Only Nancy Marsh, only now.

He remembered.

The video jumps as he approaches the young woman, her slim frame hunched over a white and pink iced birthday cake with nineteen candles. She blows them out. Camera catching a glimpse of her breasts. The video image blurs, sharpens to a close-up. His naked body lifting weight, muscles bathed in sweat. He can see the veins and sinews pulsing, can feel his blood surging like a cobra. He spits and writhes as he struggles with the weight. He knows it is training for what he must do.

Even closer, his eyes fill the screen, fluttering, then rolling up into white balls. They engulf the lens.

He is plunged into darkness. Into Nancy.

She died in this house.

This next part he loves.

A white blank blur becomes a white ceiling. Fading back, adjusting the focus, it is the ceiling. The camera drops down abruptly. Nancy Marsh is there. She is thrashing, crying, turning to him as he stands over her. He says nothing, smoothing her hair as she tries to rise. The camera jerks back and there is a room. White tiled walls and floors. A stainless-steel table. He walks to the camera, his naked body obscuring the shot, blackness. Then he walks back to the screaming girl.

He notices now in the scene he is firm, excited.

He feels it here too.

Injecting her, the girl's body goes limp, although she is still screaming. Shrill screams.

Nancy Marsh is wet with perspiration, gleaming in the light he has installed overhead. Her neck rising up, wildly. Eyes roll, then focus on him. He walks to the camera. The screen goes black.

Darkness hides many sins.

Light again. It is focused more clearly now. The tripod has been moved closer so he can tape her face. Remembering the first time he decided to tape her face, he realizes only now the reason he did so. It was to relive his grandmother.

He closes his eyes and remembers the first time.

"Santa," he says. It was what he had always called her.

Opening them, he is hovering over Nancy. Cutting. His hand coming into the picture from the right, holding a long stylized knife, its blade gleaming. First there are the numerous small incisions, each one a release for him. He can hear his breath, lumbering and heavy from the camera.

He licks his thick lips as the images play out.

As he approaches the last wound, the one to the abdomen, his hand is shaking. Knitting his brows, he holds it still. He can cut the life right out of her with one blow. Yet she is alive. A dark spot below her buttocks spreading, arms and hands doing nothing, the drug having taken its toll. The screams are there.

Darkness like a sea around him, transporting him. In this room, he is covered in sweat, although the air conditioning continues to purr. Tongue running against small teeth.

She is dead now. Propped against a sycamore bush, her head dangling. A brown blur turns into a black blur as he curses, moving to the tripod; he steadies it and returns to her. Carefully, he arranges her, head facing toward the sea, to Newport. That way she can see La Blanca forever. Share it with him.

He puts his hand on wet skin, taking himself in his palm.

She is with him. Here. Now.

Arranged, her body resembles a scarecrow. Nancy Marsh under a sycamore bush, splayed out for all the world to see.

He comes into the picture from the right, moving slowly, effortlessly, as if on air. He wears a coat now, blood-smeared. With gloved hands, he takes her limp, lifeless arm, putting it around his neck. Lifting the lobbed head, he grins in the direction of the camera, holding the pose for a good ten seconds.

He wants to make sure this is captured on video.

He watches himself and Nancy in an embrace.

Forever.

SEVENTEEN

Which way I fly is Hell; myself am Hell;
And in the lowest deep a lower deep
Still threat'ning to devour me opens wide,
To which the Hell I suffer seems a Heav'n.
—John Milton, *"Paradise Lost"*

hat same day, Cat got word from the FBI in Chicago. Boston, Miami, New York, and San Francisco had come up dry on this guy's MO. But Chicago, well, that was a different story.

Cat immediately decided to fly into O'Hare. Richmond disagreed. "Cat, you're needed here. Without you who'll oversee the forensics work, photo analysis, the evidence handling?"

"Agent Gray is well versed in FBI procedures. And anything he can't handle, Sanchez can. From there, anything that needs further decision can be handled by me." She lifted her cell phone in the air. "I'll be reachable."

"But what can you hope to gain from going to Chicago now?"

"I don't exactly know, but I mean to find out," she said. She was supremely cool yet anxious to be on her way. "Will you drive me to the hotel, to pack some clothes? Then the airport? I've got a six o'clock flight on United." Cat cursed herself again for not renting a car yet. What kind of life was this, begging rides here and there?

"I see no reason why not."

"Good," she responded in a knee-jerk fashion.

"You sure Gray and McGregor can handle it? What if we get another body?"

"James is as competent a medical examiner as I have seen. You get anything major, you call me."

Within five minutes they were in Richmond's car, a Mercedes 500 SEL. Cat surveyed the car. "Police work must pay well."

"Just appearances. It's a lease. I don't own one of these, probably never will."

"Oh, I don't know about that. I see big things in your future." Cat knew it sounded like polite small talk, but she was telling the truth. "You've got a good way with the media, and your men respect you. That's more than I can say for a lot of chiefs I've worked with."

They headed toward the Hyatt, Cat tucking her black doctor's bag firmly between her ankles. "Any aspirations of higher office?"

"To be honest with you, I haven't thought about it since my wife's death."

Cat wondered if she should ask then decided on it anyway. "How did Emily die?"

He took a gulp. "She was killed at night coming back from a fundraiser in Brea. Hit by a drunk driver on Brea Canyon Road. Guy fell asleep at the wheel." His words were shaky, quick, as if by speaking of it he relived each second. "His pickup truck crested a hill, already over the center line. Hit my Emily straight on, doing seventy-three miles an hour. She didn't have a chance."

"That's horrible. I'm sorry." It was one thing to deal with death daily, strangers' deaths, innocuous bodies on a slab. It was another to listen to a personal account.

"She was beautiful, my Emily. Always giving of herself, even till the day she died." His face reddened. She could see he was fighting tears.

They sat in silence till they reached the Hyatt. Cat ran in and five minutes later reappeared with an overnight bag. In the time she was gone, Richmond gathered enough strength to continue the conversation.

"What about you? You must have someone special in your life."

Cat wondered about his intent; he probably meant nothing. "I have a son, Joey. He is six, almost seven. And an ex-husband who I'd rather not talk about."

"Difficult divorce?"

"No, actually we get along pretty well as far as my son is involved. It's just that Mark isn't part of my life. I don't need him anymore." Cat watched the sun setting.

"Do you need anyone?" Richmond asked.

"That's a strange question."

"No, it's an honest one," he said as they turned onto MacArthur Boulevard, left toward John Wayne Airport.

"I don't know, Robert." It was the first time she had called him by his first name.

Pulling up to United's departure terminal, he asked, "Do you think you ever could?"

"I don't know. Never thought of it."

"Well, think of it while you're gone, Catherine. And keep yourself safe."

She grabbed her bags and was gone.

News of the Burning Man Task Force made the *Orange County Register*'s front page. He settled down with a Blue Mountain coffee in his favorite overstuffed chair.

From his Laguna Beach house overlooking the midnight blue Pacific, he could see the water outside swelling, waves growing larger and more prolific. In keeping with the island's secluded aura, Catalina appeared to emerge naturally from its surroundings in the distance.

Night was just giving rise to day.

He opened the paper, amused to see Dr. Catherine Powers on the front page. Thinking of her was quite common to him now.

Surrounded by his white-on-white Turkish rugs, paintings by Medved, he relished this sanctuary. This house. He'd called it La Blanca, "The White," and outfitted it in all white. He sat in the one object in the house which was any other color, a blood-red-hued chair.

It was pleasing to let Catherine into his house. The only woman, other than Maria, the maid, who had shared this space with him for the past fifteen years. He beamed as he thought of her, his eyes studying her news photo once more.

"Catherine," he whispered to her, his words barely a purr. "Catherine, welcome to my world." He lifted his arms. "This is my world."

He took the front page and splayed it out on the white carpeting. "My Catherine, beautiful Catherine," he said, eyes dancing over her photograph, taking in a three-stranded pearl choker, cobalt blue suit, pearl earrings, elegant and understated. "Like the woman herself," he added, his voice soft, controlled.

He felt the excitement rising in him, his pulse quickening.

It was so exhilarating to share himself with this woman. Finally, after all these years. He could see her here, walking casually among his McGuire furniture, towel drying her damp auburn hair after a brisk morning shower.

A shower they would share together.

He took scissors, carefully cutting out the photograph and the article. He studied the words they had written about her: "'We intend to catch him, pure and simple.' That's the quote from Dr. Catherine Powers, 38, the FBI's chief forensic pathologist out of Quantico, Virginia. Dr. Powers will head the Burning Man Task Force from Orange County, a statewide FBI dragnet. Calls have also been put out nationwide. The task force will call for the cooperation of over 100 law enforcement agencies working in unison. Dr. Powers, a doctor of psychology, brings her special talents in forensic medicine and criminal psychology to the investigation…"

Looking at the photograph, he noticed a lock of hair was pulled behind her right ear. A nervous habit? Right-handed, no doubt. Blue suit buttoned so high around her neck. The last time he had seen her, she had been wearing a gray sweat suit. Despite the informality, signs of Catherine's clout were evident to him—the way she commanded the media, the coterie of politicians who trailed in her wake, the diamond solitaire ring she wore.

"I wonder who gave that to you?" he mused.

More perceptible, even from this grainy color shot, was the way she held herself. Head high, back straight. Catherine had become a lightning rod of the public's perception of problems with violent and uncontrolled crime. A Madonna for all that was wrong in the world. From the aggressive fire in her eyes, she relished this role.

"I like a woman with a little fire," he murmured, remembering how Consuelo Vargas tried to scream. "But you are lagging behind. I expect so much from you. I know you will get there soon."

He lay on the floor, seeming to be asleep, his head propped under one hand. The newspaper clipping lay on his chest. Almost imperceptible breathing. The only real betrayal of each breath was a slight rise in his chest. He could control it. Had many times before.

Opening his emerald eyes, sitting cross-legged on Berber carpeting, he returned his gaze to the photo, pressing supple fingers against the print. He kept reading. "When asked how long the investigation will take, Dr. Powers replied, 'As long as it takes. What's important is that the women and children of this community feel safe.' Dr. Powers herself is the mother of a six-year-old boy."

"Ah yes, my little friend, Joey," he said smoothly, controlling each syllable. He let excitement wash over him. Anxiety tingling in his fingertips.

He would know the boy better before the day was over.

Without meaning to, he sucked in a deep breath.

What would the boy look like today? Those long eyelashes. His innocence. Laughter.

He laughed himself, small white teeth showing.

"I read all your stories, Catherine. Each is more interesting than the last. More…" He hesitated, then instantly found the right word. "Passionate."

He looked up from the paper, watching dawn break. The real beauty of Laguna lay in the daily discovery of its hidden gems, he thought. Its roaring surf.

Small children playing in sand down below. He loved to watch them from this vantage point. Like a hawk watching his prey, from high above. Silent, unseen, deadly.

An uncanny orange sunrise. He wanted to share these things with Catherine. Surprises at each corner, surprises with each light glimmer that painted these white walls.

Surprises that she could not possibly imagine.

He wanted to share this perpetual backdrop of ocean and sky with her. "Yes," he said. "Catherine, one day soon."

Taking a sip of coffee, he read the articles again. Catherine said she cared about the people who lived here, and he believed her. But what would she know about the overwhelming bond that he held with her? It was imperceptible to her now.

But soon it would not be.

When all the talking ended, when she had protested his actions and was stunned by their result, then and only then would she understand their bond.

He had never been bitter about his mother. Hated her and loved her, yes, but never bitter. She taught him some good lessons. How to deliver on a promise, how to be productive during the day, and how to feel so engulfed by the night that he felt he was thrown into the sea.

At times it was scary. He didn't deny it.

But with each day, he set his heart and mind at developing his talent. With each minute he invested in making it real, the investment paid off. Each woman he killed felt better than the last, the prior one a fraction as fulfilling as her successor.

Laguna Beach was of course the perfect place for such fantasies. A community of upper-class gays, artists, and liberals, it seemed to personify the free-flowing easy mentality that was Berkeley in the sixties. This town was tucked just below Newport, but people here were not into Porsches and Beemers. One could just as easily appreciate a 1964 mint-condition Mustang with gleaming chrome trim, top down.

He fit in here perfectly. Fancied himself a mastermind at portraying what was expected. He appeared the liberal yuppie, carved from the ranks of men who named their kids "Sebastian" and "Tyler."

He could not foresee himself ever leaving this place. La Blanca. Soon enough, Dr. Catherine Powers, his colleague, would share it with him.

EIGHTEEN

Endure, and preserve yourselves for better things.
—**Virgil**, *The Aeneid*

It was impossible. Dr. Catherine Powers handled Flight 411 from Orange County to Chicago's O'Hare as well as could be expected, white-knuckling her way through. Her anxiety worsened as the plane descended. She could see no land down there, no horizon. A glimmer of lights like pin dots. Then only pitch-black nothingness. Turbulence over Texas was unbelievable. This plane seemed at the air currents' mercy.

Cat broke down and ordered a double scotch. She didn't care if it was nine o'clock at night. If it took a double to take the edge off this flight, then so be it. The scotch washed over her, the alcohol creeping through her veins, numbing every cell it came in contact with. It felt good.

Her mind wandered to thoughts she normally shunned—about her role at the FBI. In a business embroiled in blood and bodies, Cat could foresee the day she would leave it. Walk away. Despite the Behavioral Science Unit's success, funding was being cut. The entire US government seemed to be "downsizing." In California alone, major defense industry players like Boeing and Lockheed had taken huge cuts in spending programs thanks to Uncle Sam and the California budget crisis. Cat wondered what her future with the FBI would bring.

More importantly, she wondered about her future with Joey. In the last year, she had earned twice as much as she had the previous year but had spent a fraction of her time with him. Yet she loved the boy dearly. Wasn't there some saying about absence making the heart grow fonder? Right now, she was sure that was true.

Mark, of course, was far less sentimental about her work. "You can't be married to your work and be married to me," he had told her when they separated. Now she knew that applied to Joey as well. "You can't have your work and Joey too." She could almost see the words pouring out of Mark's mouth, although he had never spoken them.

It came from somewhere back long ago. The need for family, for roots. Maybe the relationship with her father. A sentimental fool, she did not see that what she wanted, she was tearing down. Solid ties with her son, with her family. She had never come near what Joey wanted her to be. Now in this flight's loneliness, the scotch, she realized she didn't have much of a place in Joey's life. Maybe it would be worth it. After this experience.

Maybe that's why she was getting out.

The plane landed safely at Chicago's O'Hare. Summer's heat sweltered. Humidity in the 90 percent range. She remembered Chicago in the summer. The heat hit her as she disembarked the plane. Cat wanted to strip down to nothing.

As she entered United's expansive terminal, she heard her cell phone ringing at the bottom of her purse. She fumbled past lipstick, mints, a hairbrush for it. Finally, on the fifth ring...

"Dr. Catherine Powers."

Detective McGregor's agitated voice. "Doctor...Cat...is that you?" Static on the line.

"Yes."

"We got another floater. This one looks like it might be Carrie Ann Bennett." He tried to calm himself. She could hear his purposeful gasps for air. "From the looks of it, she's been out there awhile."

"I just arrived in Chicago," she said slowly, deliberately, trying to disguise the slight slur to her speech.

"Can you get a flight back?"

"What?"

"Can you get a flight back?"

"What are you talking about? I left a standing order for the Irvine coroner to handle the autopsy."

"Well, there's a little problem with that…"

"What?"

"We can't locate him."

"You what?"

"We can't find him. He appears to have skipped town."

Cat slapped her forehead, gathering her thoughts. What else could go wrong?

"Okay. I'll have to see if there's a return flight tonight." She glanced at the sports watch on her wrist. "It's eleven-thirty now. I'll have to catch a red-eye back."

"I'll tell the chief."

"McGregor, has anyone touched the body?"

Cat had also left a standing order that anything resembling the Burning Man's work was to be left where it was. No sheet covering it, no attempt at dignity. Nothing. Even if it was a floater.

"No, not that I'm aware."

"Where did it wash up?"

"It's near a place the locals call The Wedge in Newport Beach."

Cat nodded, recalling the jettied harbor where waves doubled back on themselves, building speed and velocity. What resulted was a hammering force, compacted sand, riptides unlike she'd felt before. The surfers loved it. On a bad day, The Wedge could kill you.

"What condition is the body in?" She knew it was a stupid question as soon as it came out.

"Pretty battered, I'm afraid."

"No one touch it till I get there. Find out who found it, but no one touch it."

"Sure."

Cat glanced up at the departure boards, found out the plane she had just come in on was leaving for LAX in an hour.

"Here's the deal. I'll be taking the same flight back to LA. It arrives at 3:35. Secure the scene, swing by the hotel for some sweats, and meet me at LAX."

"Sure thing." He could hear her sigh. "You all right, Cat?"

"Yeah. It's just I've been doing a lot of thinking…"

"Thinking?"

"About this life. All we do is react. Waiting for bodies, waiting for our families to adjust to all this madness." It was the scotch talking. She never shared herself like this.

McGregor knew what she was thinking. "It is madness, ain't it?"

"Sure is."

Bucking winds, Cat's plane arrived ten minutes late. Clutching her overnight bag and medical bag, she did not worry about what she looked like. Though she was sure she looked like hell. Instead, she worried about Carrie Ann Bennett. What condition was she in?

McGregor knew what she was thinking as soon as she got in the car.

"Long night, huh, doc?"

"Yeah." Cat kept her eyes averted.

"You doing okay?" McGregor could see her fatigue.

"Yeah, I'm fine."

"You know, whatever it is, you can talk about it."

"Yeah, I know." She would not look at him.

"It's hard, I know." He spoke from experience. "I know this all can affect how you feel. Sometimes I feel it too. Like it's all for nothing. Like for every one you catch, there's a hundred more, all ten times worse, ten times more vicious. Sometimes I say what's the use? Feel like chucking it."

Her eyes met his in the dash board mirror.

"When you get like that, you've gotta take a deep breath and look at all the good. Kids like Carrie Ann Bennett, Nancy Marsh. Without us, they might never be found. Never receive any…" He stopped, swallowed hard. "Dignity."

"I know."

"Maybe you feel like you're always chasing and it ain't no good. But it is, Cat." He took her hand and squeezed it, then let go. "It is."

Cat smiled halfheartedly and pulled herself together. It had been a long night, with no sleep. It was just going to get longer. "So tell me the condition of the body."

"It's pretty bad. Worse than the last one. The surf beat her into the sand pretty good. She's been floating for a long time. From what I heard, the people who found her weren't even sure it was a body."

"That's common if she's been out there any time. Any clothing, jewelry?"

"Nope, nothing like that. She's clean. Naked."

"What about the people who found her?"

"Older couple, in their sixties. Have a beach house nearby. Taking a midnight stroll. From what I hear, they couldn't make out what it was at first. Figured a shark got hold of a big seal or something. The man went closer in to investigate." McGregor cleared his throat. "He got within twenty feet, realized it was something awful, and called 911 from his cell phone. Paramedics and cops arrived in minutes. Cops advised against moving it, like you ordered, although the paramedics wanted to make sure it was dead. Crime scene techs kept everyone at bay, you know?"

"Yeah. I know. They didn't touch it did they?"

"Naw. Chief got the call about a minute later."

Cat listened as he continued filling her in.

"Scene's been secured; we should be there soon."

They passed over nearly deserted freeways, side streets, the ride taking about half what it normally took. Just turning off the freeway, Cat looked at him.

McGregor rocketed the car down Balboa. A mile ahead, she could see the luminescent glow of yellow and blue revolving cruiser lights. Her excitement rose.

As McGregor swung the car into a paved opening of palms, beach, and a police mob, Cat put her hand on his.

"Don't tell anyone about our conversation earlier, will you?"

"You don't have to worry. It's between us, Catherine, and it'll stay that way."

"Thank you."

Cat bent under the yellow crime scene banner, its letters twisting in the sea breeze. The air was heavy with the smell of salt and death. Above the horizon, daybreak.

The chief nodded to her, watching her emerge from McGregor's car. She wondered why she felt a funny twinge when she saw him.

The older couple was sitting on a Medevac van's bumper, the man's arm around the woman's shoulder. Her face was illuminated in the lights. From the look of it, she was crying. Paramedics packed up their gear, realizing they could do no good here. McGregor stood with his hands deep in his pockets for a while then walked over to where the older couple sat. Cat knew he would go over everything they had already told the authorities fifty times before. It would do no good. They hadn't seen anything.

The only one who had seen anything was Carrie Ann Bennett.

Cat ducked into the back of McGregor's car, which was parked in a dark spot. She quickly changed into sweats, thankful more morning light was now showing in the sky. Light would help her search for evidence.

Evidence was an ally. Wading into the water didn't scare her. Not finding any evidence did.

Thankfully the waves this morning were calm enough for her journey. Only about a foot high. Cat wanted to be able to take a look at the body before anyone else did.

Here, there was no need for compassion, no use for decorum for the dead. The dead were dead. Any attempt to drag the body in, to bring it ashore, to shelter it from shocked eyes was useless to her because it all destroyed evidence. Without evidence, she would never catch him. Perhaps he knew that. Perhaps that was why he was now dumping into the ocean. It had a way of erasing everything, fingerprints, skin, hair, fibers, semen. Literally, the ocean did its job of washing the body clean. So often, moving a body onshore only made matters worse. What little trace evidence there might be below the fingertips was lost in the sand. What little epidermal skin was left was dragged onshore.

Cat wouldn't let that happen to this girl. To Carrie Ann Bennett.

She wouldn't let it happen to her evidence.

Couldn't give the bastard the advantage.

As she waded into the water, her medical bag floating behind her on a makeshift raft, she thought of the girl. Right now Carrie Ann Bennett was only a number—number five in these killings.

Seagulls swooped, carried on the wind around her, their *awk-awk* cries resonant over the waves. She watched as a few brave birds dive-bombed the body. Waist-deep in water, Cat moved forward and back slightly with each wave, keeping her eyes focused on the floater, her bag trailing behind her wrist like a sport fisherman tied to a bowline. The Pacific's water was clear and cool, as was the morning air on her cheeks.

Cat braced against a weak riptide every now and then, digging her feet into the sand for support.

Around her, this idyllic Newport Beach surf spread out in both directions, blue and aquamarine. Below water, Cat watched surfperch zip by between floating kelp clumps. Even with this current, this was a place of life. Above water too, the air was filled with gulls and the sun's warmth. Twenty feet away, Carrie Ann Bennett floated in conspicuous contradiction to her surroundings. Bloated from internal gases, she appeared a bulbous mass. Arms, legs, intestines splayed out like a starfish, above the smooth blue horizon.

Cat wondered how something so horrible could exist in a place as full of life as this. Looking over her shoulder, she could see McGregor and the others watching her from shore, their bodies growing smaller with each step she took.

About ten feet from the body, she was thankful it hadn't been moved. Removing the corpse from the water would have exposed it to air. The stench would have been unbearable. At least here Carrie Ann Bennett lay protected in a watery cocoon. Conceivably for that reason, the body did not smell that bad. And because of the Vick's rub she had put under her nostrils before wading out.

Cat beat back one of the screeching seagulls overhead. Carrie Ann Bennett appeared inhuman. Her midsection had blown up to three times its normal size, skin glossy, several layers having sloughed away. Floating face-up, the girl's grotesque, irregular features contradicted any notion that this was once a lovely young woman. Forehead, cheeks, chin appeared a doughy white mass, much like risen bread before it's baked. Eyes gone from their sockets, a likely meal for crabs, fish, microbes.

Now Carrie Ann Bennett lay open to the elements, sun baking down on her. Arms and legs floated out to the side, each mushroomed in size. Attached to her left arm was what appeared to be a black serpent. For an instant, Cat was taken aback. Then she realized there were ropes, like black tentacles, leading off from her torso in three directions. With each soft wave, a whitish splotchy film that encased Carrie's body gave way, a little more of it floating toward shore.

Staring down at the body, at that film, Cat remembered her first floater. In medical school, there was a saying that "one never forgets their first floater." Cat had not.

In the small town of Key West, Florida, the ocean crystalline and calm much like this one, authorities had dragged a fifteen-year-old out of the salt marshes. Although they had not known it at the time, the boy's body had floated back to where it belonged, to the shore. Cat remembered the ballooned appearance, the unbelievable stench, the way the hair had simply fallen away from the boy's scalp. He was a victim of foul play. His friends dared him to walk outside the wooden pier's protective guardrail. Drunk on booze, the boy lost his footing and fell fifty feet to his death in the middle of the night. Receding tides had taken him out to sea, then back in, where he had been impaled on sharp rocks offshore. During the night, his friends had dragged the body in and dumped it in the local salt-marsh mangroves, hoping no one would find it but the herons and gulls.

Cat had performed testing which showed the saline levels in the lungs and skin tissue were entirely different. Cause of death had been a broken neck. Local authorities, given this information, re-questioned the boy's acquaintances on the night he disappeared. One of them cracked and told everything.

Disquieted, Cat remembered her exuberance for this job in those days. How she had tended to the boy as if he were still alive. Speaking to the body as she autopsied him, telling him what she was doing would cause him no pain. What happened to that person? Had death become so routine to her that she simply didn't see people as people anymore? Just hunks of flesh that could be ripped apart by a lightning strike or a gunshot?

Sometimes she wondered how she would die. Would it be investigating one of these cases, or something as simple as a car accident? She had learned so much about medicine, but so little about human beings all these years. Life was a precious thing, but in all this, that conviction seemed to be slipping away from her.

A squawk from overhead brought her back. Carrie Ann Bennett rolled closer to Cat with each wave, bobbing on the ebb tide. Cat positioned herself in the water sideways to the incoming current so that she could float along with the girl's body. From the looks of it, she had been floating a good ten to fourteen days. Ropes twisted around the wrists and left leg, two, maybe three times, tied down so tight it appeared the girl's appendages had been noosed.

Cat leaned over the body and began working, averting her face from the stench that rose up when the wind came in from the east. Lacerated, the girl's skin, even what was left of her hair, had been bleached white by the sun and salt. Rancid-smelling adipocere floated from her stomach cavity, waxy and yellowish-white in appearance.

She tried to get close enough to work, but not to touch the body, or have it rub up against her. Critical evidence could be lost to the teeming surf, from the slightest pressure from her skin. Expertly, she took advantage of the current to bring the naked body closer.

It was funny how the ocean, the giver of all life to the world, also harbored death, as if trying to resurrect it. Cool aqua waves lapping against the corpse, fish swimming by below, oblivious to the horror. The sea filled up each of this girl's cells, trying to infuse her with life, trying to bring back what was already gone.

Assessing the hands first, Cat saw that only three nails remained on the left hand, two on the right. The body's expanding gases and the formation of adipocere had caused most of the nails to pop off. They were now lost to the sea. What struck Cat first was the fact that what remained had been washed clean. Any trace evidence—blood, fibers, hairs—would be long gone. But still the girl's nails had a story to tell. Although bleached white, the nails were not torn or jagged. She had not fought her attacker, had not ripped into him. When his cutting began, thankfully she had been unconscious, perhaps drugged.

Cat took a clear plastic Ziploc baggie from her tethered floating medical bag. Carefully and quickly, she removed a nail with tweezers. It gave way instantly from the jellyfish-like hand, slipping easily from the flesh. She placed it in the bag and went over the seal twice with her fingers, making sure it was closed. She labeled it with a wax marker, tagged it, and continued with the other nails.

With gloved fingers, Cat examined the hands painstakingly. Each finger resembled a slimy white waterlogged cigar. She handled each gingerly, afraid the finger would simply tear away and be gone.

It was as if the body was liquefying right before her eyes.

Scrutinizing each hand, she was looking for any lacerations, contusions, or abrasions that would indicate the girl had fought for her life. Picking up the flesh, which hardly held together in her hand, Cat found a blackened mark on the anterior portion of Carrie's right hand. Mentally Cat noted there had been a struggle. Carrie may not have clawed her assailant, but at least she had gotten one good lick in. Good.

Fighting against the ocean's growing surge that wrapped her legs, tugged at her footing, Cat took a hair sample, both from the head and pubic region. Skin tissue samples were taken from various sites of the corpse, each to compare the decay, to determine exactly how long Carrie Ann Bennett had been at sea. Toxicology and DNA testing would tell Cat much about the girl's time of death and whether she had been drugged, poisoned.

Cat's chest pumped up and down, fighting for clean air. The water had done its job, preserving the body, relieving the stench. But every now and then the chest was left bare so that an unbearable stench rose up.

Having collected what she could in the water, Cat noticed the body floating close to the barnacled jetty. She did not want any further secrets lost to rocks and surf. Carefully she held the pulpy mass, turned with the waves slapping against her, and pulled it ever so gently toward shore, steering clear from rocky outcroppings.

"Come on now," she coaxed the girl, "I'm taking you home."

NINETEEN

Be patient toward all that is unsolved in your heart.
Try to love the questions themselves.
—**Rainer Maria Rilke**, *Letter to Franz Xaver Kappus, 1903*

Testing at Quantico headquarters confirmed Marlin Bennett's worst nightmare. His baby had come home. Tissue matches substantiated beyond a shadow of doubt that the poor soul was Carrie Ann Bennett, all 133 pounds, 5-foot-3 inches of her.

Cat found conducting Carrie's autopsy difficult. It was never easy with a floater, but having brought this one back to her mother, her father, had made it even tougher.

Cat went through the motions, as before. Further tissue samples were taken, although Cat was certain the ones at sea had been enough. Still, one couldn't be too careful. Mercilessly, the sea had taken almost all the girl's hair, to the point that her own father had not recognized her. When dental records and DNA had confirmed the worst, he had simply stood there, mute for a good long while. Then, as if a sudden wall of grief had struck through an impenetrable dam of disbelief, he allowed himself to cry.

Now it was Cat's job to learn as much as she could. Invariably, in a case like this, questions only led to more questions. How was he luring them in? What was the attractant? How many more were there out there floating, left for dead?

Looking at the custard-colored mass in front of her on the stainless-steel table, it felt odd being in Dr. Conrad James's facilities without him. She had grown accustomed to him by her side.

He still could not be located, although the Irvine PD had checked with staff and friends. Cat wondered if he had lost it, or decided to get away from this case. She had heard stories about medical examiners cracking under pressure, but she'd never actually seen it happen. Now Cat had two of his assistants helping her with this corpse. They looked forlorn, also wondering where their fallen leader was. One, appearing in his thirties, had the most intense eyes she had ever seen. The other faded into the woodwork. They both stood there, hands clasped in front of them, waiting for her orders.

Gowned, gloved, and receiving clean oxygen through forced vents above, Cat went to work. Peering over the body, she gave the standard information: apparent age, sex, condition of the body. Normally she would have been able to report eye color, obvious race, and age. But with a floater, all of these things were obscured, as if the ocean was playing its own game of hide and seek with her. For this reason, the tissue samples and evidence gathered while Carrie Ann Bennett was in the water was even more important.

It was a perverse irony that only God seemed able to understand: how a girl could be so beautiful in life and so wretched in death. Cat recalled the girl's photograph her mother provided the police—flowing hair, warm smile, the innocent allure of a girl turning into a woman. She felt a twinge of nostalgia. In life, Carrie Ann Bennett had not been beautiful enough to draw a crowd, but pretty in a fresh, down-home sort of way. Cat imagined she was the type of girl who liked to take her daddy a tall glass of lemonade as he cut the grass on the front lawn. Now she would never have the chance again.

Remembering the warm smile, she could feel the girl's presence hovering, Cheshire cat-like, over her remains. Posthumously, Carrie Ann Bennett expected more of herself than most. She expected to tell Cat more than the others.

During the hours that had lapsed between the body being recovered and the present, Cat felt as if she had been caught in a whirlwind. It was always that way. The forbidden excitement from death, like a palatable force, never disappointed. The hype and expectations never fell short of what she knew to be true.

People had a real and unrelenting fascination with death's gauntlet. That was why they slowed on the freeways to gawk at accidents. That was the grounds for the popularity of television shows like *CSI* and its cousins—they dealt unabashedly with the curiosity about death.

Coincidentally, that fascination as a child was what led Cat to this profession. Knowing what she did now, she wondered if she would have made the same career choice. Questions without solutions seemed to play havoc with her mind, her self-confidence. As with the other autopsy, Cat began, speaking into the hands-free mike. This young woman, like the other before, was in much the same condition. Still Cat owed it to her to be equally careful in her observations and her descriptions of what she was seeing. She could not overlook anything.

Cat's two assistants simply stood like sentinels. She wondered if this was their first floater.

Cat turned her attention to the eyes, or lack of them. "The eyeballs are missing, having been consumed by sea life. Sphenoid is visible; a centimeter of tissue is visible attached to the interior orbital fissure…

This girl had teeth that appeared in good condition. "Dental work to the bicuspid molars were evident, three silver fillings total." Describing this, Cat knew Carrie's dental records were a match.

Once gain, over the entire body, the skin appeared translucent, blanched white. Cat struggled to properly describe the bleached mass. "The skin has none of the familiar patina to it, there is no ruddiness, no evidence of color at all."

Cat moved in over the skull, examining the little hair clumps that clung precariously to the skin. Slipping her gloved hand under the head, she lifted it and felt something notched below her fingertips.

Feeling her pulse quicken, she turned off the voice recorder.

"What is it, doctor?" one of the assistants said.

"I've got something back here." Her assistants moved forward, one of them slipping his hands below, the other with his hand under the girl's back. Instinctively, they could tell what Cat needed them to do. "Help me turn her over."

Carrie Ann's fatty, jellied corpse did not want to turn, clinging and squishing stubbornly away from their grip. It was as if she were still floating, not wanting to give up her secrets.

"One, two, three," Cat said as they simultaneously put more effort into flipping the body. It wasn't so much that the corpse was heavy. Far from it. Any heavy muscle tissue had long been replaced by decaying fatty matter. It was that they didn't want to lose any of her. Cat remembered touching a floater at room temperature when she had interned, watching a glob of fat slip through her fingers and plop on the floor. When she thought of it, the image still terrified her. She would not allow that to happen here.

"Careful now, careful…"

The corpse was halfway turned, some of her body weight borne by her mercilessly swollen tree-trunk arm. Soggy layers of skin give way, coming free from bone in one quick movement that they hadn't anticipated. One of the assistants gave a look of sheer disgust.

"I'm losing her!" the other one shouted.

Before his words were over, the featureless putty that had once been Carrie Ann Bennett was flopped on its stomach, making an odd splat sound. Even before that, Cat looked at the cranium, searching for what she had felt.

She didn't search long.

Even as bloated as the head was, Cat could make out the word. Someone had carved "WANT" into the back of Carrie Ann's head.

TWENTY

For of all sad words of tongue or pen,
The saddest are these, "It might have been!"
—**John Greenleaf Whittier**, *"Maud Miller"*

Y ou mustn't blame yourself," McGregor said.

"But he is sending me a message. Don't you see? He is killing them now for blood sport. It has become an even greater game since I entered the picture. This whole national search thing. It's a load of crap." Cat looked at McGregor sideways. "Don't you see, by escalating our search, we are feeding his sick fantasy. And who are we kidding? This guy doesn't live in some backwoods trailer in South Carolina. He's right here, right under our noses. And he's rubbing our noses in that fact every second."

"How can you tell that?" McGregor tried to remain calm, to soothe her. He'd seen this type of reaction before. A combination of getting too close to the case, too little sleep, and too many suspects.

"We can't find him. He leaves us too little." Pent-up frustration came through. "What kind of sicko enjoys this?"

McGregor shook his head. "Cat, maybe you should take some time off the case for a little while."

"What?" Her temper flared.

"It's just a suggestion. You've been out here for two and a half weeks. It's plain to see you're on edge…"

She wheeled around to look at him, stop him from going any further. "You want me to chuck it? Leave it to you local guys?"

McGregor understood that he underestimated Cat's passion and her toughness.

"You think that would be fair?"

He said nothing.

"You think I'd just walk away from this? You think I possess that kind of righteous disregard for my investigation to have someone else simply take over? That's ridiculous."

"I'm saying others are capable, Cat. Someone not as close could be more objective."

She felt her pulse throb in her neck.

"He's sending messages to me. How could I possibly walk away from that? 'I want.' What the hell does that mean? I want what? I want to live, I want to die. I want to do this to every woman I meet."

Anger, like a cascading flood, poured out. McGregor knew better than to say anything more. This was a catharsis. He'd hit a nerve. He would let it ride.

"You wonder about my sanity, think of his. How sane can someone be who writes messages into corpses' heads and then sends them on their watery way?"

Her question reverberated in the car that Tuesday morning as they sped toward the home of Dr. Caldwell Hamilton Marsh.

"How do you think I feel?" There had been a leak from the coroner's office and the papers had plastered the fact that the Burning Man was carving messages into his victims. This had earned Cat a dubious honor. "How do you think I feel when I walk down the street? Everybody saying 'There she is'? Asking me what it's like to be the object of this bastard's affection? Everyone wants to know if I'm enjoying it?"

"People are curious, Cat. You, of anyone, should know that."

"I do. But for the first time, my personal life has become intertwined with a case. And I don't like it one single bit."

Newspapers were filled with speculation about what it was he could want. Her job, money, more victims, compassion, forgiveness, a place in her heart. Cat knew he wanted none of these. He wanted to be understood for being himself.

Not just the public persona which he so carefully cultivated and crafted, but the warped, wretched side of him that only she could understand.

It was like looking at a Picasso or a Van Gogh. One could not begin to understand the artist without first studying the brush strokes…the use of color, line symmetry, light, dark.

With the Burning Man, she could not begin to understand him without studying each of the corpses, blood work-up, toxicology, his modus operandi. With each new killing, he was leaving her more clues, but they were leading nowhere specific.

His killing fever was growing. She was running out of time.

She sat sullen for a minute as they headed along Jamboree, up into Orange Heights.

Soon they came to Dr. Marsh's home. Set back from the road, Cat could nevertheless see a sprawling English Tudor-style home, painted cream and brown. To one side, a turret speared up into the sky. In front, a proper English garden flourished—Pacific giant delphiniums, late-blooming David Austin Roses, an array of sedum and lamb's ears. At first blush, the house seemed quite large, austere, a massive combination of wood, concrete, steel covered by a wood shake roof, which looked somewhat in need of repair. On closer examination, the house, like the man who lived there, seemed warmer, more modest than its exterior. Complexity and simplicity in one.

Dr. Marsh answered the door. From his looming exterior shone appealing eyes, a firm handshake, a sheltering persona. She understood instantly why he was a famous doctor. His sheer size made one feel protected, his personality nurturing. He did not have the "God complex" that many surgeons had. Instead, he welcomed them in easily and warmly.

"Sorry to bother you, sir," McGregor said.

"It's not a bother at all." Dr. Marsh quickly pulled off gardening gloves, rinsed his massive hands under the sink. "Would either of you like something to drink?"

Both McGregor and Cat declined.

He ushered them to a formal living room, done in monochromatic furnishings, leading the eye naturally to Santiago Canyon's hills beyond, now painted green by the summer's rains. Cat could hear the sounds of birds, wildlife outside. She supposed the point of the room was just that—

to allow nature's sounds to be the star. Magnificent white orchids dotted the room.

Cat touched one of the flowers, not believing it real.

"One of my hobbies, raising them," said Dr. Marsh.

"They are beautiful." Cat ran her fingers across the delicate petal, wondering how God could create such perfection in a flower and such evil in a killer.

"They are my babies. Well, at least one anyway." Sitting on the edge of the chair, he spoke at a fast clip. Despite his size, she was sure he was the type who never sat still. It was visibly killing him to sit now.

McGregor pulled out his notebook and got to the point. "Doctor, I know you've read the papers. Heard of the terrible condition of the latest..." McGregor caught on his words. "Victim."

Dr. Marsh's face showed emotion for just a millisecond.

Before McGregor could say anything more, Dr. Marsh began talking, his voice tragic, hushed. "It's really my fault. Nancy wanted to head off to UCLA. She was a bright young woman. She'd been offered a partial scholarship there to study English literature. After a liberal arts education, we had talked about law school for her, maybe Loyola."

Cat watched him wring his big burly hands as he spoke.

"Her mother had accepted the fact she would be leaving. But I could not. She was my only girl. My baby. I wanted her to stay. Convinced her to do a year at Chapman, said it would be good for her. In a liberal arts education, the units would transfer. Hell, I had friends at Chapman who'd make sure they did. I just couldn't bear to lose her yet. We had so much left to do."

He refused to look at them, focusing instead on his hands.

Cat had seen this before, this guilt and self-blame that followed a parent around for the rest of their life. Knowing if only a different decision had been made, their child would be with them today. It was clear that Dr. Marsh would carry the scars the rest of his life.

"Doctor, I know we've asked you this before. But it's really important now. We have reason to believe that the killer has medical training." McGregor paused, ready to write down whatever came out of the man's mouth. "Is there any one of your colleagues, associates, who might have wanted Nancy..." McGregor let his words trail off, the obvious implication hanging in the sunlit room.

"No. Not that I remember. Nancy was a charming girl. Most of the men I work with had watched her grow up. We're a tight-knit, close family. The people at Hoag are an extension of that. For all the money that's been pumped into that place, the doctors and nurses there are still real people. We all work together to preserve, not destroy—" he stopped, tears welling in his eyes—"life."

"I know that. But maybe there was someone who took a special liking to Nancy. Someone who showed her special attention."

"Everyone showed Nancy special attention. She was that kind of person. She could charm a flower into opening early, could sing the birds down from the trees." He looked out across the white carpeting, through the glass doors and concrete pavers to the hills. "You could look straight through that girl, just like you can this house. She didn't have a bad bone in her, not one. And I remember…her laugh."

His gaze returned to his hands.

"You see that garden out there." He looked up toward a backyard filled with perennials, annuals, all in bloom. "That was her favorite spot. We designed it together, to blend in with the wildlife."

Cat looked up. Indeed the carefully manicured lawn and flowerbeds did give way to towering trees, a babbling creek, probably filled with tadpoles and crayfish.

"On a Sunday morning, we would sit out there. Just the two of us, with our coffee, talking. Sometimes fighting over who got the sports page first. Usually she'd win, be up first. She'd be sitting out there, her feet propped up in her white bathrobe, hair slicked back wet. We'd start our Sundays that way."

Cat saw tears in his eyes.

"Of my three kids, she was the one I loved the most. And I couldn't protect her. From him."

"We don't know who he is. Is there anyone you can think of at all who might have had it in for you? Someone you pissed off?"

Sunlight poured in through the south-facing window, cutting a path across the man's face. As he looked up, wet trails stood testament on his cheeks. "There's no one, no one at all."

TWENTY-ONE

There is no great genius without some touch of madness.
—**Seneca**, *On Tranquility of the Mind*

There was no hurry.

Sunrise in Laguna, the surf was still and the yellow sun gleaming.

He sat in his favorite red chair, his face orange in the sunrise. He picked up the paper. A quick glance through and he found her name, her face, lingered over it for a time.

Excitement rose and fell in him when he saw her.

He would not allow himself to look at the photo again today.

By ten he had worked out with weights to near exhaustion. He satisfied himself with his vigor, watching his pecs jump up and down. Sitting in the red chair, his torso pumped from the workout, he watched the surf roll in and out.

There was no hurry.

His flight to Virginia did not leave till noon.

His sense of power engulfed him all the time now.

From the newspaper, the Irvine Police Department and the Burning Man Task Force said what they wanted. But the bottom line was the same: no progress.

Turning on the television, he thought by now there might be some breaking news. They had found Carrie Ann Bennett.

Stretched out in the red chair, he smiled. Catherine was in a group of microphones. Flanked by cops, perhaps a bodyguard, she said, "This man's savage butchery will only make us work harder."

He snorted. *Go ahead.*

But it wouldn't help the next one.

She was already dead.

The newspapers were calling him the Burning Man. He liked the name. Thought it appropriate. After all, what death did men fear most? Death by fire.

Intensity and heat. The words suited him.

Passion too, just like his Catherine.

He watched Catherine's face, studied it. He had DVD'd her. Now he could freeze-frame her at any time. Enjoy the delicate eyes, the way she squared her jaw when she was angry.

Today he would bring her closer to him.

He wanted to tell her what would happen. Wished she had one inkling of what he wanted most. He tried to send her messages. But she had no sense of his presence. When this day was over, she would. He would share himself with her. But she could not have it and live. Still, he wanted her. She was the only one who could understand him.

TWENTY-TWO

For they have sown the wind, and they shall reap the whirlwind.
—**Hosea** 8:7 (KJV)

know, it's all political. You and I both know that, McGregor. But isn't that pretty much what we're doing anyway. These news briefings aren't getting us any closer. They're just making the politicos look good."

Cat and McGregor walked out of the Irvine Police Department building in late afternoon.

McGregor nodded. "Just keep doing what you're doing, and I'll do the rest."

Cat was asked by the chief to stay. The request had been predicated on Cat's building a more detailed profile, so the city could put more black-and-whites on the street in affluent neighborhoods. She didn't buy it.

"And, besides, we don't have anything new to build a profile with. The black nylon rope that was tied around her, it could be bought at any local Ace Hardware Store. Then there's the electrical tape he used. Same thing, buy it at any local home and garden store. Don't you see, he's toying with us. Leaving us with jack—"

"They want you to stay, Cat," McGregor said, squinting into the sun. Donning his sunglasses, he added, "It might not be a bad idea."

"Covering their asses is what they're doing. They're stepping up foot patrols, cars in all the rich areas, thinking that's where this sonofabitch will strike next. But everyone forgets about Kim Collins. She doesn't fit that victim profile. Neither does Consuelo Vargas for that matter."

McGregor knew she had a point. "What if we get another floater?"

"The assistant medical examiners here can handle it. Just make sure they do a thorough job."

"You think there'll be more don't you?" McGregor said.

"Yes. But I don't know if they will be floaters. He seems to work in twos. We've had two upper- to middle-income victims, two floaters. Then there's Kim Collins. God help the politicians if he chooses a poor one this time. With all the manpower concentrated in Irvine, Orange, Newport Beach, he could hit the back streets in Santa Ana. If that happens, you can be sure they'll blame it on my profile. No way."

"You think it's just as likely he'll strike in the lower-classed areas?" McGregor asked.

"It's just as likely. He'll strike wherever he thinks he can get away with it. But there's no reason for me to sit around and wait for it."

"You think it's a good idea to head to Chicago right now?"

"It's the only lead we've got. Someone's got to follow up. Something tells me it will give us something. And anything is better than what we have now. I don't give a damn what the Justice Department is saying, or my superiors. Someone's got to follow up on this. And with my background, I'm the best one."

"I guess you're right on that one."

"Stick with me on this, McGregor. Something's gotta break open soon enough."

TWENTY-THREE

When we remember that we are all mad,
the mysteries disappear and life stands explained.
—Mark Twain, *Notebook*

Would you like more coffee, sir?" a flight attendant with pouty lips asked. He had sat in silence for ten minutes, watching the descent into Virginia, its rolling hills stretched out before him on this Tuesday afternoon.

"That would be fine," he said, lifting his empty cup. She moved forward slowly. He felt the gentle curve of her hand brush his as she poured. A strange and heavy fragrance. It was her perfume—lavender. It reminded him of his grandmother.

"Would you require anything else, a blanket perhaps?"

"Yes, that would be lovely."

He stopped his breath as he watched her back arch upwards, breasts straining against her white cotton blouse. A radiant heat to her. It was here now. He could smell it.

He closed his eyes, taking in her lavender smell.

"Here you are."

He opened his eyes and she was there, her face so close he could feel her breath on his cheek. "I'm sorry, I didn't mean to startle you."

"You surprise me in many ways, my dear," he said, his eyes dancing over her.

She blushed and was gone on a waft of perfume.

He turned his attention back to Virginia below, to thoughts of the boy. Visions of the child reflected like tiny points on a movie screen in his mind. He slept.

Cat heard the bolt slide open. The plane's steel door swung left in front of her. Chicago's O'Hare presented itself. Unwelcoming and still hot.

She looked out. At that angle, she could not see the Sears Tower and the Hancock Building, but she knew they were there, towering over this city.

Cat wanted time to brace herself for the heat, but there was none. It felt like being dipped in the Amazon jungle. At times like this, she wondered why people lived here. The city seemed a city of extremes.

With her overnight bag on one shoulder, she grabbed her suit bag and headed for a cab. Within an hour she had unpacked at the Drake on Michigan Avenue. One of Chicago's finest hotels, she could see nothing had changed. The lobby, still outfitted in marble and velvet, felt so old world. The service discreet, impeccable. Like the first time she had been here.

After she and Mark divorced, she'd had a brief affair with a doctor. As head of the American Medical Association, Dr. Gregory Taft wielded power with reckless abandon. When they had first met, she pursued the singular opportunity to study with him. It was so rare to meet such a supremely confident man. Perceptive, with a brilliant mind, and even more brilliant hands. She recalled how he touched her when they made love. It was as if each touch contained his every thought, his very soul. She longed for a touch like that again.

It had been a long time. As much as anything else, she realized only now that renewing that affair was her reason for coming here.

But first there was business to attend to.

After an hour-long cab ride into the city, she settled into the room that would be her home for the next few days. Sometimes the travel got the best of her, making her feel like she was always packing and unpacking, longing for her small bungalow in Quantico. She sat on the bed and called down to the front desk. Her rental car had arrived.

She had prearranged a meeting with Dr. Phillip Stall, the chief of staff of the Illinois State Hospital for the Criminally Insane. Her preliminary research into this case had shown that he had treated a boy years ago, a boy they called simply Eric.

From the little Cat knew, Eric had been convicted of murdering his grandmother and a cousin with acid, sulfuric acid, when he was only seventeen. That was twenty-one years ago. Eric had been institutionalized, judged insane, incapable of assisting in his own defense. After years of therapy, drugs, and eventually a trial, the jury had found him innocent and he was released. He had disappeared. That is what Cat feared the most.

She thought carefully of what to wear to this meeting. Should she change her normal blouse and skirt and heels to something more mannish? Or would that communicate to Carl Stearbourne that he had already gotten in her head? Should she wear perfume or not to her first meeting with him? Hair up or down? She decided that anything contrived would be immediately apparent to him as soon as he met her. It would show in her demeanor, and he would pick up on it right away. And why not simply dress as she always did? So he would admire her legs in black high heels. Carl Stearbourne wouldn't be the first man to do so and he wouldn't be the last. And by not changing her appearance for him, she would signal that she was not intimidated by him or his insanity. It might actually prove to be a way to communicate that she considered him a person, as opposed to an animal.

The more Cat thought of it, she was sure she had made the right choice.

As she drove the rental, she prayed that somehow, some way, the killings would stop. But like all the serial cases she had worked in the past, she knew that was a fantasy. Barring something unexplained, the murders would not stop. In her opinion, the killer had not been born a serial killer. He had been manufactured, his murderous fantasies a result of a traumatic home life beyond his control. From what she knew of Eric, his home life fit that profile. All through childhood, the boy's life was orchestrated by a grandmother whose hatred for him fueled Eric's all-consuming rage. As a child, Cat thought, the killer had directed that rage against the domineering female figure in his life, his grandmother. He was directing the same rage again.

Only this time it was indiscriminate.

From what she knew, Eric fit, maybe a little too well. Arriving at the institution, it looked more like an Eastern Seaboard college than an institution for the criminally insane. Other than high iron gates and fencing, it gave no indication that it housed Illinois's most insane.

Dr. Stall met her at her car with a firm handshake. "We are so pleased to have you, Catherine, or should I call you Dr. Powers?"

"Actually, Cat is just fine."

"I was so pleased to hear you'd be coming. I've been following your case with great interest." Stall wore coke-bottle-thick glasses that obscured his pupils. Cat did not like being unable to meet the man's gaze.

He ushered her inside the austere brick building, into his office.

"Please, have a seat." He directed her to a leather chair and then took a seat behind his desk. The room smelled like lemon polish. It was small, cramped, thin ribbons of dust visible through a single sunlight shaft from a window above Cat's head. Books and copies of *The American Journal of Psychiatry* lay open on his desk. Efficiently, he closed the case file he had been working on, stacked it to his left, and folded his hands in front of him.

"The FBI really appreciates any help you could provide."

"We are glad to provide it. Now about the meeting with Carl."

Carl Stearbourne had been Eric's roommate of sorts, sharing the cell next to the boy. He was the only man Eric would speak with, himself a murderer of women. On one level, the relationship between the men seemed superficial; but on another level, both understood each other's overriding fantasy to rid himself of a domineering mother figure in their lives. While the doctors and psychiatrists merely analyzed, Carl understood.

Catherine would be Carl Stearbourne's first outside contact in over a year.

"Please don't misunderstand me, doctor. We are more than happy to cooperate with you, but there are a few ground rules we follow with Carl. Everyone follows them. Do I make myself clear?" The small-boned man rocked back and forth in his chair, as if the mere mention of Carl Stearbourne made him nervous. From the looks of it, any mention of Eric's name made him even more so. He still wouldn't meet Cat's gaze.

"Carl has been here for thirty-one years. In that time, he has mellowed. However, the risk still exists that he may—" The man hesitated and rocked harder. "Engage you. It is very important that you not provide him anything sharp."

"For obvious reasons."

On the flight, Cat had read about Carl. Anyone who studied psychiatry had. He was the consummate prisoner, until you gave him an advantage. Then he turned predator in the most cunning and malicious way. Convicted of stabbing his mother to death with her garden shears, he had splayed the corpse out on her bed, had sex with it, dissected her in the family bathtub, then calmly bagged her remains and sat there, waiting for someone to find the horror. He and Eric had much in common. Cat had read that a year ago, one of the guards had made the mistake of thinking Carl was ill. After being escorted to the infirmary, Carl had calmly turned to a nurse. Requested a kiss. When she refused, he yanked his IV out and jabbed it into her fifty-four times. By the time the guards got hold of him, he had snapped her neck. Not just broken it, but slit it ear to ear.

"Yes, I recall reading about the incident," Cat said smoothly though her pulse was racing. "And he has been diagnosed with a personality trait disorder, passive-aggressive type."

"Yes." The rocking receded.

"Any signs of schizophrenia?"

"None. He knows exactly what he is doing when he does it. He is not delusional."

"Is he currently medicated?" Cat was thinking ahead. If he was overly medicated, an interview would mean nothing.

For the first time, she could see Stall look her up and down. "He is not. That is even more reason to be careful. You should not get too close to him. As handsome a specimen as you are."

"I have studied and dealt with men of his kind before, doctor."

"You may have dealt with his kind, but I can assure you there are few like Carl." Stall pushed back from his heavy, scarred desk and stood. "And I promise you, you will not understand him. I myself am no closer to understanding him. I have studied him for fifteen years."

"Why do you believe that, doctor?" There was an honest curiosity in her voice. Stall could tell she was thinking the same thing of her own killer.

"It is just that his kind is so rare. The rest of us, we look for reasons for behavior. For him, there are no reasons, no explanations. One minute he can be cooperating with you in a session, the next he is on you." He pursed his lips for a moment. "I once asked him why he killed them, when I had first arrived here, thinking I would get a rational response."

"And what was his response?"

The man held his chin between his thumb and forefinger, thinking. "Many serials we get, they blame people. Blame their over-worrisome mother, an aggressive father, the system. They blame because they feel guilt, remorse. At least they know what they have done is wrong, in society's eyes. Therefore, they want to crawl out from under the shame, displace it onto something, someone else." Cat read concern in Stall's face as he spoke.

"What was Carl's response?"

"With Carl, we never got any of that. No voices, no bad childhood, no abuse. When I asked him the question, he simply said he did not understand how he did it. But he knows he did. And he makes no apologies for that. Given the chance, I have no doubt he would do it again."

"I understand." Cat had heard enough. She wanted to speak to Carl herself. "Does he know I am coming?"

"We told him he would have a visitor, but we have not told him your identity. We did not want him to get keyed up."

"Yes. By the way, do you have a photo of Eric? It might be something that we could age progress to see what he would look like today."

Dr. Stall shook his head and looked a little guilty. "I'm sorry to say the only photo we had of him as a boy burned up in a fire about seventeen years ago. Those were before the days of laptop computers and everything being digitized like they are now."

"I understand. Thank you for your time." Cat rose and offered a handshake to the doctor.

Stall looked her in the eye over his frames, his pupils tight, constricted. "I do not want to promise you anything, doctor. He may provide you no information at all. At times he is impervious to any line of questioning. There are other times that he will speak, but it is all lies."

"I have had sufficient experience to be able to tell the difference."

"I hope so."

Behind her, Cat heard a maximum security steel door slam home with a resounding clang. Behind it, over her shoulder, two similar doors, both operated remotely as well as by keyless entry, stood as testament to the monsters housed here. Holding a tiny tape recorder, a steno pad, and a pencil, she walked past what appeared to be glass cases, though Cat knew them to be reinforced multi-inch-thick plastic. Inside, displayed like bugs in a case, were society's most horrific killers.

Each cell contained steel bars about two feet back from the clear partition. A small flap, six small holes, was the only way she and Carl Stearbourne shared the same air. Behind the barriers, men were in various stages of daily routine. Some sleeping, reading, playing cards. In here, they almost looked normal. Partitions and bars reminded her they were not.

Cat had always been fascinated that there were no women here. It seemed only the male of the species harbored enough rage and frustration to rape, murder, and maim. Or perhaps it was society's notion that women were still the weaker sex, that somehow they were not to blame for terrible crimes they committed. Therefore, they were never sent to a place like this.

She thought of what she knew of Carl Stearbourne as she walked. The case had been taught regularly at Quantico. She knew all the facts but didn't have any idea about what made this guy click.

Carl Stearbourne was born in 1934 in Milwaukee, Wisconsin, the only son of a widowed music teacher, Kathleen Stearbourne. His early childhood was marked by signs of genius. Before he could walk, he was reading the classics, Homer, Aristotle, the works of Emerson. An accomplished violinist by age five, he had an uncanny ear for music. The boy's mother was an overbearing perfectionist. Perhaps seeing a child with this much natural talent only brought out the worst in her. She forced him to practice for hours on end, pawning him off to school only when she had to. She had a mean, sadistic streak. Conceivably in an effort to gain more control over the boy, she dressed Carl in bright clothing and sent him off to school, challenging him to be "the man of the house."

By the time he was six, Carl had been expelled, a ripe candidate for Kathleen's particular brand of "homeschooling." His young adult life was marked by the all-consuming affection and attention of Kathleen, yet when he did not play to perfection, she poured hot oil over his hands.

From what Cat had read, he'd never called her mother. Rather he addressed her only by her first name, which he sometimes pronounced with a lisp. At the age of twenty-five, Carl Stearbourne had had enough. On the night of August 12, 1959, he broke into his mother's bedroom and slaughtered her with her tree-pruning shears. When he was finished, he left her intestines coiled neatly beside her body.

When asked by police why he did it, he only answered, "I just wondered what it would feel like to stab her." The fact that he had done nothing to hide the body indicated to police that he had no inkling that what he did was wrong. That reality still persisted in Carl Stearbourne's mind today. He had never taken responsibility for his acts; therefore, he had never been freed.

Cat calls and whistles increased as Catherine got closer to Carl's cell. "Hey, Carl, looks like you've got yourself a visitor, pretty one too. You gonna cut out her vocal cords, or play nice and have a conversation?" She looked at a strapping guard standing at the hallway's end. His eyes flashed white. His forefinger massaged the weapon strapped on his shoulder.

Cat nodded to him, acknowledging his protection.

Apparently, with Carl Stearbourne they had taken extra precautions. Behind the see-through partition was another one, twice as thick as the first. In front of her, a single folding chair sat waiting for her audience. At first she was angry about it. She had wanted to surprise him, catch him off guard. Cat thought about it and resigned herself to these arrangements. There was really no chance of surprise. He knew she was coming. She drew in a breath and stopped in front of his cell.

Carl Stearbourne appeared to be reading at a bolted-down desk. The book, Jean Cocteau's *Le Rappel à l'ordre.* He spoke to her without lowering it from his face.

"This book speaks of Barabbas. Are you familiar with him?"

Cat's hair bristled. "Yes."

He read from the book, his voice a controlled, deep baritone. "If it has to choose who is to be crucified, the crowd will always save Barabbas."

Silence followed as Cat tried to figure out where he was going with this.

Carl slowly lowered the book so that only sharp tiny pupils showed, his eyes focused on her. "Do you believe I am Barabbas?"

He was, of course, referring to the biblical character freed by Roman governor Pontius Pilate instead of Jesus—who was crucified. Cat wondered if he considered himself a savior, like Christ.

"Do you believe you are, Carl?"

"What I believe is not your concern, is it, doctor?"

"Oh, but I believe it is." Taking a seat, careful to keep her distance, she hit the record button. "Do you mind if I tape?"

He waved his hand in the air. "You may. Every day I am taped, every hour." He looked up to a recessed video camera artfully tucked in a back corner, protected by plexiglass. Cat hadn't noticed it. "I do not understand what they hope to gain."

"Perhaps to understand," she said, feeling her palms sweating.

Carl put down the book, stood and came closer. He sat on a chair that was bolted to the floor two feet back from the metal bars, looking her square in the eye for the first time. His eyes were unlike anything she'd ever seen. Black pupils and black irises melted into one. It was as if his eyes were an abyss. "I have been waiting for you, Catherine," he said. "How do you spell that? With a C or a K?"

He leaned into her. Cat involuntarily felt her body move back a half inch. He sensed it, enjoying the game.

"How did you know I was coming?" Her words were quick, carefully chosen.

"I have been following your career for some time. It was inevitable that you would come to *see* me. To *speak* with me. To *be* with me." He placed one finger over his pursed lips. "It is a pity we could not have met on the outside." His face was blank as he said it, but she understood the implication.

"Yes."

He looked at her, his eyes traveling from her Ferragamo shoes to the conservative Anne Klein pearl earrings and back. Cat forced herself not to squirm.

"You are quite beautiful, doctor. The photographs in the paper. They do you little justice."

She did not smile. "Thank you. You have been following the case?"

"Yes. A daily paper is one of the few luxuries they allow me. When your case went national, I began to follow it."

"Really?"

"But I have been following *you* for quite some time." His emphasis on the word *you* gave her the creeps.

Cat felt he was staring through her, as if she were not even sitting there. Yet his eyes seemed to swallow her up. Consume her.

"Yesss." He let the "s" sound purr like a kitten off his lips. "I knew you would come eventually to ask me about Eric. He was quite an unusual boy."

"How so?" She asked open-ended questions to elicit the most information from him. Occasionally she glanced down at the recorder to be sure the tape was still moving.

"Do you really think I would tell without some sort of arrangement?"

Cat was surprised he wished to bargain. From what she had heard, Carl Stearbourne considered himself an elitist, on a much higher social strata than the others she had studied. This lack of bravado was out of character for him. But it could also be a ploy of some kind.

"You may do as you please, Carl. I am not here to make any promises."

"Understood. And I am not here to provide *you* any answers."

"I do not believe you are in a position to bargain, Carl," Cat said, listening as her voice got tenser.

"I have something *you* want, which I do not have to divulge. I am in a far superior bargaining position."

"And if I do not bargain with you?" Cat's stomach somersaulted as she asked.

"Then more girls die, don't they, Cat?" He said it with a crooked smirk, his black eyes focused intently on her for any reaction at all. She refused to give it.

"What is it you want, Carl?"

"I would like music. Mozart. Perhaps some Rachmaninoff. It would drown out the constant sound of that video camera zooming in and out." Cat could not hear it, but she assumed Carl's acute senses picked up everything around him, from the smell of her hair to the weave of the tights she wore.

"I believe that can be arranged."

He sat back in the chair for the first time. "When I saw you for the first time, doctor, there was one word that came to mind."

"What was that?"

"Passion." He sucked in a deep breath. "You are a most passionate woman."

"How do you gather that?"

"The way you look at me, the photographs, your press statements. We share that." He studied her response. "Don't we?"

"We share nothing, Carl."

"Oh, but I think you are wrong. We share many interests. Music, the arts, an innate perception of evil. I also share that perception of evil with Eric."

He said nothing for a minute, his eyes bearing down on her.

"Tell me about Eric," she said.

Carl thought for a moment. "Eric was unlike the others I had known, unlike my other acquaintances. He was capable of such raw emotion, yet such a quiet boy, really. He would be forty-six years old now. Blending quite nicely into society, I assume."

"Why do you believe that?"

"Eric was that way. He had a kind, genteel face. Clean cut, invoked visions of mom, apple pie. You know the type?"

Cat nodded.

"And they believed he took responsibility. Once you take responsibility, you can write your ticket out of this place. Eric did what he needed to do to survive. Do you do what you need to survive, doctor?"

He peered at her with his black eyes, jawbone set, jutting forward.

"No."

"Then what do *you* want from me?" He lowered his chin and looked away. It was obvious she had angered him.

"I have some photographs to show you. Would you step back please?"

He did so. He knew the routine, had been following it for most of his adult life. Cat put forty-eight horrific crime scene and autopsy photos on the sliding tray, twelve of each girl. Gingerly, she pushed the tray through then sat and waited. Carl put his hands through the bars, then the plexiglass holes, and retrieved them. As he got closer, he inhaled deeply.

"You are wearing Je Reviens. It's a very subtle fragrance. My mother used to wear that. How long have you been using it?"

Cat did not answer.

He took another deep breath which seemed to infuse his whole body with the fragrance, then turned and walked back to the chair. "It is no matter," he said softly.

"Can we get down to business?"

"Give me a moment with them will you?" As he asked, he closed his eyes and ran his fingers across the photo on top. It was as if these death photos gave him life. Cat watched rosiness flush his cheeks. "Yes, yes," he breathed in deeply, "this may be Eric's work. Shy boy. He was quite an introvert, isolated. But we became soul mates over time. Eric likes to take his time, doesn't he? When he burns them, cuts them, it is not a quick process is it, doctor? It is a painful, arduous way to die."

"Yes."

"And he enjoys watching them die in the night. Watching their blood spill, isn't that right?"

Silence.

"He takes them away, isolates them, just as he was isolated when he was a boy. The cutting is deliberate, slow, excruciatingly painful. And he is good at it, good at cutting the flesh. *You* are good at cutting flesh too, aren't you, doctor?"

Cat wanted to scream at his questions, but she kept still.

"Flesh in moonlight can be disarming, can't it, doctor? *You* know about flesh." He leaned into her again, took a deep breath. "Roses, a hint of lavender, peonies… flesh and moonlight."

"Why does he do it?"

"Why do any of us do it? We are all just children of our needs. Eric, more than most of us, realized his needs at an early age. And now he is making up for all those years he was unable to nurture and feed those needs. He is only making up for lost time."

"What about the cutting?"

"Yes, I have read about it. Extremely precise in the placement. Worries you, doesn't it? Strikes too close to home. What if it is one of our own, you think. One in the profession?"

"Did Eric have any medical training? Did he display any extraordinary skill with instruments?"

"Not that I recall." He flipped to the second photo, closing his eyes again. "This one, her name was Nancy, wasn't it?"

"Yes."

"Do *you* think she screamed?"

Cat steeled herself against his mind games. She wanted to get away from him. Far away. "I do not know, Carl. Perhaps you can tell me."

"I think she did. I definitely think she did."

"If he enjoys listening to them scream, then why did he crush the throat of the third one?"

He paused. "Give me a moment. I have not reached her photos yet." From the looks of it, Carl was still on Nancy Marsh, immensely enjoying the inhuman way she had been torn apart, displayed as if she were an animal.

"Do you think less of Eric because of these?" His black eyes met hers in a flash, then immersed in the photos again.

"I do."

"You should not. A man capable of this is far superior to many men. Not to me, but to *you*, of course. He is capable of living a double life. And I mean that in the broadest sense. Not only is he able to look the part, he is able to live the part. At an early age, Eric developed a detailed fantasy involving the interplay between death and sex. As he got older, that fantasy evolved into what I have before me." He glanced at the photos, visibly taking the brutality in. "You see, for Eric, having the partner alive is not good enough. There has been so much muck fed to him that he is unworthy of their love, that he does not believe a normal boy-girl relationship is possible for him. But when his fantasy escalates to death, dismemberment, mutilation…then that is an entirely different story. Possessing his partner's life makes up for his sexual and social inadequacies. To Eric, it is the ultimate form of foreplay."

He paused for a moment, taking in more of her perfume. Then started speaking again, his black eyes had a distant, faraway look. "And he leaves their faces alone, so he can see what they feel for him. How much they *love* him."

He flipped to the seventh photo. "I am sure Dr. Stall told you of Eric's episodes with his sister's dolls, with the family cats."

"No." In spite of herself, Cat leaned forward.

"At the age of seven, Eric told me, he loved more than anything else to play with his sister's dolls. His mother caught him at it one day and beat the daylights out of the poor boy. Eric directed the anger he had for his mother onto the dolls, cutting off their heads, appendages. It appears…" he flipped again to a new, probably more grotesque photo "…that he was practicing his craft."

"What about the cats?"

"Eventually the dolls were not good enough. You see, they did not bleed. He escalated to dismembering the two cats, leaving them hanging in a broom closet, waiting for his grandmother to discover them."

"He was not institutionalized at that point?"

"No. Eric came from a very private family. Eric's mother, who raised him, was a domineering, abusive woman. She refused to have it spoken of. His entire killing fantasy…" He flipped again to another photo. By now Cat had lost count, but she could see by the look on his face that he was enjoying himself immensely. "…revolves around women. He told me at times he went into her bedroom with a kitchen knife, just standing there watching the blade reflect the moonlight, willing himself to bring it down into her skull. He could not. That is where he and I are different."

"How so?"

"I could do it." He sat quietly, having put the photographs down on his lap. "I would be less than honest if I told you I did not like Eric. He was a friendly, open, sensitive boy, given the right setting."

"I thought you said he was shy, introverted."

"He is that also. Quite a chameleon really. If you met him on the street, you would ask yourself 'How could such a charming, articulate man do such a thing?'" Carl Stearbourne grinned. "I can assure you, doctor, it is in our nature… to deceive."

Cat had heard enough. She glanced at her watch and feigned another appointment.

"May I keep the photos?"

"I don't think that would be a good idea."

"I have not had the opportunity to look at all of them. And how can I assist you further if you do not provide me the tools?"

He had a point. "All right, I will ask Stall before I leave. If he doesn't approve, I'll be back for them in five minutes."

"All right then," he said, black eyes focused on her, clutching the photos close to his chest.

"Next time you come, doctor, please wear something more revealing. We are all purveyors of the flesh, aren't we?"

"Thank you for your time, Carl. If you need to reach me, Dr. Stall has my number."

Cat picked up the recorder, clicked it off, and rounded the corner toward the heavy steel doors. For the first time, she felt like she was locked in a cocoon. In her head, the hollow drumming of Carl's words.

"Purveyors of the flesh," he said again softly as Cat waited for the steel doors to open. She felt dirty, like she was carrying a piece of him with her outside. As if breathing the same air had polluted her thoughts, her judgment. Wide-eyed, she flashed a nervous look at the guard; he nodded back, his expression unchanged. She believed he had seen this behavior from others who visited Carl Stearbourne for the first time.

Outside the maximum security wing, she collected herself. Breathed the fresh air, straightened her skirt. Assuring herself she was all right. Within a few minutes she had Dr. Stall paged, and he said it would be acceptable for Carl to keep the photographs.

"Don't worry. He will do nothing to them. They are his favorite kind of art."

She told Stall about the deal she had struck, and he smiled approvingly. "You know he will want to see you again?"

Although Cat was opposed to the idea, she knew it was true. Now that Carl Stearbourne had someone listening, he would keep playing the game.

In one sense at least, Cat needed all the help she could get.

TWENTY-FOUR

And cometh from afar.
Not in entire forgetfulness,
And not in utter nakedness,
But trailing clouds of glory do we come
From God, who is our home:
Heaven lies about us in our infancy.
—**William Wordsworth**, *"My Heart Leaps Up"*

This day that would change Catherine Powers's life began several hundred miles to the south. At a McDonald's in Quantico, Virginia, he waited for hamburger and fries. He stood, eyes focused out the window, feeling steam rise from his coffee.

Outside, a storm was brewing in the late afternoon. Clouds, balled and tight and angry, knitted the sky. The wind picked up now, bending maples, oak leaves flying. The air had that magnetic quality he could not quite describe, only knew he could feel it.

The food came. He neither smiled nor frowned at the pimpled teenager but walked with his tray to a corner table and sat quietly. Opening the bun, he squeezed

161

mustard out of a plastic packet and placed the bun back on top. It was a mechanical action, for his mind was elsewhere.

Nostalgia came quickly and left him as he watched the children across the street. He scrutinized them at recess, laughing at their silly games, remembering himself years back doing the same gyrations on the monkey bars. Perhaps he was feeling misty-eyed because he knew too much, or too little. Whatever it was, the feeling soon departed.

Listening to the painfully boring background music, he knew himself a veteran of this sport. There was no mystery to his success—a vast amount of patience, careful planning, thinking of every eventuality. He would not be disappointed this time, as he had not been in the past.

Normally he would be agitated by now. But this week, long self-imposed hibernation was healthy for him, if he got what he wanted.

In any case, he wouldn't have to linger much longer. For a week he had been poised in the shadows, waiting to benefit from his current challenge. Gentlemanly, he had been lying low, for many reasons. Some personal, some not. It was the first time he would take a child, the first time he would become the demon that had haunted his own childhood. A predator of children.

But it had to be done.

It was necessary to bring her to him.

Besides, he equated slowness with wisdom. His methodical plotting had never failed him before.

He sipped his coffee through steam, watching the one called Joey.

"Are you finished with that?" A red-haired teenager was standing over him, her hand poised on his plastic tray, waiting to whisk it away.

He turned to her, snatched French fries off the tray. "Yes, I am."

Sitting on this hard bench seat, he hunched his shoulders and watched the schoolyard. Kids moving like leaves in the wind.

Joey had a sort of rounded body, with a big head, large pale eyes.

He stared at the trees, eyes open, slipping a now-cold French fry into his lips, watching.

In his mind, he was holding the boy, not hurting him, just holding him. He smiled. When he touched the boy, his flesh was warm, smooth. He could sense the child on his fingertips, even here. Could smell his scent.

He was good at imagining. Imagining had gotten him through the hard times in his life. Locked up, he had been deprived of anything that would stimulate his mind: books, magazines, movies. They thought they were punishing him. In fact, they were making him stronger. He turned in on himself, learning that the mind is man's most powerful tool. In his mind, he painted fantasies.

One of them went something like what he was living right now.

Joey Powers was swinging back and forth on a Jungle Gym swing set, his hair tousled by the wind. Wearing blue jeans and a bright yellow windbreaker, the boy was thirty feet away; the only thing separating them was glass and a chain-link fence that towered over the child's head.

Suddenly Joey stopped swinging. There was stillness, even in the wind, and a stare.

The boy could feel his eye contact.

Averting his eyes, he stared at the gray, angry sky, the band of low clouds quickly filling the horizon. Casually, he ate another French fry. He looked away to safeguard himself.

The boy must not know he was coming.

*   *   *   *   *

Joey Powers sat on the swing, his small fingers wrapped tight around the cold chains that supported him, feeling the wind picking up. At the playground's corner, he watched tall elms bow. The sandbox appeared a tornado of sand. Beyond it, beyond the fence, a lone man sat at an orange and brown plastic bench and table, next to the glass at McDonald's. He'd been there for an hour, slowly eating something.

Joey wanted to tell the man to quit watching him.

As Joey watched the man, he could see the man quickly get up from the table, throwing his fries away. The man blasted out the front door, head down, hands shoved in his pants. No jacket on.

Something about the way the man moved told Joey something was wrong. He kept his eyes on the man. Watched as he turned around, their eyes meeting. Joey thought, only for a second, he might know him. The hunch to his shoulders, the head, eyes, long limbs, seemed familiar. Like one of Dad's friends. At this distance, he couldn't be sure. Couldn't get a good look at the face from this far away.

Suddenly a dust cloud picked up right in front of Joey, blinding his eyes. Squinting them closed, he felt the dirt burn. Tears flowed as he rubbed his eyes.

When he opened them, looked up, the man was gone.

The clouds were coming in.

A heavy, steady rain started to fall.

Joey stepped inside his first grade classroom, moved to the window that faced the McDonald's.

There was nothing there.

He stepped away from the window and took his seat. The room was full of color. Walls painted bright primary colors: cherry red, bright yellow, cobalt blue, Kelly green. Mrs. Miner had taken special care to place one of each of the children's artwork across a banner that stretched above the blackboard. Small wooden desks, even smaller plastic chairs. An area for playtime indoors.

It was bold and bright.

Joey loved it very much, even with the sky blackening outside.

He couldn't help it.

Wouldn't change anything about it even if he could.

Except the man.

Mrs. Miner, a thin, tall, funny woman, rallied the children together for nap time. She cut the lights in the room to half wattage. Each child lay out on their mats, their limbs falling into slumber in minutes.

All except Joey.

Joey could hear the rising and falling of her breath in his direction.

"Mrs. Miner," he whispered to avoid waking the others.

At the head of the room, she got up and started toward him. He could hear her shoes on the floor.

She knelt beside him on one knee. The fuzzy cardigan she wore made him feel safer. Just having her near, he felt safer.

"What is it, Joey?"

"I can't sleep."

"Well, that's plain to see. Is there something bothering you, something you'd like to talk about?"

"Yessth."

His lisp came and went, so she hardly noticed it anymore.

"What is it, hon?"

Joey looked out the window, his eyes faraway. "When I was outside, there was a man. Watching me."

"Outside when?"

"Just now, today."

"A man?" There was disbelief in her voice. At six, children had vivid imaginations, she was used to that. They could see imaginary friends, playmates, dogs, cats. One little girl in the class carried her imaginary friend everywhere, named her Samantha.

"Yessth."

She knelt on both knees, tucking her feet under her. "And where did you see this man?"

Joey stared out the window facing McDonald's. "He was out there. He was staring at me."

She smoothed his hair, her voice cooing to him. "Now, now, Joey. There's nothing to worry about. It's just the rain on the ceiling, a little pitter-patter. Nothing to be scared of, really."

There was no reproach in her voice. After all, she was used to the children being scared every once in a while. Some were naturally more sensitive than others. Joey was one of the sensitive ones, she knew.

She petted his hair and sang a lullaby.

It still took him ten minutes to fall asleep.

Mark picked Joey up right on schedule, three-thirty. He was one of a growing number of dads who picked up their children at The Oaktree School.

"How's it going, tiger?"

Joey ran to his father's arms as if they hadn't seen each other in weeks. "Dad!" He held up a picture of a racecar, his favorite subject, the colors not perfectly in the lines but pretty close. "Look what I did."

"That's great. Your coloring is getting better than mine."

Joey grinned like a Cheshire cat. Mark tousled his hair.

The boy moved to a large windowpane and stared out at the rain.

"Can I have a word with you?" Mrs. Miner's face was neither cheerful nor worried. She pulled him aside.

Mark grew worried. "What is it?"

She was careful in her choice of words, occasionally smiling encouragement at the other children as they left with their parents. Her voice had some intensity. To a woman who lived her life for these children, her look troubled Mark tremendously.

"What's wrong?"

"I don't mean to alarm you. Joey was watched today by a man. We don't know who he was. By the time security investigated, he was gone."

"A man. What man?"

"We don't know who he is, or was. Just that he sat there watching Joey for some time."

"Sat where?"

"At the McDonald's across the way. It upset Joey. I checked it out with some of the other kids, and they confirmed his story." She knitted her brow. "You didn't send anyone, did you, to watch him?"

"No one. What did the guy look like?"

"No one at the McDonald's remembers. Just keep an eye on Joey tonight, will you?" There was genuine concern in her voice. Joey was one of her brightest students.

"I will. And thank you." Mark looked across the room to where Joey was standing. "Come on, sport, it's time to go."

Outside, the storm had strengthened, the rain coming like bullets from an ever darkening sky. It looked more like night than day.

Mark thought of leaving Joey in the sheltered alcove and running to get the truck, as he watched parents with death grips on their children's arms running for shelter. Given the events of the day, he thought better of it. It was better to be wet than…Mark would not think of it. Besides, Joey was a resilient kid. A little rain wouldn't hurt him any.

People were speeding through the parking lot as if the rain put the fear of God in them.

"Come here, buddy." Mark hoisted Joey's windbreaker-clad body into his arms.

"Let's go!" Joey said, enjoying the free ride. He held on tight to his father's neck. Mark sloshed through puddles, feeling the cold permeate his leather loafers, socks, toes.

Joey was jovial, enjoying the adventure. "Yahoooo, Daddy. It's like we're sailors at sea. We're caught in a shipwreck. Man overboard!" His small frame pumped up and down in Mark's arms as if he were really caught in the thick of the action.

"Shiver me timbers, matey. Is that our car I spy? Or could it be a Spanish galleon, full of gold doubloons?"

Joey was breathing hard through the water washing against his face. "It's a ghost ship! Let's go aboard." He laughed.

Mark saluted with one hand, the other fumbling with the alarm and keyless entry. The Chevy Yukon chirped, then the doors automatically unlocked with a pop so they could slide into safety. Mark secured the boy in the back passenger booster seat, then tossed Joey's backpack in the backseat. Hurrying, he slammed the truck door and shook as if he were a wet dog trying to get his fur dry. Joey laughed again. Leaving the school, Mark drove past a man in a raincoat standing on the sidewalk. He was hatless, his hair drenched, obscuring his features. Head bowed, making them even harder to read.

The man glared at them.

Joey busily scribbled in his soaked coloring book, not paying attention.

Mark motored cautiously through what had now become drizzle to the east side of town. Cape Cod-style homes stood on perfectly manicured lawns, each one looking like a putting green, never used. Towering maples gave up leaves to the sluice of water, their late summer color already yielding to autumn's yellow hue. Car lights ahead appeared as streaks of gold and white on a rain-smeared windshield.

"I'm not afraid of the rain, Dad."

"I know. Neither am I." Mark smiled at the boy sideways, keeping his eyes on the winding road. He thought of asking Joey about the man but decided otherwise. It would do no good to bring up the memories, only trigger nightmares.

Instead, he'd just let it go. For now.

They got home and heard Clifford barking in the garage. As the automatic garage door opened, Joey scrambled out of the truck to the dog. Clifford, a fawn-colored golden retriever, licked the boy twice in the face and headed back to the shelter of the garage.

Joey did too. He was inside before Mark pulled in, calling for Charlie, his lizard.

Mark gathered all the wet things from the backseat, his briefcase and laptop, Joey's backpack and colored pictures, a signed Mike Trout "Kid Fish" Junior baseball Mark had ordered on the Internet. Joey's favorite baseball player. Mark hadn't said anything about it. It was going to be a surprise.

Going inside, he hit the automatic garage door, listened to the mechanism whir, watched the door close tight. It was a comforting feeling. At least here, they were safe.

He waited. His rented black Cadillac SUV's engine pinged and knocked. Coffee was cold now. Rolling down the window, he poured the last of it out into the steady rain, cursing as his sleeve and shoulder got drenched. Stretching his muscles as best he could, he put binoculars to his eyes and followed the shiny wet sidewalk up to the west.

He'd been sitting about five hundred feet from the house for five minutes, with the heater going, blowing into cupped hands, trying to get some circulation going. Already he missed California.

But he knew this would be worth it.

From the looks of it, the house was modest for what this family made. A Cape Cod-style clapboard with three dormer windows on the top story. Early Americana influence. An American flag flapped in the wind outside what appeared to be the kitchen window, a dim light illuminating that part of the house.

Neatly trimmed pots stood outside the front door. The Cape Cod was set back about a hundred yards from the road, encased in an ivy-covered red brick wall crowned in brass lantern peaks. The four-foot wall reminded him of an undulating snake. Its height didn't really matter. No fence or security system would protect this family today.

He watched a new Chevy Yukon pull left into the driveway, watched it stop. The little boy got out, lit up for a moment in the headlights. A dog came running out, licked him, and then made a smart move. Headed for the garage.

He watched as the portico light turned on.

A cypress tree caught the wind.

He waited.

A minute later, a figure in the kitchen's bay window: a man dressed in a white business shirt, his tie already pulled loose, half off, dangling like a dead serpent. He looked of average build, hair the color of sand. He watched the man lower the blinds in the house's bay windows till only slats of light emanated into the wetness.

He put the binoculars down, settled back, and slept.

He had time. At only five-thirty, there was plenty of time.

TWENTY-FIVE

In memory, everything seems to happen to music.
—**Tennessee Williams**, *The Glass Menagerie*

He watched for two more days. Establishing a pattern. Mark and Joey came and went, unaware of the man's presence, as he was even more careful than before.

Then, on the third night, it was time.

A five o'clock, he positioned himself behind the gate to the dog run, crouching, small teeth shining. Clifford lay to the far end of the run, the golden retriever's throat slit. In the streetlight's yellow glow, the dog appeared an immovable pile of fluff, as if it were sleeping. He realized his coat smelled of blood and dog kibble.

Damned dog took one good bite at him. Rocking his hand back and forth at the wrist, it hurt, but he could move it. Teeth marks oozed dark and ugly in the little light he could find. Turning his hand over, he could see three puncture marks on the top, just next to his index finger, two matching wounds in his palm.

Pain means nothing.

They will be here soon.

Looking around, above the fence, he waited for the neighbor's downstairs lights to come on. Glancing up, he waited for some sign of life on the second floor, for eyes peering through blinds or curtains. Nothing. The neighbor's house remained black. There was no movement. Thankfully, they weren't home.

Like the other nights, a slow, steady rain began to fall. He crouched under the eaves but put his hand out into the stream, letting the cool water cleanse his wound. The fire started to subside…he had no time for it anyway.

Through a tiny vertical slot in the wooden slats, he watched double white lights speed by, reflecting on wet pavement. Crouched down on his haunches, his calves tightened, cramped. He pulled his raincoat closer.

Squatted and small, he couldn't help but remember.

"Sandra!" he screams her name. "It's dark in here."

He is not sure how long he's been in the basement, shackled to a hard wooden chair. He knows his limbs have fallen into a kind of languishing. His belly aches for food. Eyes burn with tears that have come and gone.

What day is it?

He has no answer, nor does he know the time.

Steal cuffs rubbing into raw skin at his wrists, ankles. A thick rope circles his waistline, then crosses in the back and doubles back over each leg. She has tied it together below the wooden seat and taped any of the rope's stray ends down with electrical tape.

Though he has tried, he cannot reach the tape's edges.

The rope has begun to fray from his pee, the sticky stuff on it giving way to the soreness, the stickiness he feels in his pants. Sitting in pitch blackness, he feels a spider crawl over his big toe. He screams but there is no one to hear him. He thinks to crush it with his foot but decides against it.

At least someone is with him down here.

At least something cares for him.

"Sandra, I know you are up there," he chokes, then swallows his tears. "Sandra, get down here now." His voice is stronger now, defiant. He rocks on the chair back and forth, straining against the shackles.

A loud hollow crash, a thud.

Success. He has wobbled the chair enough for it to fall over. He is lying on his side now, nearly in a fetal position, his sore bottom finding some relief.

He wonders if he has crushed the spider. Prays he has not.

Above him and to the left, the basement door opens with a hard clap against hardwood floors. Squinting, he can hardly see through the light.

"Sandra," he whispers, seeing her huge frame fill up the light. He can't see her face, but he knows she is angry. She is always angry.

The silhouette moves closer till there is only the hint of light in the room cast through her thick ankles.

She is standing over him, a two-inch-wide stick slapping rhythmically against her palm. The sound of it slapping, thump, thump, thump. It is music. It takes him out of this place.

Whump. Hot, tingling fire across his thigh brings him back. Pain in his stomach. He feels he will vomit.

Regrettably, the music stops. She stands over him. He is far more frightened than when he was alone.

His eyes adjust to the light. He can see the spider made it, is still alive. The creature saunters along, oblivious, just a half inch from the boy's eyes. He smiles.

"Wretched child," she scorns him, the thump, thump never stopping in her hands. He cannot see the stick but knows it is there. His body shows the scars from wars with it.

Pulling against the cold steel shackles, he listens to the chains go tight, hears the chair scrape against the cement floor.

No escape.

Stepping forward, heavy black orthopedic shoes come down right in front of his eyes, filling his frame of vision. Her left foot crushes the spider.

His eyes widen but he says nothing.

His urine and excrement have combined to form a foul odor. He notices it only now, for reasons he cannot explain. Terrified, he is sure she smells it too.

"You think I am here to clean up after your garbage?" Her voice booms over him, accompanied by the thump.

He closes his eyes, tries to think of the music, but it will not come.

She kicks him in the groin. Instantly, his body buckles over on itself, though still restrained. Vomit comes in small retched lurches. Black dots in front of his eyes, a strong, shrill whining.

"Answer me," she commands, her voice bouncing off the hollow, empty room.

He says nothing, still coughing, gasping for air.

"Answer me." He has no choice this time. It is a command.

"Sandra, I…" His voice is low, sheepish.

Thump, thump gets faster.

He knows what it means, braces for another blow.

Trembling, he answers her. "I didn't mean to do it. It was a mistake."

"I've checked your bed. Wet. Third time this week." He hears her swallow. "You think it's funny me cleaning up your piss?"

A clap of wood. His right forearm takes the brunt of it. Thankfully, the blow only brushes his ribs.

He is sobbing.

"I'm sorry. It was an accident." He forces the words, his voice meek. Then the orthopedic shoes are gone, replaced by her ugly, horrid face, down on the floor with him. Leaning into him, she is barely a half inch away. Sour breath laden with scotch blows into his eyes, stinging them. Spit flies like a shower as she screams, "You're a good-for-nothing dirty little bastard. I do my best with you, and this is what I get?" She holds up his soiled sheets to his face, then takes them away.

Coughing, gagging. Stinking cotton. The pee leaching into his eyes, stinging them.

"How does it feel?" Her tone is suddenly gentle now. He prays the worst of it is over.

"I…I…" He chokes words but they will not come. More than anything else, he is angry for that. He wants to kick her, curse her, bash her head into this hard cold cement, but even words betray him.

His body trembles.

She draws back and claps him again, this time on the bottom. The blow is so hard it draws blood. Can smell it. Metallic, lingering in the air. Can feel it trickling down his bare leg.

Blood seems to appease her, if only for a second.

"Ain't nothing wrong with you a good lickin' won't fix." She turns away, the thump, thump, thump still echoing in his ears as she goes.

He wants the music to come. Where is it?

Like everything else, it has abandoned him.

Then the cold rage is back as suddenly as it left.

The thumping has stopped. He is thankful.

Grabbing his throat with the full force of one massive hand, she wrenches him up off the floor and plunks down his body, the chair upright.

"Please don't," he pleads, chin quivering.

"You know what comes next, don't you, boy?" It is horrible in here. Her voice is a monster's voice. Low and growling.

"No, please," he cries softly, between a new wave of tears.

"Now sit still, boy."

He feels her heavy hands on his crotch.

He waits for the music.

TWENTY-SIX

A woman's hopes are woven of sunbeams;
A shadow annihilates them.
—**George Eliot**, *Felix Holt, the Radical*

n all the world, Cat couldn't remember feeling this content. In front of a soft smoldering fire, she sat staring at Dr. Gregory Taft. Firelight and soft neoclassical lighting cast a glow on Greg's face. Others refer to him as Gregory, but to Cat, he is Greg. From the looks of it, the years had been good to him.

Chez Paul was a Chicago landmark of fairly recent vintage. Though the building itself was over a hundred years old, the restaurant opened two decades ago. It had quickly made a name for itself with Chicago's moneyed elite.

Solid mahogany doors led to a small salon with coat check. Thick carpets and drapes masked this inside sanctum in sheer opulence. Up a winding wooden staircase to the second floor, Greg had requested their best table, tucked into a secluded corner with its own fireplace. Cat savored the fire's warmth, the company, and the sheer relaxation of this moment.

Mahogany-trimmed emerald walls, huge cut-crystal chandeliers...the place reeked of power but had an unhurried pace. Service was discreet, yet excellent. Starched waiters in white gloves appeared and disappeared without so much as a noise. Chez Paul was Dr. Gregory Taft's favorite dinner spot. As soon as they walked into the restaurant, Michelle, the head hostess, greeted them, assuring Dr. Taft that everything was in order.

Now Cat simply sat, immersed in this, his world.

A chardonnay was poured. She savored the flavor of sun, oak, a hint of apricot on her tongue. Cat put down her glass and looked directly at Greg, taking him in. A few more wrinkles, same hair, green eyes, he seemed to blend in with his surroundings. "So, Greg, how long has it been for us?"

He put down a shrimp-laden fork, thought about it. "It's been at least seven years. You were here in, let's see, 2007, I believe."

Cat gave him a questioning look.

"Are you sure? I was almost positive it was 2008?"

He took her hand, rubbed it, and looked at her deeply. "I remember it like it was yesterday. Remember taking you to the Museum of Science and Industry. You were like a kid in a candy store. Worse than a five-year-old," he teased.

Cat's face glowed. "I love those hands-on exhibits. Reminds me of when I was a kid."

A waiter appeared but was dismissed with a short wave of Greg's hand.

"Now tell me, what brings you to our city?"

Cat popped in a broiled, marinated shrimp, chewed. "I'm here following up a lead on an investigation."

"Ah yes." He poured her more wine casually and sat back in his chair. "The Burning Man investigation."

"You know about it then?"

"All I know is you're investigating a case in California. But that doesn't explain what brings you to Chicago." His lips curled in what she could not quite describe as a smile. Simultaneously, she felt his leg brush hers under the table. Instinctively, she knew he wanted her to say it was to see him.

Gregory had always had a big ego, perhaps rightfully so.

This was a man who wielded power in an effortless way, headed one of the most powerful associations in the country, was respected among his peers. A man who no longer needed to practice medicine, yet medicine needed him. He had lobbied against Obama's ballyhooed healthcare reforms and won, in some respects. The rollout had been a disaster. The American medical system, with all its padded billing, secret euthanasia, second-class mental healthcare, was safe. At least for now. Dr. Gregory Taft had seen to that. The medical community was eternally grateful.

Still, Cat admired him. He was a hands-on fellow, much like her. Unafraid to jump into the thick of things.

They'd met years ago when they had worked together on a horrible plane crash in the Florida Everglades. She had been summoned from Key West to assist in identifying bodies pulled from the swamp. He was there treating survivors, trying to do what he could to preserve life. Jointly, they had a role in comforting the families. So little was left of the plane, perhaps their first affair had been spawned from comforting each other too. The death toll had been over 80 percent.

Cat forced herself to smile.

Regardless, he could read the pain on her face. "What is it, Cat?"

"I'm just remembering when we met. Sometimes I wonder if the only reason we are together is because of pain."

He leaned forward, took her hand, concern in his eyes. "What do you mean?"

She gave him an incredulous look. "Do you ever wonder if it's worth it, Greg? I mean all this. We have the admiration of our colleagues, careers, but when it comes down to it, when you're lying in bed at night, staring at the ceiling, do you ever want for more?"

He pulled his hand away. "Yes, of course, but I am a selfish man. Or perhaps I haven't found the right woman." He smiled warmly. "What do you feel at night, Cat?"

"Lonely mostly, like I'm missing out on something, though I don't quite know what it is." Cat's eyes roamed the dining room.

"Joey, right?"

She nodded. "I just wonder if I'll ever be able to replace the times I'm missing with him. Memories I've missed, they can't be replaced."

"No, but you can make new ones, ones that are uniquely your own. He doesn't expect anything more." He took a sip of wine. "He's a child. He doesn't differentiate the days and weeks that you're gone. He only remembers the trip to Disneyland from yesterday. That's how kids are."

"I know." She looked down at her half empty plate. "I just feel I'm missing out."

"Look, Catherine. Your work is important too. You safeguard society against the worst it has to offer. You make the world safer for kids like Joey, for all of us. There's something to be said for that too."

"I know. I guess I just have to find a balance. And lately it feels all one-sided."

"Because of this case? Because of this trip?"

Cat casually looked at the heavily draped window, at the Chicago night. "Yes, I'm here checking a lead that seems to pan out to a similar MO."

Gregory leaned in. "Tell me…"

"Not much to tell really. Young boy, same type of pattern. Killed his grandmother and a cousin. They let him go years ago."

"And how does it fit for you?"

From the looks of it, Gregory Taft wasn't interested in the standard line Cat fed everyone else. He was genuinely interested in what she really thought. He wanted the truth.

Cat's eyes met his and stayed locked for five seconds until she went back to her food.

"Well, the thing is, I spoke with this man, and I use the term loosely, who knew the boy. Anyway, Carl Stearbourne—"

"Whoa, you spoke to Carl Stearbourne, face-to-face?" She could hear the surprise in his voice.

"Yes." Cat did not know what else to say. "He and this boy, Eric, were close. Real close. Like they could read each other's thoughts. Eric developed such an affinity for Carl that he wouldn't speak to anyone else."

Gregory was captivated. "Was Stearbourne as bad as they say?"

Gregory and Cat finished their shrimp almost simultaneously. A waiter appeared and whisked the plates away. Within seconds they were replaced with lemon sorbet, in small silver bowls.

Cat took three bites and the silver servers were removed once more, replaced this time with pâté de foie gras. She broke off a tiny bit of a toast point, spread it with the smooth mixture, and continued talking, nibbling in between words. "He's a classic passive/aggressive. I thought a sociopath, but they say no, he knows exactly what he is doing at all times. Very direct, slightly confrontational. In a passive sort of way. Carl Stearbourne's most powerful weapon is his mind. They can restrain his body, keep him locked away. But even in death, I don't think that mind would die. Somehow he would find a way to keep it alive. That and the power he wields with it."

Gregory sipped a French Burgundy. "Why do you think that?"

"Greg, he defines himself in no other way, although I understand he can be physically strong as well. Snapped some poor nurse's neck a few years back with his bare hands…" Her words drifted into the air.

"Yes. I remember reading about it in the papers."

"To look at him, you would never know. He is of average build, slightly pudgy in the middle. It's the way he holds himself. Those eyes. He's the ultimate liar."

"And that diagnosis is based on…"

"He deludes himself into thinking he is not a killer. He believes himself like other men." Cat stopped. "No. You know what?" She chewed in between words. "On second thought, I'll take that back. He believes himself better than other men."

"How so?" Gregory said, sipping his wine.

"He's killed eight people, three for no other reason than he felt like it. On the other hand, most of the men there have killed over love, revenge, money. You see, Carl Stearbourne does not see himself as a high-priced liability to society. He has the talent to market himself. That is how he keeps the journals doing stories, year after year. He packages himself as the most bizarre lunatic the world has ever seen, because he appears sane. Completely sane."

"That's what you think of it?"

"Put it this way, even the guy's own doctor, a man who's been studying Carl for years, treats him like he's an enigma."

"What the hell do they care? He's in for life, isn't he?" Gregory's eyes roamed the dining room, then met Cat's.

"Don't you see? There is a prestige factor to housing Carl Stearbourne. And the journal articles aren't bad publicity either."

"So what you're saying is this lunatic's been able to engineer a marketing machine to sell himself from inside his cell?"

"Precisely. And the doctors don't even know it."

"What's his motive for it? He doesn't get paid."

"He gets something even more precious to him than money."

"What?"

"Recognition and control."

"So what's all this got to do with your California killer?"

Cat's voice was passionate. "I believe the personality we are looking for is almost identical."

Gregory looked astounded. "You think there's a Carl Stearbourne loose on the streets of California?"

Cat scrutinized his face for a full minute and then let a breath out slowly. "Yes, yes I do." The pitch in her voice raised. She looked around the restaurant quickly, feeling foolish. *Back at your old games again, Gregory. Goading me to make a point. Then backing off.* Was he playing a game? Or was Gregory just testing her theories the way he always had, knowing she'd eventually have to take all this public.

She was being silly. These propositions sounded farfetched. Gregory was testing their strength and her commitment to them. Still she felt it, like an ache in her gut.

Cat lowered her voice and leaned in closer to Gregory. "Carl Stearbourne and Eric had the closest ongoing relationship of two inmates in that place. As a society, we want to believe there couldn't possibly be another Carl Stearbourne. We couldn't have one incarcerated and one loose. Hell, that would be too much—the fact that society could create two such demons in one generation. But I'm telling you, he's out there. Simple as that. Carl Stearbourne wasn't the first and he won't be the last. I've been considering this for some time, Gregory." She went to take a bite but didn't. "Long before I ever started talking with you tonight."

Gregory chuckled softly at her.

Cat looked at him. "What the hell are you laughing at?"

"It's just I love it when you get mad. You're passionate as all hell." A tugging smile at his mouth turned into a full-fledged grin.

The item came on Tuesday afternoon in a large manila envelope addressed to Dr. Cat Powers, c/o Burning Man Task Force, Irvine.

McGregor was sitting in the back corner of the task force room. On the far wall, photos of the girls loomed. For each one, two to three shots of full-faced, confident young women. Beside these, death mask photos. Details of each body's condition, where it had been found.

The smiling faces of innocence.

A dry vote of confidence.

Appreciated, though nothing was moving forward in the investigation.

McGregor noticed the envelope, conspicuous in its size and bulk, against business-sized envelopes on Cat's desk. A twinge in his stomach.

Something wasn't right with it.

Slipping on gloves, he pulled the envelope out of the stack. It was as if it did not want to come. Gave some hesitation. A lingering formaldehyde odor hit him. He brought the envelope to his nose. A stronger smell.

Some gung-ho rookie walked in, working late, trying to score brownie points. McGregor didn't want to be in the task force room with this envelope when he opened it. Richmond's empty office was better light. He went inside, closed the door, and sat at the desk, clearing a hole in the paperwork.

The envelope looked standard size and weight. Probably could be purchased at any one of a million locations. Placing it lettering-side down on Richmond's desk, McGregor tweaked the metal clasp and ran his finger slowly under the gummed seal.

As the envelope opened, the smell of formaldehyde intensified.

McGregor held his breath.

Putting two fingers on the envelope's back left corner, he tilted it to a forty-five degree angle. Something heavy inside. Dead weight, like what was in there didn't want to come out. Choosing a pencil, he stuck its sharp point in the envelope to draw out what was inside. It slipped out.

McGregor put his head between his knees until his ears stopped ringing, spots disappeared from his vision. He took a deep breath and picked up the phone.

⁙ ⁙ ⁙ ⁙ ⁙

He tried Catherine's cell phone. She wasn't picking up. It went to voice mail.

"Dr. Catherine Powers, where the hell is she?" McGregor screamed into the receiver, spit covering it in minuscule wet spots.

"Sir, I'm sorry. I've tried her room. She's not there."

"Look. This is police business, an emergency."

"Hold the line and let me see what I can find out."

McGregor heard a clunk as the phone was placed down. Dead noise in his ears for thirty seconds, a telephone ringing, shuffling, then the voice back on. "I spoke to Judy; she's on before my shift. Dr. Powers checked her messages before leaving for dinner with a gentleman. He picked her up around six."

"Did she mention who it was?"

"Hold on."

Dead line, but McGregor could make out a garbled conversation with someone who must have been Judy.

A female voice got on the phone. "Sir, can I help you? This is Judy Kennedy." Although she said the word *help*, it was clear she was annoyed.

"I need to find Dr. Catherine Powers. You saw her last?"

A few seconds passed before a response. "Sir, we respect the privacy of our guests."

McGregor exploded. "Look, this is police business. Life and death. You get my drift?" He took a breath and made himself settle down.

"Yes."

"Do you know who she was with? Did she mention a name?"

"She mentioned a doctor. Task, or maybe Taft." The woman's voice was small. "She said they were going to Chez Paul for dinner."

"Did you see the car she left in?"

The woman sounded tired, frightened. "Yes. A cream-colored late model BMW sedan."

"She didn't leave a forwarding number for messages?"

"No, sir."

"Thanks. Do you have a number for Chez Paul?"

"Yes" She gave him the number, he wrote it down and called it right away.

After 6 rings, someone answered the line. McGregor again explained the urgency of the situation but was told that Cat and Dr. Taft had already left. He asked the obnoxious sounding host if she would be so kind as to provide the good doctor's phone number if they had it. The woman provided it after some coaxing.

This was taking too long. He wished Cat was here. Wished he could protect her from this. Useless, childish thought.

McGregor called Taft's home number. He was so keyed up the babysitter at the end of the line couldn't understand him.

"I'm calling from the Irvine Police Department in California. You the babysitter?"

"Huh?" a cracking teenaged voice said.

"Look, I'm trying to locate a Dr. Catherine Powers."

"Who?"

McGregor was tired. He'd had it. Too much time was going by.

Stop getting angry and think. He slowed his voice, purposefully took breaths between words.

"Shut up and listen. I'm trying to locate Catherine Powers. She's a doctor who is out with Dr. Taft. Did he leave you a number where he could be reached? The name of the place they went? Anything? It's real, real important."

"Yeah, I got the cell number here. It's 569-3428."

"Thanks. Thanks a lot."

Quickly, he hung up the phone a third time in as many minutes and dialed the 619 area code and number, asked to speak to Cat. After a long empty pause they were connected.

She sounded surprised. Surprise turned to worry.

"What is it?" she said.

McGregor's voice was shaky, uneven. "It's another body, in a manner of speaking."

"You need me to come back?" Cat was saying into the phone, reading his signals all wrong.

"No, Cat. I'm looking at it."

"You're what?"

"I'm looking at it. Jesus, Catherine. There's no body this time." McGregor sounded shell-shocked, the kind of voice you heard after people survived things they shouldn't. "He sent us a piece of her."

"What?"

"Some poor girl's scalp, in a Ziploc bag, addressed to you."

"Oh God…"

"And he's left us a message, carved in it." McGregor sounded odd, far away.

"What does it say?" Cat begged, her voice barely audible. She heard a deep, purposeful breath from McGregor.

"Joey. He wants Joey."

TWENTY-SEVEN

If you will it, it is no dream.
—**Theodor Herzl**, founder of political Zionism

Mark hears the gate open, feels an unknown presence. Automatically he smiles, waiting for the boy and the dog to run through his headlights. Metal clinking, the garage door opening. Greenery. The soothing smell of rain.

To the right, through the open passenger door, Joey's grunt. Mark turns, seeing small, hunched shoulders, a close-cut head filling up the light. A shout.

Mark screams "Run!"

The man has Joey by the throat.

He is inside the passenger-side door now, coming headlong through the opening.

Mark hits him in the face then feels the blow before he sees it, unable to turn from it. An impact punches him backward into the truck window. A halo of impacted broken glass left where he hits. Blood on his forehead, the smell of oil.

A singular thought runs through his mind.

Joey.

Mark wants to scream "Run!" to him again, but the words will not come out. Only a groan escapes. A blackness descends over him, the presence. The man is there. Mark can feel him moving on Joey.

Say something.

Blood is trickling down his cheek, out his nose. Trying to shout, blood rises in his throat, leaves his mouth. Pain like a river of nails.

Far away, he can hear Joey crying. Out the corner of one eye, he can see him struggling, pushing the man away.

Please dear God, let someone drive by and see this. No headlights round the corner. It is a black night. Rain is pouring. No one will come.

Must make an effort to move. Left shoulder blade moves half an inch, excruciating pain. Mark vomits through blood. Eyes roll back wild. Wetness at the top of his forehead.

Must focus on the boy, on the man. Memorize some feature for later.

Let there be a later.

Stupid thought, there must be.

In a heap, but keep your eyes on Joey.

Joey is out of the vehicle running. The man catches him. The man has one hand on the child's throat, lifts him off the weathered brick paver driveway.

He twirls the boy in the air effortlessly. Brings him down on the passenger seat, facedown, gets Joey's arms behind him, although the boy is writhing, fighting.

Mark can hear electrical tape being pulled out of a spool, above the rain's gentle patter. Catches a glimmer of dull gray metallic. Joey screams, jerks his head up off the seat.

Half-sensible, Mark manages a smile, eyes shining bright, at his boy.

Tape around Joey's wrists and ankles, in quick successive circles.

Joey is crying, screaming, fighting.

Mark cannot fathom this madness. Far away, inside the house, the phone is ringing.

Lifting his head with much effort, Mark looks down at his neck, chest. Red all over him. He doesn't want Joey to see him like this.

The man is over Joey, just inches away.

Joey says the words just a bit louder than the rain, "I'll be all right, Daddy."

And then Joey is gone.

TWENTY-EIGHT

Reality is a staircase going neither up nor down,
we don't move; today is today, always is today.
—**Octavio Paz**, *"The Endless Instant"*

The thump of the man's hand carries through Joey. He is lifting, straining, pumping against this strength clamped on him. Head forced upward, trying to use it as a battering ram. But the man is bigger, stronger.

"Stop," the man says.

Startled by the voice, Joey stops. It is not a voice he expected, not at all like the movies; it is a calm, controlled voice.

Still, this hand at his throat. No, he has not misjudged the man, he decides. It still hurts.

Joey turns his head sideways in a quick, jerking motion, feels something in his neck snap. In this, he gets what he wants—glimpses his captor's face. The man forces his head straight.

"Don't." Joey's voice comes out raspy.

Not speaking, the man simply smiles sheepishly.

A discomforting smile, as if he knows what time will bring.

Demons in the man's eyes. Eyes the color of glass, seemingly able to reflect everything around him. Joey glimpses himself in those eyes, snared like an animal.

Desperately, Joey's mind strains with his body. Think of a way out. He has not been cut, he is not bleeding. It is his way to fight, but he cannot, his hands, legs bound like a prisoner. Struggling against tape, his muscles produce only a dull ache. It is no good.

Joey hears his own heart beating.

Clifford is dead. This man has killed him.

Suddenly he is afraid.

He thinks of his father in the truck, eyes open, unmoving. There is a hollow emptiness inside.

Fear saps his strength. He crouches into a ball and groans. Around his neck, the clamped hand grows tighter till it is hard to breathe. Above, low street lights glimmer. Around him, a deep, chilling rain falls harder. Joey wishes the rain would camouflage him, simply make him invisible to this man. He curls up tighter.

From inside the house, he can just barely hear the phone ringing. He supposes it has been ringing all along, though he is not sure why.

Joey wants to turn his face from his dad's Yukon, but he can't. His hands are fighting each other now, if only to wipe tears. Light seems harsh. There is a giant sound in his ear, like the sound of gushing water. Cold, shaking, hair matted, rainwater running over his lips like a river, Joey feels his stomach muscles bunch up. Wants to just curl up and go to sleep.

Rain and tears on his jacket.

Pain rushes in like a wave. Terrible pain.

He is up off the pavement.

Time has slowed. It is as if each raindrop takes minutes to fall.

A hard, thick hand.

The calm voice commanding him to walk.

Cannot get his legs to do anything, like his bones are gone. The man drags him, new sneakers scraping on wet blacktop.

There is an SUV not far away, a big black Cadillac Escalade.

The man commands him not to scream because now they are in front of the neighbor's, the Grahams' house.

Do as you are told.

Practically on his knees, he's being pulled, then a sudden surging force and he is inside something. Metal slams hollow over him.

Blackness. He is in the back of the SUV, shoved into the space that holds the spare tire. There is metal above. He can feel it with his fingertips. He tries to get up but hits his head. As the SUV takes off, Joey lurches forward, then back.

Above, a great expanse of nothingness. He looks at it for what seems an eternity. Eyes tiring of focusing on blackness. Tiny finger reaches through black to the metal, working over grooves and fissures that feel like rivers and canyons.

Tears come again.

Focus on the last clear image he had before this began. Read the face, but it will not come clear.

His father's face is splattered red.

His mind is full of possibilities of what is about to happen. The unthinkable already has; his father is dead.

Joey struggles up, balancing weight on the small of his back. Inside this place, it smells of mold, grease, dirt. Below him, what feels like a small thin mattress, sharp metal springs jabbing his thighs, buttocks. He can almost taste the rusted metal springs.

In this instant, he wonders if he can disappear. Make himself invisible. Will it, as he has willed other things. Then the pain would leave him too.

And things would be as they were.

Time stretches into nothingness.

His only companion, brakes squealing. Muffled sounds of the man talking to someone, above the liquid violins. A rapid rush of blood to his head. Could there be two of them? He does not remember two, but it could be. Concentrating, he realizes there is only one voice. No one speaks back.

Thoughts of his father…

I want to see my mother. Thoughts of her flow immediately after thoughts of his father. If he closes his eyes hard enough and long enough, he can reach up and touch her. His mother destroys men like this. He wants her here now.

Outside, the SUV is idle, then roars out. Forced down into the mattress, which smells raw, ragged, dirty.

Joey will not shrink down. Arms to his side, to brace himself for the next turn, he makes sense of it. The small man with the calm voice driving; he must be the one Mom is after. But why would he come here? Why to him? Each passing second brings more questions.

At his age, Joey thinks death is unimaginable. Life is infinite. There had only been one exposure to death in his life, the day his Grandma Sasha, a wrinkled figure with cloudy eyes, passed away. She was seventy-nine. Joey remembers holding the brown speckled hand, cold, crooked fingers for a long time, listening to her breathe soft and shallow. She had known he was there with her; he could feel warmth, followed by a slight squeeze, then gradual coldness. Joey had been led out of the room by his mother, and he had not seen Grandma Sasha anymore. She'd gone to live with the angels.

Whispering "Stop this, stop this" to himself, to the man, but the man does not hear.

The SUV is moving—one corner, then another. Its ride is jarring and rough.

How far would it be before they are out of town?

He wonders, but he can't tell without a window. There is no way to know. Joey wants the sun on his face, fresh air. Here there is none of that. Only darkness. But he will fight it, he must fight it.

Pulling knees up to chest, he holds on, kicking with all his might. The metal will not budge. He kicks again and again, but nothing moves. Only now does he realize he has lost his shoes. Feet wet, cold through damp socks. How did he do that? Maybe when the man yanked him in here. Maybe they'd find them on the sidewalk.

How long till they find Dad?

Closing his eyes, he focuses on his father's face, blood like a crimson mask, red stains. Joey is scared. If death comes for him, how will he know it? Will it be painful, like the look on his father's face, or will he simply fall asleep and never awaken? Or will it be this never-ending blackness? He wonders when it will happen.

Joey wants to scream but shouldn't. In the movies, if you scream they kill you. In the movies, you are scared but can't show it.

Joey hears the music. Immediately he shies away from it, a gut reaction.

But it's only the radio, only the sound of violins. Classical music. The man is quiet.

Joey slams his feet against blackness. Sudden wrenching pain, like a firecracker, dull aching that goes through ankles, shins, thighs.

Grunting, Joey tries once more, crashes his feet into his makeshift prison, harder this time, sucking for air as he hits.

The SUV brakes hard, swerves, stops. Violins stop playing, hollow footsteps coming closer. A metal click in the lock, just above him. The latch releases.

In that instant, he's going to die. He's sure of it, fiercely conscious of his own mortality. Closing his eyes, he imagines flying high and away from this.

The trunk opens, light flooding in.

Joey's afraid to open his eyes, look up, but he does.

The calm voice, not as soft as before, coming from above. The man stands before him, shirttails out, raincoat billowing around his body so he looks bigger than he is. The air is cold. Something glimmering in the man's hand catches the sunlight shafts filtering through clumping, gray clouds. Joey knows instinctively what it must be.

He wants to control his rapid gasps but can't.

The man looks different in sunlight. Eyes light and unmoving; balding, shaven head; an odd twitch to his right cheek.

The man comes headlong at him through the opening, though Joey is still squinting into the brightness.

He can see the whole face now, like a sun that fills up his horizon too quickly.

He feels the sharp tug at his hair. A violent, jerking motion that snaps his head back into an unnatural position, exposing his face to a cool wind above the field. He cannot bear to open his eyes, instead keeps them tightly closed, waiting for the pain that will signal his end. There is no pain, only the horrible sound of the voice. A demonic voice that goes to the very heart of him, fills him with terror. Joey's shrieks are carried on the wind, out into the greenness for no one to hear. Joey stops.

Acrid breath on his face, the man's stench. "You do that one more time, I'll slit your throat."

There is no anger in his words, just a sure confidence.

Joey leans back, small hands clutching tightly to carpeting, nodding.

"I'll hurt you," the man says.

Joey lifts up, just inches, to get a glimpse of his world. His last look, he's sure of it. Yet he will not go to heaven without knowing.

"Who are you?" Joey asks, his words barely a murmur.

"Consider me a friend of your mother's," the man says slowly, laughing a wicked, low laugh that crackles out into the molten sky.

The man's hands aren't big, but he is rubbing them together like they are cold. One is swollen, red. Dried gray and brown dots on it. As the man touches it, he winces.

"My mom doesn't have friends like you," Joey says, sitting up further. Only now, he can see they're on an unfamiliar two-lane highway, cornfields to his left, husks barely taller than the man blowing in a growing breeze from the direction of the setting sun. No other people in sight. The rain has stopped.

Realizing what the boy is doing, the man laughs louder. The kind of laughter that rolls out, sweeps over the landscape. Joey shivers.

The man reaches in his front pocket, takes out a hard pack of Marlboros, lights one up. Joey can see the side of his face, only now realizing: I know this man.

"You're the one that was watching me?" he asks.

The man takes one puff of his cigarette, throws it on the ground, stomps it out, and grunts. "I've been watching you for a long time."

With that he pushes Joey down and slams the metal thing over him. In the pain of darkness again, Joey listens to the motor turn over, gears shift, the SUV rolls onto the highway. These sounds will be Joey's personal hell. He knows that although he wants this demon to go to hell, he is not ready to go live with the angels.

TWENTY-NINE

You can do very little with faith but you can do nothing without it.
—**Samuel Butler**, Rebelliousness, in *Notebooks*

ain was falling when Cat got there four hours later. It was a cold, irritating rain that dampened her spirits. Sky the color of slate, a kind of sky that conjured visions of Armageddon, as if Satan himself would descend from the clouds. Three months later, and these clouds would have brought a blizzard. Nature had a way of choosing her own course.

Cat got out of the cab and stood silhouetted against police cruiser headlights, hands stuck deep in her raincoat pockets, looking through a sea of heads for McGregor's.

Like her, he'd taken the first flight out.

Yellow crime scene tape fluttered, slicked shiny by rain. She bowed under it, willing her legs to keep moving. In front of her, Mark's house, a place she once called home. Gray siding reflected blue, yellow, the red of the crime scene van's lights. Everything and everyone was dripping wet. A kidney-shaped bed of dark petunias she'd never noticed seemed beaten down by rain.

Guys with FBI jackets everywhere, block letters emblazoned in bright yellow across their backs. She caught one of them by the arm, his face reflected in an ugly blue flicker from one of the squad cars. "McGregor?" She couldn't bring herself to get the word out with much force, but the stone-faced man understood.

Turning, he pointed in the Chevy Yukon's direction, its passenger door gaping open.

At this point, she did not know what had happened. Only that something had happened to Mark and Joey. With Mark's truck sitting there, both front doors splayed open, Cat couldn't bring herself to comprehend the worst.

Like a shrill cry from inside, suddenly she knew what it all meant. A singular note of confusion catapulted through her. Like a crescendo, it brought her down. McGregor was moving toward her, his face motionless, evasive.

"Dear God, no." She couldn't find any air, couldn't see what was ahead.

She wanted to hold back this despair, make it go away. But it flooded her, taking all her sanity with it. She focused on McGregor's face; he was in a full run now, moving faster through the crowd, wearing a worried expression.

Cat heard a hopeless cry that seemed to come from afar. She realized her mouth was hanging open. It was her cry.

In that instant, she wondered if she would ever be all right again.

Was it possible that God had taken both of them? It could not be so. It could not. She simply would not allow herself to believe it.

She crouched down, shivering hands in the rainwater, touching the blacktop, though it seemed so far away. With effort, she wiped water off her face. Crickets, the screeching of bugs louder. The air suddenly thicker, icier.

It felt like everything was falling down.

A clap of thunder in the distance; twenty seconds later, a sudden brilliant flash of light.

Find the strength. One foot in front of the other. You have done it before, she told herself. But her legs would not respond. McGregor was there now, his arms around her. Simply holding her. Cat could feel his heartbeat.

"Let it go, Cat, it's all right," he whispered. "Let it go…"

She shuddered.

"Mark's gone, Cat."

She watched the coroner remove Mark's body. Mark, this man she'd known well, with whom she'd shared hardships and rewards, a man she'd grown distant from. There were so many opportunities left unfulfilled, things she'd never be able to say, words of forgiveness still to convey. They'd come so far, but there was still a long way to go with Joey.

Pushing back from McGregor, her eyes searched his for hope. Cat identified little there but pity. She needed to know, even though she could not bear the thought. What about Joey? Inquisitiveness overcomes any need for self-preservation. Where was her child? Watching the zippered body bag, she blocked any thoughts of her butchered child.

She closed her eyes, fought a terrible yearning to know. Finding strength, she performed the simplest of miracles and opened them. Repugnance at bay, she scanned the Yukon's inside, ghastly blood soaking the driver's seat.

McGregor was cradling her. Her legs failed and he slowly brought her up. Resting her full body weight on him, Cat inched forward. Blood splatters covered the inside windshield, the driver's-side window displaying a circular crack. Red soaked a six-inch puddle in beige, matted carpeting. Even with this carnage, she could see her little boy was not there.

Euphoria.

But not yet. Cat would not allow herself to feel it yet.

Her eyes scrutinized the interior once more, eagerly this time. For verification. No other blood, no other signs of a struggle.

Sudden elation sprang in her, like a sweetness she'd never known. Sheer jubilation.

Joey's gotten away, she thinks. *He couldn't save Mark, but he has gotten away. He is safe. He'll come back when he realizes it is safe here. When he sees me.* Her mind was reeling.

Cat turned away, leaning against McGregor less now, starting to find her legs. Magic was etched in each pore of her face, a look McGregor had never seen before. As abruptly as it came, the look was gone.

Cat's eyes gazed past clusters of officers to a few men standing down the street, about three hundred feet away. They were stooping over something, picking it up gingerly off the wet pavement. Others stood looking on. It appeared they were talking, consulting. One scratched his head.

She froze, feeling her knees start to buckle. "Please, please, please, oh God, no…" The words came in silent prayers, like her screams, as she got closer to the men huddled. They gestured to her to stay back, McGregor's hands on her, but she thrust forward. One of the men, wearing a tweed sports coat, stepped to the side, dark bags like painted circles under his eyes. His face was solemn. He walked toward her, charity in his eyes.

She could see inside the streetlight's circle of light.

Cat exhaled quickly, furiously, as if she had been punched in the gut. She froze, features carved in thick stone, holding her breath. There was a pounding in her head. Unexpectedly, street odors—rain, pavement, oil, smoke—took on a life on their own, overwhelming her. There was another smell. Musty, savage. At first she could not identify it. It was her own sweat. Although the air was cool, she felt heat in her chest.

A permeating heaviness pierced her breast. Cat was uncertain when it first came, the numbing sense of loss.

It was the last thing she saw before collapsing, an image stuck indelibly in her mind.

Joey's ragged, scuffed sneakers.

THIRTY

Progress imposes not only new possibilities for the future but new restrictions.
—**Norbert Wiener**, *The Human Use of Human Beings*

A clicking sound and the metal is gone. Then a grunt. Joey turns, feels the man's presence there, the man with the soft movements, even softer voice. Today his motions are even more subdued in the otherwise still air. The stale smell of the Cadi's trunk gives way to fresh air.

In almost total blackness, Joey listens to the sound of leaves, imagining the rhythm of the land.

Raising his head, he strains through a tiny flood of light under his left eye.

From the duct tape's corner, there is sunlight, just a glimmer of it, and Joey twists slightly to the left, just a millimeter, to get all of it he can. Enough to get a glimpse of a strangely rounded head, the close-cropped scalp.

Shoes scrape on blacktop, a dark, elusive shadow over him. A quick rustling of leaves, cool breeze against his cheek, the babble of a brook. All these things are out of sight, but he knows where they are.

Just as he knows where the man is. Coming headlong at him, he sees a large, wild shadow. It is vague, silent, ominous. Though Joey holds his breath in the open trunk, the odor of the man overwhelms him. The smell of old sweat and whiskey lingers, overtaking the good clean smells of nature.

Another smell too. He tracks the smell to the man, clothes damp and wet, combined with the animal smell of leather, Joey supposes, coming from the car's seats.

Joey, terrified and dazed, can't make out any features, only this man's vague malevolence directed at him, which seems to rise and fall like a cascade of misdirection with each passing second. Unwittingly, Joey realizes the man's hatred is directed not at his kind—not at boys in general, not that at all. Rather, it is that he is a particular boy, someone's son. That is the reason he's been taken.

In this breakthrough second, Joey Powers knows he is just a boy, but this demon sees him as so much more than that. To this man, he is deliverance and meaning, all rolled up in one. At the same time, finding his breathing in cadence with the man's shallow respiration, Joey knows he is hated for everything this man has never had—love, kindness, innocence.

Joey is dimly aware that his chest is moving to the tempo of the man's breathing. The sun feels warm on his face, and he turns to soak up what remnants of it he can before the detectable gloom of night forces him back into darkness.

An obscured figure casts darkness before the sun.

Through his meager light shaft, Joey can see the man is coming even nearer, just an inch away, looking closely into his eyes for a long time. He dares not move, watching the knife come up through his tiny portal, the man pressing its sharpness against his throat. Moving the blade down, it touches Joey's clothes but doesn't pierce the nylon fabric of his jacket. Lower now, on his chest, between his ribs, down to his stomach. He is sure the man can feel his small chest heaving in quick, short gasps.

He closes his eyes and is oddly aware of the cold pressure of the blade on his abdomen, pressing through blue jeans. It seems to last forever, fear and anticipation beyond anything Joey has ever known.

Joey tries to move away from it, to break from the paralysis the knife has spun over him. Suddenly, it is as if something hard is holding him, the feel of cool metal encircling his wrists, a clinking sound, then a snap.

As he moves his arms painfully, the unnerving clink of chains. Can only go so far before the metal circles restrict him. Handcuffs.

Maybe, maybe, the legs would move further. Stretch out one leg, just a little. He is careful not to move his abdomen against the knife's pressure. Through the deafening beating of his chest, Joey is aware that the man's breathing is gone. Where is he? Is he looking? No. He can barely make out the man's head. He is staring out at the horizon, not this way.

Stretch, oh God, pressure there too on his ankles. Same coldness; that smell.

Hand shackles and leg shackles tight.

Unerringly, the blade hasn't moved. The air seems to take on a life of its own, seems to throb, constricting in his lungs. Seconds later the blade's coldness retreats and Joey feels the sharp tip behind him, slipping between his wrists, his ankles, cutting the electrical tape, releasing him from his bindings.

Anger seethes through every muscle in his body. To be released only to be imprisoned in something more restricting. Cold, heartless hatred directed at this indistinct figure. The man's head is turning now; he is looking this way maybe. Can't tell. Then Joey can feel the man's eyes on him, raping him of his dignity with a stare.

It all seems to continue without end.

Joey does not know how long it has been, how many days.

By the time he is aware of the man being gone, pitch blackness surrounds him like a shroud, whiskey stench no longer sickens him, violins are playing, and he is exhausted, empty, and alone. In the darkness.

Fluttering her eyelids open, to the pain from bright lights overhead, Cat wondered how long she'd been here, even where she was. The smell of antiseptic lingered as she stared past the light to the square perforated ceiling tiles. A dull ache all over.

A beep, beep, beep she recognized as a monitor. Turning her head from side to side, she could see her right wrist was wrapped in tape, an IV administered via a Hep-Lock. From the looks of it, they had recently drawn blood.

Momentarily, she searched for fragments of memory, trying to put the pieces together. She could remember only a hint of time, standing in front of a gray Cape Cod house. More vividly, she recalled the Yukon, its interior splattered with blood. Tiny white and blue tennis shoes.

"I've got to get out of here." She threw the sheets back, the IV stand lurching jerkily behind her swinging arm.

"Now, there will be none of that," a heavyset nurse, half her age, said, trying to get her back into bed.

The tiles were cold on Cat's feet, but she just wanted to get her clothes. "You don't understand," came her automatic response. "I'm a doctor."

The nurse looked exasperated, apparently unimpressed. "I don't care who you are, now get your ass back in the bed. You're being released soon anyway." Her voice had a smoker's throatiness to it.

"Soon's not good enough."

"Look, missy, I don't give a damn what you think. I'm calling a doctor, getting you a sedative." She hacked a cough, then intercommed the nurse's station to have Dr. Barker paged.

"Dr. Barker, he admitted me?"

The nurse nodded.

"You've got to get him in here, he'll understand. He knows what I do for a living. He'll see what's going on." Cat waited for some of this to register on the expressionless face, but nothing did. Not even a shrug of her shoulders; it was as if she were a robot going about her business.

She held Cat's arm still, pulled out the IV, covering the spot with clear tape and a white gauze wad. Cat noticed for the first time that her right arm and shoulder were black-and-blue.

"Now you get up on this bed till the doctor gets here." Dark pupils flashed at her. Cat did as she was told.

McGregor entered the room, wearing a sports coat that looked as beat as he did. When he saw her eyes open, he smiled widely. "Hey there. We missed you."

"How long have I been out?" Cat's words conveyed urgency, directness. She managed to prop her body up. Instinctively, McGregor reached behind, drawing two flat pillows to the arch of her back. With the movement, she felt soreness permeate each fiber…her right arm and shoulder hurt the most.

"What the hell did I do?" She gave McGregor a quizzical look.

He chuckled in spite of himself. "You fainted, went down pretty hard, knocked your head."

She said nothing, rubbing her shoulder. "How long?"

"They've had you here overnight, just for observation. Barker said you look like hell, haven't been taking care of yourself."

"Anything broke?"

"Nope, you didn't bust nothin' up, just bruised a few spots. You got some fluid in your lungs. They think it might be a bronchial virus or something."

"Then why won't they let me out of here?"

"You needed the rest, Cat. You've been working on this case night and day for weeks. You haven't been sleeping at night. You're a wreck. You need rest."

She considered his statement, the lines around his eyes, mouth, more prominent than before, etched with worry for her. "How can you ask me to rest at a time like this?"

"I can't ask it, or expect it. I'm just telling you what the doctors say."

"Screw the doctors."

Just then Dr. Barker walked into the room. By all appearances, he was a man given to excess, just as Cat remembered. A forty-five inch waist, large hands, six foot three, he was the kind of man who made an entrance. One couldn't mistake, or ignore, his huge girth or charming smile. His eyes danced over her. "Well, Catherine. Finally awake are we?" He smiled halfheartedly at McGregor. "Let's have a listen, shall we?"

Dr. Barker stepped around McGregor, leaning Cat forward with one massive hand so he could place the stethoscope to her mid-back. It felt cold on her skin; she felt gooseflesh rise across her neck. He commanded her to exhale and inhale normally a few times as he moved the device, listening. Then he leaned her back on the pillows, doing the same in front just below her collarbone.

Cat felt embarrassed having McGregor there; she didn't want him to see her like this.

"Now, I understand there's been some talk of you walking out of here. Impetuous, aren't we?"

He let his words stand in the air for a moment, a broad smirk painted on his lips.

Cat would have none of it. She was dead serious. "Doctor to doctor, okay? I'm taking up a bed. Prescribe me some antibiotics. Amoxicillin or a Z-Pak will kick this. You don't need me to be here, and I don't want to be here. I've got things to take care of."

McGregor offered no support, staring out a window that looked onto the street below.

Cat gave him an angry sideways glance.

Dr. Barker cleared his throat. "You ever heard the saying…"

She wouldn't let him finish the line. "I know, a doctor makes the worst patient." Each voice mocked the other, words mirroring so well it made McGregor take his eyes off the road.

"Come on, I'll slow down if I'm not feeling good."

Dr. Barker looked unconvinced.

"Okay, here's the deal. McGregor here's with me most of the time, like a regular watchdog." Cat studied him to see if he was paying attention. True to form, McGregor looked like an obedient puppy. "He'll take care of me. I place my care in his hands. If I'm feeling lousy, he can bring me right back here, I won't protest." She looked at Dr. Barker matter-of-factly.

He knew she was playing a game, but he couldn't make her stay. This was the next best thing. Dr. Barker turned to McGregor. "You'll kick her ass if she doesn't take care of herself?"

McGregor's face brightened. "It would be a pleasure to kick her ass." He flashed a mischievous grin.

"Good, all right then. We have a deal." Dr. Barker placed a corpulent palm in the detective's. They shook.

Cat looked up to the heavens. "Thank God for small miracles."

"I'll have you released within the hour. Your clothes are in the closet," Dr. Barker said, walking out to the hallway. Before he said it, Cat was out of bed, already gathering her things.

THIRTY-ONE

The race is to the swift;
The battle to the strong.
—**John Davidson**, *"War Song"*

C at heard the brakes squeal. The lights of Quantico faded slowly in the back windshield. Gradually, the scene along the freeway had moved from a concoction of inner strip malls, fast-food restaurants, and small houses packed too close together to a green agriculture, apple trees, orchards. The air smelled sweet with ripening fruit. Farther out, giant elms and pines filled up the dusk, casting shadows down on the road.

Then on to the Beacon Hill Estates, two-story three- and four-bedroom homes that sat in neatly trimmed culs-de-sac behind a lapping waterfall that continuously cascaded in back of polished brass letters that announced the development.

Cat sat in silence as they passed it, listening to the car rumble under her feet. It was the second time in two days she'd passed it, and she hoped never to see it again. With the silence thick, oppressing, McGregor had to know how she felt.

Cat rolled her head on her shoulders to ease the stiffness in her back.

"Thanks for getting me out of the hospital," she said to McGregor.

"No problem."

He had an odd look on his face, like he also was dreading going back. For Cat, there was a great risk in returning to this place, but the prize she sought there was the power to understand what happened. If she could do that, she could move forward. And she could find Joey.

Cat knew she didn't have to dread this house. It was not the house that had done her harm; it was the man that had been there. The more she thought of it, she knew there was a link between the man she'd been stalking in California and all this. Anything else was too coincidental.

Blinking back tears, she let the blame fall squarely on her shoulders. And yet there was strength in her belly now, born of sheer will—the will to know, to make things right.

She thought of what must have happened. Hiding in the bushes, he had waited for them. In her mind's eye, she could see Joey walking up the driveway, sneakers skipping along, finding Clifford. Mark in the truck, engine running, unaware, waiting for the garage to open. Joey running out, terrified. This man, this stalker, over him, already on him before Mark could do anything. A struggle. Followed by a fatal blow to the head. The crushing force. Cat wished Joey hadn't seen it, though she was sure he had.

Although she dealt with criminals every day, the worst of humankind, up to this point she had always felt secure. Now she wasn't sure she could ever feel that way again. The brutal reality, that she and the people she loved were the hunted, haunted her. She'd been a fool to believe anything less.

McGregor watched her hollow gaze, knew what she was thinking. Like the time he found Nancy Marsh.

She only wanted to save what was savable.

McGregor stopped the car at the end of the cul-de-sac, drawing up too close to the curb. A high-pitched squeak as the tires rubbed the curbstone. McGregor turned left, parked in front of the Grahams'.

Across the street, canary yellow crime scene tape had broken, fluttering in a light breeze, the letters unreadable.

Two cars were parked in the Grahams' driveway, one a white Chrysler, the other a late model Mercedes, Mrs. Graham's pride and joy. Much of the house was dark. Cat could see a dim light behind frosted glass and mini blinds in the living room. She heard voices in there, one she recognized as Patsy Graham.

Cat rang the doorbell, listened to the *boing-boing* on the other side.

A woman's footsteps coming. Patsy Graham answered the door, pulling it back to peer through a latched opening. From the inch exposed, Cat could see she was wearing no shoes. "Hi, Patsy, it's Catherine Powers. This is Detective McGregor. Can we come in?" Patsy mumbled something. Cat could hear a chain unlatch, tinkle against the heavy door.

"Come on in. We got time before dinner." She spoke in forced pleasantries, as if it really were an intrusion. Cat was sure the gossip mill had started about what had happened the day before, why Cat hadn't been there. Laying blame where it might well belong.

Cat stepped over to the hearth. A pungent cabbage and corned beef odor. The house was as untidy as she remembered last time. Patsy moved quickly, stocking feet quiet on the smooth floor.

"Have a seat." Patsy led them to the formal dining room with its blue wingback chairs, attempt at fine art on the walls. Cat felt uncomfortable for intruding, assured the woman they wouldn't take up much of her time. From a side room, she glimpsed Patsy's kids, *WWE Monday Night Raw* blaring.

"Turn the damned TV down, we have guests," Patsy hollered through the doorway. A pimpled teenage boy, not much heavier than a paperclip, scowled at his mother but did what he was told, turning down the bad wrestling TV show. Cat noticed his left leg in a full cast.

"Thank you!" she shouted in a condescending tone. She turned to Cat and McGregor, put her hands on her knees. "Now, what can I do for the two of you?"

"You know about Joey?"

Dismay washed over the woman's face. "Oh, my God yes." She reached over, put her palm on Cat's knee. "I feel so horrible for you. Poor child. Do you know who did it yet, any leads?" As she said "leads" she looked at McGregor, trying to impress. This woman had been watching too much *True Detective* TV.

"I know they went over everything with you on the night of the kidnapping, but I was wondering if you saw anything unusual." Cat asked.

Patsy scrunched up her nose. "What do you mean by unusual?"

"Like out of the ordinary. Anybody hanging around?"

"Can't really say. Anyway, I'm at work all day. Retail job doesn't pay jack, and I'm on my feet all day." As if by instinct, she rubbed a hosed foot that she'd curled almost underneath her frame. "The one to ask would be Jimmy." In the next second, without waiting for a response, she shouted, "Jimmy, get in here. Mrs. Powers wants to ask you something."

The paperclip thin boy emerged from the rec room, leaning his frame against the doorjamb. Thin waxy arms, a flash of red hair. He wore black jeans three sizes too big. Cat couldn't tell if they were faded purposefully or just plain dirty. A white T-shirt emphasized his pallor, three angry swelling pimples just above his collar. Now that he was standing upright, Cat could see the boy's cast went all the way from his hip down to his foot. The only semblance of skin that materialized was three white toes.

"Come over here and sit down," his mother commanded, patting her hand on the seat beside her. The boy practically fell on the sofa, twirling himself as he went, landing with his butt just barely where he wanted it, not on the floor. Both hands down, he pulled the heavy cast, straightened his back.

"Jimmy, you remember Mrs. Powers…"

"Uh-huh. Who's this guy?" His eyes flashed at McGregor.

"A detective," his mom interjected. "Isn't that exciting?"

"Uh-huh."

Cat hoped the conversation would become more intelligent over time. Scanning his cast, she asked, "How'd you manage that?"

"Football. Some defensive back decided to have a field day with my leg." Said it without remorse but with revenge. Cat wondered what this twig of a boy could possibly be plotting.

"Fractured?" McGregor questioned.

"Yeah, in three places. They just let me out of the hospital last week."

"I can relate to that," Cat said.

"So what do you guys, I mean, what do you want?"

"Just a few questions. Your mom says you're the resident homebody around here." McGregor took on an easy manner. Years of working interviews, some tougher than others, had taught him how to read people fast.

"Yeah, really sucks. Can't go back to practice for another month till things heal up." With the first full sentence the boy had put together, Cat could tell he was still going through the voice change that marked puberty. Unintentionally, syllables cracked and lurched out of his lips.

"So you been hanging out?"

"Yeah, just watching the tube, dumb daytime TV stuff, soaps…" He grimaced as he said it. "Reruns, you know…" His voice trailed off with a croak.

As the boy scratched behind his ear, Cat noticed tattoos on his fingers. Knuckles inscribed with WAR.

Nice neighborhood, she thought, praying Joey hadn't hung around with this kid.

McGregor leaned into the boy. "You notice anything unusual last night or over the past few days?"

The boy's face went blank, disengaged. "Huh?"

Open-ended question, open-ended answer, thought Cat. McGregor obviously thought the same thing and got down to the nitty-gritty.

"The kid across the street, Joey…"

The boy chuckled, a mean laugh. "Yeah, little fart kid, always over here, asking to borrow my skateboard. Loaned it to him once, he busted his ass…" A laugh just long enough for a swat on the backside of his head.

The boy straightened up, eyes averted to the carpeting.

"You see anyone hanging around? Watching the house? Especially last night? Before the police showed up?"

"Yup. Black Cadi SUV been parked on the street for a few days at places up and down. Windows tinted. I only saw the guy once. Not real big, kinda, you know, he looked like a fag. Small-boned. Real pris."

Cat caught her breath, looked down at her hands. Unconsciously, she was rubbing them on her knees trying to get the sweat off. "You saw a man?" she asked. Take small gulps of air, she told herself, try to control your ragged breath.

"Yeah, guy looked in his thirties, early forties maybe. Never seen him round here before." The boy picked nervously at one of his pimples.

"Can you describe him for us?" McGregor asked intently.

The boy squirmed, apparently uncomfortable being the center of adult attention.

Cat white-knuckled her clasped hands, her mind full of the possibilities of what the man might look like.

"He was, like I said, white, maybe late thirties, early forties. Close-cropped hair, like a buzz cut sorta. Couldn't really see his eyes, but they were light-colored.

Medium to smallish build. Kind of guy, I could kick his ass if I wanted." He smiled naughtily, looked at his mother, met her disapproving gaze and kept talking. "Maybe weighed 160, 170 max."

"Height?"

"Don't really remember. Five seven, five eight maybe. Like I say, I only saw the guy once."

"Did you catch a license plate number, anything unusual about the car?"

"Nope, didn't really pay much attention. Just thought the guy was sorta odd. Like a goof, ya know?"

McGregor nodded. "You said a black Cadi. You remember the make?"

"Yeah, an Escalade, like Ms. Sullivan drives at school. Four-door, I think. No spinners on it though."

McGregor was scribbling it all down in a little notebook.

"Anything else you remember about the guy?"

"Nope. Just a weirdo. You need me for anything else? I wanna go watch wrestling. I'm missing the best match."

"No, thanks. We might give you a call later on in the week. And I'm gonna leave your mom my card in case you remember anything. Be sure to call us."

The boy was already up off the couch. "Uh-huh, sure thing," he called back over his shoulder.

THIRTY-TWO

We have left undone those things which we ought to have done; and we have done those things which we ought not have done; and there is no health in us.
—Book of Common Prayer

G et a composite artist out here for a sketch?" McGegor looked at her disapprovingly.

"Got any other smart ideas?" Cat said, rolling her eyes. She was a little too tired to deal with his doubts at this point.

"Yeah, for starters, we check with all the area rental agencies and used car lots. Check to see if anyone's rented or bought a used black Escalade in the last few weeks."

"And…?"

"Cross-check those names with passengers on flights coming into Quantico from LAX and South Orange County over the last two weeks."

"Okay…that might narrow the list to ten names. And do you think I have time to track each one of those names down? Speak to each of them in a nice 'I'm so sorry to bother you, my kid's out there with a madman and we're trying to track him down' investigation?" Cat was seething, not really angry at McGregor per se, but angry with the time that was passing, unable to slow it down.

208

"I know this is killing you, Cat, but it's the best we can do at this point."

Sitting in the rented car, Cat felt the weight of the universe on her shoulders. It was as if nothing was what it should be, yet everything was the same.

"There is something I can do. I mean, it doesn't make sense for the both of us to be out here. I get the impression this guy had some reason we're not focusing on for picking Nancy Marsh as his first victim. He didn't just pick her out of the blue. He knew her, watched her for some time, just like he did Joey. I know it. There's got to be some connection with the girl that we haven't clued in on. You do what you need to do here. I'm going back to California to see if this hunch checks out. There's got to be something, something so casual, so insignificant in Nancy Marsh's life that we are just overlooking it. Someone that matches our profile. I have a gut feeling the killer knew Nancy personally. That's the reason she was the first. He felt safe enough with her to allow her to be his first."

Maybe she was crazy for believing in this, but right now it felt good to believe in something. And her instincts were the only thing she could trust. She was taking a great risk and she knew it.

A small crease appeared on McGregor's forehead. "Catherine, I think you're going out on a limb here, but if you want me to handle the job out here, I can take care of it."

Dr. Catherine Powers heard the flaps of the giant 727 moan down. Newport Beach's lights appeared slowly below the plane's black wing. Under her feet, the landing gear thudded into a rush of oncoming air, locking down.

Her fingers clutched the armrests to ease the tension of the powerful touchdown.

Coming back to California.

She'd taken a great risk. Coming back, possibly slowing down the search for her son. Risking never seeing him again. The thought left her startled and helpless as the plane came to a stop. Still, in her gut she believed there were clues here which had not been uncovered.

But in her heart she knew she did not have to dread the future. Whatever happened, she had Joey in her heart. No matter what happened, she would always have that. She didn't have to worry about that being stripped from her.

From the terminal, she called Dr. Marsh. Initially the line was busy, then she got through.

"Dr. Marsh. This is Dr. Cat Powers. I've just returned from Quantico, Virginia. I have reason to believe that a kidnapping there may have been committed by the same man who took Nancy. Do you have some time to see me this evening?"

The doctor agreed. The thought of Joey tied up, tortured, or worse occupied Cat's mind all the way to his house.

The English Tudor had not changed, except perhaps the climbing rose arbor was more in bloom, or maybe it just seemed that way, with spotlights to capture the beauty of each bloom and bud. The cab parked on the street; Cat paid him and he sped away. She tried to structure what she would say to Dr. Marsh so as not to sound hysterical, or purely absurd. She'd tell him why she was there, wait until he finished thinking, and take careful notes of what he said. At least now she had some information to jog his memory. Maybe the little she had would be enough.

Only a few lights were on in the house.

Cat approached the front door, passing under the climbing roses, the blaze variety from the looks of it, deep crimson blooms perfuming the evening air with their sweet, faintly citrus aroma. She rang the doorbell and listened to footsteps inside.

Dr. Marsh opened the door and never looked up, taking her coat and inviting her into the living room. It was as she remembered it, except for boxes neatly piled in one corner, tagged in black magic marker.

"Moving some things?" Cat asked.

"No, just figured it was time to pack Nancy's things in storage. They're coming to pick them up tomorrow. Can I interest you in some coffee? I was going to have some myself."

Dr. Marsh wore a pair of Dockers and one of those thick woolen sweaters that she was sure was from New Zealand. The bulk of the sweater added more size to the man's already enormous frame. The house was homier than before, a fire blazing in the hearth.

Cat agreed to coffee. Within five minutes, they were sitting face-to-face.

"Now, you said you have some new information?" he inquired, his brows knotting in the middle of his forehead.

"Well, yes and no."

Cat fought the tears she felt welling in her eyes. A feeling of pure sorrow hung all around her, as if in human form. In front of the fire's wavering light, she could feel her resolve not to show emotion wavering too.

When Dr. Marsh looked at her, for the first time in his eyes she could feel his grief. His torment showered over her in hopeless, ringing blows. Without her saying a word, he understood and started the conversation.

"I know about your son." He tilted his eyes to the floor, holding her hand, her slim fingers disappearing under his hefty palm.

"How do you know?" Cat felt sadness wash over her like a tidal wave she could neither quell nor fight.

"I called the station while you were gone. They told me." He was not apologetic, but understanding, in his words.

Possibly, he was one of the few that understood, having gone through the same disquieting uncertainty when Nancy had been taken, before her body was identified. As he looked at Cat, there was a warm luster in his eyes, the kind of look that made women weep their souls away.

Cat wondered if she was destined to carry the same sorrow in her eyes for the rest of her life. Far off in a tiny niche in her mind, she felt guilty for pitying this man, yet grateful for his understanding.

He continued speaking, a clear, unequivocal strength in each word which he imparted to her with his strong, heavy touch. "Catherine, listen to me. There are terrors in this world we can neither understand nor explain. You, in your line of work, should know that. I, being a doctor, have seen the utmost savagery that one man can inflict upon another. I have seen bodies emptied of their bowels at the hand of another. Bodies and lives empty and gone. I know you have too. But before we let that vision encompass us, we must have faith. Faith in the memories of our loved ones that can never be stolen from us. Faith in the sanctuary of our own good lives, that we must go one living."

She acknowledged his words and he kept speaking, his grasp bearing down tighter on her hand. "These men, if you can call them that, they do not mean for you and me to survive. As much as they take your son, my Nancy, they mean just as purposefully to take our sanity, whatever slim, wavering hope we have in goodness that is left. They mean to engulf us in horrible memories of our children's last hours, memories which they hope are as cold as stone, memories from which we never escape. That is what they want for us, Catherine. But we cannot, we shall not, grant them that satisfaction, shall we, Catherine?"

"No, I guess not, but somehow I feel I am giving in." Her voice was barely a whisper.

"I know you are. I can see it in your eyes. But you are not a broken woman, Catherine. I will not let you be. You won't give in to this self-imposed punishment."

"It's been days," she said, her voice hollow, monotone, lifeless.

"I know how slowly time passes. With Nancy, I waited for days too, not knowing if she was dead or alive. Each day I would wake up and pray to find her in her bed sleeping. I'd lay my hands against her bedroom door, every fiber in my body wishing and hoping and praying she was on the other side. When I opened the door, it was always the same. My Nancy was gone. He had taken her from me."

Dr. Marsh's thick shoulders shuddered, giving the appearance of stone crumbling, his forehead clammy with sweat. Cat felt his big arms encircle her, holding her, if only for a moment. How long was she there in silence letting this man hold her, for no other reason than shared horror and grief? She was not sure, for it was as if time had frozen in his embrace. All around her, the living room fell away and she knew she was safe. This man understood. She strained to withstand the wish to stay there longer but pulled away.

He acknowledged the confusion on her face. "I'm sorry. I didn't mean to offend you."

Cat sobbed, rubbing her face. "There's nothing to be sorry about. You're the first person I've cried with since he's been gone. Haven't allowed myself to cry, to feel, anything."

"I know how that is. Denial is a terrible thing. We think of it as a benefit, but it is not. It only makes the grief harder to wade through. My mother had a saying. 'Grief is like wine,' she used to say. 'The longer you bottle it up, the more intense it gets.'"

"I know. Do you still think of Nancy?"

"Not a day goes by, not a second, without me thinking of her. I see a girl on the street, the way her hair swings side to side, and I say in my head, 'there's my Nancy.' Little things like that, you know?"

"I do."

He sat back and steadied himself. Cat saw then that he too had cried, tears reflecting the fire's glow.

"Now, what did you come here to tell me?"

Cat regained her composure, sitting up straight, collecting her thoughts. "Like I said on the phone, we have a description of the man who may have taken my son in Virginia. I don't know if he was acting alone or with others, so I don't know if his description will mean anything to you."

"How old is your son?"

Cat fought back a fresh round of emotions. "He's six."

"Is he like his mother?"

"I guess so." Cat looked puzzled. "Why?"

"If he is, then he is a fighter."

"Thanks." She felt her lips quivering to make a half-smile. "The man we know about is white, late thirties, early forties. Close-cropped blond hair, slim, wiry build. You know anyone who looks like that? Any of Nancy's friends, boyfriends, fit that description? Conceivably even one of your colleagues at the hospital?"

"There's no one I can think of off the top of my head."

"Think carefully, please."

"There are so many people I work with at the hospital. A lot of the interns are young, that age. Even the guys in the lab. Can't think of anyone with blond close-cropped hair though. You don't have a better description than that?"

"Not at the moment. I have a sketch artist working with the witness now, but nothing more."

"No photograph from the looney bin?" Dr. Marsh asked.

"No, they had a fire a few years back. The only intake photo they had of Eric went up in flames." Cat looked apologetic. "Just one other thing. Anyone you know drive a black late model Cadillac Escalade?"

Dr. Marsh scratched his chin, thinking. "Not that I can think of."

"Would you be able to get me a list of the hospital personnel falling within that age range and gender?"

"I don't think that would be a problem. Why don't you meet me at the hospital tomorrow morning at ten or so?"

"That would be fine. In admissions?"

"Yes. That would be great."

"Does Hoag keep a photograph of each employee on file?" Cat asked.

"Yes, I believe they do. Everyone wears a photo ID. Security, you know?"

"Yeah, sure. So I'll see you tomorrow at ten."

"Let me let you out then." Dr. Marsh was already up off the leather sofa heading for the front door.

"No, it's all right. If you could just call a cab, I'll wait in the foyer and let myself out when it arrives."

"I'll hear nothing of it. Where are you staying?"

"Well, I hadn't really called ahead, but I'm sure the Hyatt in Irvine has a room."

"All right then, I'll drive you," he said, moving toward the open door. "And, Cat, remember what I told you." He took her chin and tilted her face up to meet his gaze. "We are survivors. Survivors always win."

Cat nodded, trying to believe it was true.

⸺ ⸺ ⸺ ⸺ ⸺

Cat checked into the Hyatt at 11:27.

She was given Room 427, just a few doors down from the room she had before. She'd seen so many hotel rooms in the last month, she just wanted to curl up in front of her own fireplace in her cottage home in Quantico.

Dropping her bags, she took out only the bare necessities for bed.

Plopping herself down on the bed, she stared at the bedside clock, thinking what a long, tiresome day it had been, wishing for answers, wishing to hold Joey in her arms.

She changed quickly into boyish, checked flannel pajamas, pulled back her hair, and washed off her makeup. Before settling down, she called local headquarters for messages. Hitting the appropriate keys, the mechanical voice told her she had three messages. One was from McGregor indicating that the Graham boy was working with a sketch artist and that they would have something faxed to her by morning. The second was earlier, Dr. Marsh expressing his sympathy for her situation, saying he had heard what had happened. She was beginning to wonder if he hadn't a different motive for his attentiveness. Cat was most spooked by the last message, from Carl Stearbourne—even though she'd given him permission to call her.

She listened as the slightly European accent came on the line and identified itself as Carl Stearbourne. Somehow, even without the name, from the first word on the phone, she knew who the message was from. His control over every syllable unnerved her.

"Catherine, I've so missed you, *our* talks together." The line went quiet, then he spoke once more with a calm aloofness that irritated Cat. "The smell of your hair, your perfume."

She cringed.

"*You* are getting closer to him, Catherine. I know. You see, he called me yesterday. Told me he has someone very dear to *you*, someone whose shrieks I could hear in the background."

Cat felt she'd be sick. She doubled over, sliding to the floor, but held the phone to her ear, desperate for any sign of where Eric and her son were. How long she lay silent in this position she didn't know, for time was frozen in place. In place and listening.

"Eric has only taken what he needs. He needs to bring *you* to him. To have *you* understand. That is why he has the boy; he wants nothing more of him."

The madness of each word took hold in Catherine's heart.

"He will see *you* soon in California, with the boy."

Cat closed her eyes. Not a trickle of light entered her vision, her senses— nothing but Carl Stearbourne's barren, relentless words.

"And in the end, Catherine, *you* will see that it is just as it always has been. Soon the raw, unyielding love that is Eric's only true gift to the world will be yours for the asking. The real question becomes, Catherine, how much are *you* willing to give?

Ragged breathing was the only sound. Cat heard the line click dead then focused on the erratic beating of her own heart. It was odd, but that sound was a curious comfort…

Catherine knew then the fight she was in for, unsure of exactly how it would unfold, but sure about one thing. She was in for a showdown with a madman. And only with hope and sheer will would she and her son survive.

THIRTY-THREE

Reason can wrestle and overthrow terror.
—Euripides

Morning's sky was clear and so bright it made her squint. The sun rained down on a grassy border dotted with impatiens that led into Hoag Hospital Admissions. Cat waited, watching the time, then saw a blue Jaguar convertible speed by, Dr. Marsh's hefty frame seemingly stuffed into the car's small interior.

He honked the horn, acknowledging her presence, and she figured he'd park in the physician's lot behind the ER. Personnel was tucked to the side of one of the admitting areas, a small series of offices done in warm rose and green tones, like most of Hoag. Colors meant to evoke a feeling of comfort, Cat thought, though she didn't feel comfortable as her hands touched the first personnel file. She and Dr. Marsh had been ushered into a small room. They sat now with what looked like a hundred files in front of them, stacked high.

Cat separated the pile, gave half to Dr. Marsh, and began thumbing through. "Anyone that fits our profile goes here." She pointed to a blank spot on the table. "Probably quickest to check the photo first."

Dr. Marsh nodded.

She made short work of the first twenty files, each one not fitting for one reason or another, wrong height, wrong build, wrong race, wrong gender. Then she began to slow down and really look at the photographs. Could these be the eyes of the man that had her son? She scrutinized each photograph, looking for signs of what, she didn't know, still having the feeling that the Marshes had to know the man. There had to be a connection.

Dr. Marsh did the same, taking his time, though quickly discarding those that obviously didn't fit. He stopped at one longer than the others. "Wait, I know this man," he said.

Cat looked over his shoulder at the photo. "Who is he?"

Dr. Marsh appeared shaken. "Nancy went out with him once or twice. I think we had him to her birthday. Nothing serious though. She said he wasn't her type."

"A colleague of yours?"

"Yes, a young ER physician—his name is Charles Dupont."

Cat looked closely at the photograph. No blond short hair, but the eyes certainly conveyed something cold, elusive. They were a light, almost icy green. Cat fought a shudder as her fingers traced over the photo. She'd seen these eyes before but couldn't place them. Yet she knew their shape. Maybe she did need some more sleep.

"All right, he's our main guy, but keep looking."

Four and a half hours later, they were left with twelve files. None of the others looked remotely like anyone that Dr. Marsh knew. Cat pushed all but the Dupont file aside and studied the photograph. From the looks of it, he was about the right build, wiry and long. Height average, hair color in the photo didn't match the blond, close-cropped hair the boy in Virginia had described. But that could be changed, cut and dyed.

Cat flipped past the paper-clipped photo to the personnel file. It showed Dupont was an ER physician. His application paperwork was blank for the most part, making reference to his CV, which was clipped behind. Dr. Charles Dupont claimed to have studied at USC Medical School, done his residency at a hospital in Northern California, and then apparently decided to head south again. His hometown was listed as Willits, California. Cat had never heard of it, figuring it was in Northern California someplace.

"Ever heard of Willits?"

"Yeah, it's up past Sacramento, in Bear Valley. Nancy and I took a ride up there once to check out the wildflowers off State Route 20. Pretty out of the way place really."

"Want to take a trip up there with me?"

"Sure, what are we looking for?"

"We need to know if anyone's ever heard of Charles Dupont. And in the meantime, you think someone can let us into his office?"

"I'll see what I can do." Dr. Marsh was already out the door.

Within five minutes they were being let into Dupont's office. Upon entering the space, Cat felt odd. The room looked as if it hadn't been used, not like other doctors' offices, with files stacked on the floor, reference books opened. Instead, this office was pristine, books carefully organized alphabetically on the shelves, everything neatly tucked away or in its place. On the desk sat a closed black week-at-a-glance calendar. Cat opened to the day Joey had been taken. It showed no appointments…three days earlier it indicated that Dupont was to be present at a physician's conference in Atlanta. There, someone had jotted a phone number next to flight information.

Cat dialed. On the other end of the line a voice identified an affiliation with the American Academy of Emergency Physicians.

"Could you check for me whether Charles Dupont was in attendance?"

"We had him scheduled to be here, but he never arrived."

"Did he leave any information about where he could be contacted, a forwarding number?"

"No."

"Thanks." Cat hung up and flipped pages in the calendar, cross-referencing each of the approximate kill dates. Dupont's calendar was filled with appointments for those dates, but she wondered how many had been canceled.

Cat called Orange County's John Wayne Airport and booked two seats on Southwest Air's flight going to Sacramento. She looked at Dr. Marsh. "You mind sleeping in those clothes tonight?"

"Not at all." She could see a fire in his eyes.

"Then let's go," Cat said, taking the photo.

The flight touched down in Sacramento three hours later. During the flight, Cat and Dr. Marsh had not talked much, as if the hunt was consuming their every thought. There was no time for small talk, no time for emotions.

Cat rented a four-wheel-drive Chevy Yukon.

How, she wondered, could there be this much traffic out of Sacramento? Heading out on Interstate 5, once they cleared traffic they clipped along at eighty past low rolling hills, shimmering in a sea of bright green.

Before long they turned off the freeway, passing through a tiny town called Willits.

"You want to stop? Get something to eat?" Cat asked.

"Yes." Dr. Marsh still seemed immersed in thought.

Cat pulled into a roadside café, bought two sandwiches and two Diet Cokes. In five minutes they were back on the road, the knee-deep green fields turning gradually colorful, orange poppies invading like waves from an ocean, growing ever thicker. Cat lowered the window, letting the sweetness from blooming blue lupine caress her senses. The nineteen miles west on State Route 20 turned into pastures. She tried to forget about Joey. It was no use.

"Take a turn here." Dr. Marsh pointed to a small street sign signaling Bear Valley Road. Another fourteen miles on a dusty, gravelly road through what seemed an endless array of purple owl's clover and goldfields craning for sun among orange California poppies.

"It was like this when Nancy and I were here. She loved nature like I do."

Passing by grazing cows, Cat wondered, "Don't the cattle kill off all the flowers?"

"No, actually it's carefully managed. The ranchers don't plow over the fields, and they move the cows from pasture to pasture. It's miraculous, but the flowers come back every year, year after year."

Cat wondered if there would be a miracle waiting for them at the end of this journey.

"The town's about another five miles up, from the looks of it." Cat let the fresh air and blue sky distract her for only a moment. "We'll be there soon."

They turned off the road into the tiny town of Willits. The population couldn't possibly exceed five hundred, and that was pushing it. There was one main drag, one main store, and lodging at a small hole in the wall that charged fifty bucks a night. Cat only intended a one-night stay.

She leaned into the young man at the check-in desk and asked, "Who would be able to tell me if someone was from this town? If somebody was a local?"

"That would be Carmine Carols. She's lived in this town for eighty-two years. Seen everyone come and go."

"You know where I can find her?"

"Sure, she'd be out fishing the creeks, like she is most clear days."

"An eighty-two-year-old woman out fishing?"

"Yeah, says the outdoors keeps her young. Don't have no time for a rocking chair."

"Where can I find her, exactly?"

"There's a dirt road 'bout a half mile outside of town, takes you up into the forest. Head about five miles in and you'll see a red ribbon tied on a post on the roadside. Turn down that road and keep going..." The boy paused and looked outside, as if assuring himself they had four-wheel drive. "Anyways, gets pretty rough riding, you know, but you'll come to a lake and a clearin' with a creek. You'll find her there."

Cat didn't know whether to thank him or get better directions. But there wasn't time. "You heard the man," she said to Dr. Marsh. He nodded, sipping on his Diet Coke.

Before long, they were deep in the underbrush. Ferns, moss-covered rocks, the smell of wet earth took over from barren dirt roads. Cat could understand how a place like this could keep someone young. It was God's country.

Below them, the four-wheel drive creaked to the rhythm from uneven wet roads. Cat kept a constant, if not fast, speed of thirty miles an hour, even with ruts in the road.

Though wearing his seat belt, Dr. Marsh clapped his head on the roof as the SUV crashed through a particularly hairy area. "Hold up there, don't you think it's best if we find her with our senses still intact?"

"Come on," she laughed, "a little off-roading never hurt anyone."

He rubbed his head. "Speak for yourself."

Cat was going so fast she almost careened past the red ribbon.

Dr. Marsh slid forward in his seat as she hit the brakes and backed up the vehicle. "Did I miss something, or are we going to do it in reverse now?"

"We just missed the red ribbon."

"Where?"

"Right there." Cat pointed to a muddied red ribbon tied to a stick, protruding from the brush.

She floored the truck, heading down a barely visible muddy side road, listening to the back tires spin out. Part of it had washed out from a creek that meandered on both sides of the road. As they went deeper into the brush, that meandering creek turned into a brook, then into a small whitewater river. Ahead, through the trees, a clearing of yellow tidy tips spread out like a sea. Dappled sunlight beat its way through the cypress. At the edge of the clearing, a small figure in a red shirt waved at them, as if she knew they were coming.

Cat parked near the woman, who was waving them off. "You'll scare off the trout, dammit," she yelled. Though in her eighties, this woman looked no older than sixty-five, her frame still straight, brown hair tinged with gray, long and braided in a ponytail that protruded from a cap. She looked like something out of *Field & Stream* magazine.

"What the hell you doing here?" the woman said.

"Sorry to scare off the fish. You Carmine?"

Hearing her name, the woman stopped cursing. "Yeah, that's me. What brings you out here? From the looks of it, you ain't here for the trout fishing."

"No, ma'am, that's right. My name's Dr. Catherine Powers, Cat for short, and I'd just like to ask you a few questions if you've got the time."

The woman lifted her arms over her shoulders. "Got all the time in the world. This country ain't going nowhere; it's been here just like this since I was a little girl."

Cat took a softer tone with her. "Not to alarm you, but I work with the FBI tracking killers. This is Dr. Marsh. We just want to ask some questions about a man we're trying to track down. He claims to be from this area, though we have reason to believe that's not true. Someone in town told us you'd be the one to ask."

"That'd be right." The woman had a quickness about her, a wit that needed few words and even fewer questions. From the looks of it, Cat guessed she could size up a person pretty well from her first meeting. From all indications, she believed Cat was honest.

"What's this man's name?"

"Charles Dupont."

The woman's face wrinkled then resumed its easy glow. "Never heard of him."

"Ever heard of a family Dupont?"

"Nope, no Duponts here."

Just as Cat suspected, but she had to be sure.

"Let me show you a photograph. Maybe when he was here, he went by another name." Reaching into her jeans pocket, she pulled out the Hoag personnel photograph of Charles Dupont and handed it to the woman.

She scowled at the photo for a full minute then handed it back. "Never seen him before in my life."

"You sure, it's real important."

"How so?"

"This man may have kidnapped my son, killed his daughter." Cat looked at Dr. Marsh and waited for the woman's reaction.

"Let me see the picture one more time." Carmine took it, scrutinized it harder this time. After a full five minutes, she gave it back to Cat, a sorrowful look in her eyes. "Never seen him, hon."

<hr />

"Don't you see?" Cat talked quickly, her excitement obvious. "There's only one conclusion. Jesus, I knew it when I laid my eyes on him. Charles Dupont doesn't exist. Eric and Carl are the same person."

"How can you be so sure, just because the woman doesn't recognize him?" He wanted this just as badly, but they had to be rational, sure of what they were doing.

"Charles Dupont came on the scene physically just when Eric was released. I've had McGregor check on the med school references, the hospital he interned at. No one there remembers him. No one knows a Charles Dupont."

"Then how come Hoag didn't check him out?"

"Come on, Eric could have paid someone off to lie for him, say he went to med school. Transcripts, diplomas can be faked, especially with the kind of connections Eric had in jail and later in hospital."

"So his entire past is a hoax?"

"I'd bet on it." Cat thought out loud. "Matter of fact, I'll prove it to you." She pulled out her cell phone, checked for contact numbers, and dialed Dr. Stall in Illinois.

"Dr. Stall, this is Catherine Powers in California." She smiled briefly. "Yes, I'm all right. No, we haven't found anything yet. I need to ask you a favor. When Eric was incarcerated, did he ever use a pet name, a nickname? Did the others have a name for him?"

Dr. Stall thought briefly. "Yes, they did. Eric liked to call himself Charles. Thought it sounded more dignified. The others here just laughed at it"

"Thanks, Dr. Stall. Can you repeat what you just told me?" Cat handed her phone to Dr. Marsh, watching his incredulous expression as he hung up.

THIRTY-FOUR

Don't wait for the Last Judgment. It happens every day.
—**Albert Camus**, *The Fall*

C at heard the flaps moan down. Newport Beach's lights once again gazed up at her beneath the plane's black wing. Seven hours after their journey had begun, it was over. She heard the landing gear lock with a rumble, then a thud. Cat and Dr. Marsh were back in "the OC." She leaned forward, rubbing the tension out of her muscles, wishing the tightness out of her chest.

Coming back.

She'd taken a risk, losing time on this journey. But by losing time, she had gained power. It was as if every cell in her body was focused now on finding her boy. She had the power to bring her son home. Alive.

From the terminal, Cat called ahead to Hoag, asking them to recite the last address they had for Dr. Charles Dupont. They gave her an address in Laguna Beach, just off the Pacific Coast Highway. She thought about Joey being there, hands bound, gagged, the madman playing mind games with him, waiting for her. She put the images out of her mind.

Cat dropped Dr. Marsh off at his car. The parking lot was half empty, night working its way over the Back Bay. "You don't have to do this alone, Cat. We can bring in the police."

"We can't bring in anyone else. He wants me, not the damned police."

"You can't handle this by yourself. You're in no frame of mind—"

She cut him off. "It's not your son out there."

It took less than fifty minutes for Charles Dupont to drive through the light evening traffic to Newport Beach. The black Cadillac SUV pulled through the outpatient pavilion parking area and came to a stop as he waited for Catherine. She wasn't in the hospital—somehow he knew that—but she'd be coming for him. He'd baited her well.

He parked across from the pavilion in an open lot next to the parking structure, listening to sweet violins. Above, the clear sky gave way to a faint image of the moon. He watched each car going by, looking for the auburn hair, the outline of her face.

Only a few lights on in the hospital.

A small rented Ford went by and he knew her in an instant. She passed by, halfway across the lot, but there was something wrong. Dupont's forehead creased.

There was someone with her.

There wasn't supposed to be anyone with her.

Dupont could see the outline of Marsh's face as the Ford drove around past admissions. He heard voices; one of them was Marsh's, he was sure of it. He wasn't supposed to be here, he wasn't supposed to be with her.

Dupont froze as the Ford's headlights reflected in his direction as it pulled around to the physician's parking lot. Marsh opened the passenger door, got out, and stood there. Dupont could hear a loud exchange. They were angry with each other; he was angry with her for bringing Marsh here.

He was angry with her for going back to find him.

He knew that she knew who he was.

She knew about Eric.

Dupont moved fast, the Cadi's tires soft on the blacktop pavement. Got to move quickly now, but quietly. He put his eyes up at the rearview mirror and scanned the area behind him. No movement behind him. Good. No car lights. No one was following. She had not seen him.

He drove the Cadi down to the bottom of the hill onto Newport Boulevard and pulled over. There was no place to hide. His movement illuminated by a streetlight, he brought his face down to the steering wheel and let himself feel the full rush of his emotions. He rolled down the car's window, taking in gulps of the sea air, glancing back at the rearview mirror, ready for flight or fight. Nothing moved behind him but traffic. The Ford did not follow. All right. He sat up in the seat, leaned across it, and put a full clip in the automatic.

He wished the boy was still trapped in the back, but he'd left him at La Blanca. The SUV sat at the curbside.

He had to think this out.

Catherine wasn't coming to him alone. If she brought others, he'd have to plan more carefully. He had not calculated for the possibility of others—he wanted *only* her.

Talking to Marsh, she must have figured it out. She'd know by now who he was. Carl had said as much, not to underestimate her. Carl had said a lot about her.

She knew about Eric. She knew the who, but she didn't know the where. On the other hand, a match of Eric's personnel file would also yield an address. She'd already be heading to La Blanca. She wasn't stupid enough to come alone, or was she?

We play this your way.

And what was she doing with Marsh here, now? Dupont thought long and hard. Access, yes that's it. Access to the personnel records, to his office. By now she'd figured out he wasn't at the conference, had confirmed the appointments on the dates Eric had killed were all falsified. The appointments had been made, but none kept. He'd been absent those days. Doing Eric's work…work he loved.

He laid the automatic on the dashboard, covering it with a towel. All right then, Catherine, we play this out your way. Dupont put his hands on the volume button of the radio and turned it up. Violins filled in the questions in his mind.

Slowly he drove away from the curbside, heading toward the ocean, to La Blanca.

"For Christ's sake, Cat, what makes you think you can manage this alone?" McGregor was furious with her.

"Joey," she snapped back into the cell phone.

"And if you go in alone, what makes you think you'll come out of this alive?"

"He wants me. He'll trade Joey if it's just me. If there's police, the best I can hope for is another damned body bag."

"Think about this. He's been planning this for a long time. You really think you're going to catch him by surprise or talk some sense into him."

"I don't know what I think, but what choice do I have?"

"You can choose to let us help, Cat. That is the choice you can make." McGregor could tell he wasn't getting through.

"What if it's the wrong one?"

"It's not."

"What if he runs?"

"We won't give him the chance. Give me what I want, Cat."

"No."

"I admire what you did today. Putting the pieces together. But I can't help you if you won't let me. And you know he'll kill you."

"Shut up."

"He'll kill you, is that what you want?"

"That's better than Joey being murdered." She almost couldn't say it.

"You can't save him by yourself."

"Then I'm going to damned well die trying." She hit the disconnect button on the cell phone, listened to it ring back twice and go to voice mail, and turned it off.

THIRTY-FIVE

*The man who masters himself is delivered
from the force that binds all creatures.*
—**Johann Wolfgang von Goethe**

hlorophyll faint in Cat's nose. Darkness. Something moving in the shadows. She turns her head to the movement, squinting, her Glock drawn.

"I am pleased that you have come, Catherine." Dupont's calm voice.

She moves toward the sound. "Uh-huh."

Something small down below Dupont. A groan.

"Joey?"

"He's here. Breathe deeply child."

La Blanca is totally dark.

A minute passes before she speaks. "You've hurt him?"

"No, he's just under sedation." In the moonlight, she makes out the silhouette of Dupont lifting Joey, one hand under his arm. "There now, stand up. Try to stand up. Let your *mother* see you"

It is all Catherine can do not to rush to Joey, embrace her child.

Dupont continues talking to Joey. "Do you remember where you are?"

He nods.

"That's good."

Joey moves forward, stumbles, and goes down on his knees, Dupont mimicking him in one swift movement so that Joey is in his grasp, Dupont's hand firmly around his mouth.

Only then Joey realizes his mother's presence.

He struggles to rise but a hand on his mouth, arm around his chest, holds him down.

"Stay still," Dupont snarls.

From the looks of it, Joey's determination is back. He doesn't want to stay still.

"Joey, do as he tells you," Catherine says, both trying to comfort and empower her child.

Joey stops fighting and stands, wrapped in Dupont's grasp.

"That's very smart, Catherine. It's all over for me." Dupont is up, picking something up off the coffee table.

The glimmer of metal catches Catherine's eye. She watches him stick something up against Joey's throat.

"Put out your hand, Joey. Feel this. Don't grab it, feel it." Dupont's words are calm, almost serene.

"It's all right, Joey, do what he says."

She watches her son's small hand move across the metal. "That's right, Joey, it's a gun. A .22. You know what it can do to you, don't you."

Catherine listens to Joey quietly sob.

"Now take your hand down."

Catherine watches Dupont push the cold muzzle deeper into her child's throat.

She keeps her own aim direct on Dupont, but she can't pull the trigger with her son so close.

She hears a thump-thump above before she sees it. Light in the room. From outside. Police. *Please God, no. Anything but that.*

The chopper hovers for an instant outside the windows. Then, snatched in updrafts and downdrafts, it loses its target point. Catherine tries to wave them off, her sights still trained on Dupont. She hopes they see her. Call it off.

"I wish I could have trusted you, Catherine. I wanted to believe you."

He is crying.

"Now, I can't leave Joey to you. You know what they'll do to me."

Dupont is bawling.

Oh sweet Jesus, Catherine thinks.

Dupont's hand bolts down, grabbing the boy by the shirt collar, grasping enough of it that he is able to stand Joey up, his head in the air.

She tries to bring her pistol up at eye level to find him, take a level shot, but her sights are blocked by a curtain billowing. She has no room to maneuver.

"Help me!" Joey screams right at her. He's been pulled up into Dupont's arms now, the madman's left arm around his stomach. Then Dupont tucks the gun and delivers a blade to Joey's throat in one quick slashing movement. Blood spews out onto Dupont's pants.

"Oh shit, shit!" Catherine screams, shouting in horrified madness. For a second, she can see Dupont's face. It is christened in an exquisite rapture, watching her child's blood gushing like an open bottle of champagne all over him. Cat hears a machine gun go off, glass shattering, the thud of a bullet. Ears numb. Light washes the room.

There is nothing.

Dupont and Joey are gone. She fears this the most.

Suddenly, glass is crunching, a door swinging open to the side of the room.

She rushes forward.

Light now is all around. She feels the night air on her arms and face. Her legs perform a crazy shuffle. Out...hurry...follow them. Stepping on glass shards, she stumbles to the door. One hand with her gun. Legs tensed, she steps into the night. Stairs. She slips, falling backward, scrambling up again. Under her, the gun. Don't drop it.

Throat gripped in cold, moist air.

Outside now. Turned around. Confused. Trying to feel through the brush. Listen. Follow the trail. Left or right, which way did they go? She can't think.

"Shit, shit," she keeps saying under her breath, waiting to catch some sign of where Dupont and Joey have gone.

Something wet under her fingers. What is it? Fingers up to her nose, the smell metallic. Blood. A shuffle in the distance. Cat collapses. Up on her hands and knees now, crawling away from the house, she prays the chopper will not highlight her whereabouts for Dupont. The thump-thump-thump of chopper blades above tell her it is just off the coastline. Behind her, the house looms white against black.

She must stay low, out of sight. Breathing deep until she can stand, walk, run—until she finds them. Cat closes her eyes and turns her head left, then right, her mouth open, gasping for breath. Her hands on her weapon.

She gets off her knees, hears the sound. She hears Joey gagging. It is the sweetest and most horrific sound she has ever heard. For an instant, she is frozen. Thinking what he is doing to her son. She knows she must follow that sound. She makes up her mind not to think about it, about what he is doing to Joey. She runs forward in the brush.

Joey is still gasping. Cat doesn't want anything to happen to him, but dear God, baby, keep making that noise.

She reaches a cliff face of sorts, taking a tentative, awkward step down the steep embankment toward the cries. She wants to move quickly, to run in their direction, each small, quiet step utterly frustrating. But she has to wait for them to reveal themselves. At the bluff's top, she catches a glimpse of them a few hundred feet ahead, Dupont stumbling down the cliff face on a steep, barely defined path. His intention is clear. He will escape with Joey or die trying.

Now.

THIRTY-SIX

There is in every true woman's heart, a spark of heavenly fire,
which lies dormant in the broad daylight of prosperity; but which
kindles up, and beams and blazes in the dark hour of adversity.
—**Washington Irving**, *The Sketchbook*

Dupont scrambles down the cliff, Joey firmly in his grasp. Coastal cacti and grasses cut Dupont's legs. Joey is screaming.

Dupont's yacht is in sight, a three-quarter moon above lights the way.

Behind him, Cat is coming.

He can feel her, hear her.

He likes being pursued by her. To be near her.

Being out here is a rush.

And she is coming.

Cat-and-mouse, he thinks, smiling.

It is all a game.

Just the way he wants it. The way it is supposed to be.

Above in the not too far distance, lightning cracks. Then thunder less than a minute later. This is perfect. A storm is brewing, just as the weatherman predicted.

Someone comes over the cliff. Cat is coming.

Joey sees his mother and starts screaming louder.

Above the thunderclaps.

Dupont's exhilaration increases.

Everything is coming together just as he planned.

Above Catherine, thunder claps again, closer. But she focuses on Dupont. She can see him. She can't see Joey, but she hears him screaming.

The wind picks up, changing direction.

No longer a gentle night breeze.

Colder, more menacing.

Like the storm.

Like her life right now.

Dupont scurries to the boat.

It is big enough that if he makes it there with Joey, she may never see either of them again.

That can't happen.

Dupont is almost to the boat.

Catherine is still a quarter of the way up the cliff. She has called off the police chopper. He watches it fly away.

Lightning again.

A flash that casts Joey and Dupont into a bright whiteness.

Joey breaks free.

He runs up the cliff, his face a mask of sheer terror.

Run, baby, run.

Dupont is startled by this sudden unplanned development. For a millisecond, Cat sees his indecision.

Run, Joey.

Her child is running toward her.

Then a gunshot. Joey stops in his tracks.

Oh no…no, my God, no.

Cat freezes.

Dupont is on the downed child, grabs him.

Cat can't tell if he is hit or if he went down to avoid the bullet.

Then, in another lightning bolt, the proof is there. Joey's side is red.

But his attempt at freedom wins Cat precious gained distance.

She knows that if Dupont makes the yacht, she will have a chance of making it there too.

Thank you, Joey. These words in her head seem hollow.

Dupont is only fifteen feet ahead now.

She can hear waves crashing against the boat. She is close, so very close, her breath ragged. Dupont is only steps away. Joey is still screaming, terrified. Dupont stumbles and goes down, a clap of lightning above. She sees him at the boat now, shoving Joey aboard. He resists.

"Mom, help!"

"Get on," Dupont growls.

Joey does as he is told. Thunder rolls through the heavens. Dupont throws the child back and is at the console. Cat hears the engines start, smells exhaust fumes.

"No, no, this can't be happening. No."

Dupont guns the engines. Joey is thrown back. A towline is dangling off the back, three feet of towline. It is Cat's only hope. She lunges for it.

"Come on, come on."

As she grabs it, cold Pacific water hits her, jarring her senses, heightening them. Water surging all around. Her eyes sting with salt, engine fumes, all of it at once. But none of it matters. All that matters is Joey and getting to Dupont. The boat is accelerating. She pulls her body against the engines' tow. With three big pulls she is hanging on a side cleat. She is in the water from the waist down.

Pull, Cat, pull.

Wet fingers strain to keep hold. Dupont faces her, his eyes flashing in fury. He says nothing.

Cat pulls up, but the weight of her legs against the water is making it harder and harder to move. Her adrenaline kicks in. With one quick move, her left foot catches the side of the boat and gets traction.

Thank God for all those late-night runs. Her physical strength is a blessing.

Her arm muscles are screaming now, even though the water is cold and black. Just as she comes up over the side, she feels the boat shudder. A slight change of direction. Above her, Dupont. He has something in his hands. What is it?

Something shiny catches a light glimmer.

Lightning and thunder again over the roar of the engines. With a flash, something is digging into her hand. Pain as it makes its way through her tendons. What the…? She looks down. Dupont has jammed a grappling hook through her left hand. It is all she can do to hold on with her right hand. Her grip actually tightens. Fighting the pain, she pulls herself up and over the side. The hook is hanging from her hand. Blood everywhere. Joey screams at the sight of it. She starts to sweat.

Breathing is getting tighter.

Her field of vision is getting tighter, darker.

All of a sudden, there is not enough air in the world to fill her lungs.

She connects what is happening—shock.

But she can't let that happen.

Not here. Not now. Not like this. She fights it.

No, not like this.

There is only one thing she can do.

She has to pull it out. There is no other way.

Dupont is on her, fighting her for control.

"No, you bastard." She pushes him off, his eyes wild. She has no time to think.

Do what needs to be done. She reaches down and pulls with her right hand, trying to reverse the angle of the sharp hook, out of her hand. She feels it come out in one movement. Her legs go weak with pain, but she can't let herself go down. Not now.

Cat's hand is a mess—blood and white tendons hanging from it. She does not care. It does not matter.

Dupont picks up the hook with both hands and claps her across the face with it.

She can taste liquid metal in her mouth. Her jaw feels like it has been reset two inches to the left. "What the hell!"

She is up and on him in an instant. Her good hand is going after his eyes. He is moving side to side; he knows what she is thinking.

Her fingers find the mark.

She gouges his eyes.

He screams out, just as another clap of thunder roars.

"Take that, you devil!" she screams back.

He is over her, behind her, his arms holding her. His head butts her in the back of her head. They are tumbling together now. The boat is moving forward without a pilot.

Joey cries at the sight of his mother and this maniac covered with blood. The sound of him wrenches her back to reality. She has to end this.

The grappling hook is clanging on the deck, just out of reach.

She is looking into his eyes, his face just inches from hers.

Hatred there. He growls at her.

She holds his gaze while reaching with her good hand for something he does not see. The sky flashes again. Bright enough that she can see what she is doing. He looks at nothing but her face, her blood partially obscuring his vision.

Finally, she has her fingers around the grip.

He is over her.

Hits her again with his fist.

With one quick movement, she grabs the grappling hook's handle and slams it against his jaw. She can see shock in his wide eyes.

With the force, he falls backward. He is cursing her but up on his elbows as quickly as she is on her knees. With the blow, the hook falls to the deck. She reaches for it again.

Once again, she is too quick for him. The hook finds its mark on the side of his head.

He is down again, this time not moving as quickly.

But still he is trying to get up.

She has the advantage now.

She is over him, on top of him.

The boat continues to plow forward, moving side to side. Quickly it jaunts right and she is thrown toward the left stern. The hook clangs above her head against its side. The boat rocks in the water. She can see white surf over her shoulder even in the driving rain. With the boat's turn, Dupont rolls on top of her again. Now he is even stronger. Even angrier.

"Bitch." His face is so close she can smell his breath. Cat just wants to kill him and get out of there. Frantically she reaches up, her good hand finding his eyes again. Her bad hand is not much use. He is over her. It is not good. He is going to strangle her. Then she remembers; there is someone else in this fight. Joey.

Above the engines and the ocean and the lightning, she screams, "Joey! Steer."

She can hear him crying, but out of the corner of her eye she sees him move toward the helm. Dupont is so focused on her he does not notice.

The boat rocks farther left.

Pitches left.

She can see the black water right there. If she goes over now, it is all over. Dupont also rolls with the pitch. Then they both roll right. Hard right, him first.

She is behind him, then on him. Joey is trying to steer but has overcorrected.

Realizing what has happened, he cries "Mom, Mom!"

The hook clangs against the boat. She scrambles over Dupont, reaching for it. He has her calf in his hands, trying to hold her from it. With one final stretch, she has the hook in her hand. It is cold, slick and wet, covered in her own blood.

Above, suddenly, a spotlight.

The police chopper.

They can see her struggling with him.

Dupont is pulling at her leg, trying to pull her back. With a crack, she swings the hook wide and it comes down with force, finding its mark.

Dupont's calf.

She can see the hook go in one side and its point out the other side of his leg. He screams in agony.

For a second, he lets go of her.

She is up.

Toward Joey.

Still at the helm trying to steer.

"Come on, baby, time to go."

She has the back of his shirt, pulls him close, her arms protectively around him. He has never felt so good in her arms. She is up where the sail rigging is. Then, holding Joey as securely as she can, she jumps.

Cold black water claps her back. The air goes out of her lungs. Everything is dark, black, confusing. Joey is gripping her so tight. Then she pops up out of the water.

Joey's head follows. They are coughing.

Dupont's boat is heading off into the distance. The chopper's spotlight is so bright. She is terrified to be in the water this far out at sea. Tiny specs of light signify the coastline. The cold from the Pacific goes right through her bones. Joey's face is white; his eyes seem to lose focus.

Teeth chattering.

Hypothermia.

He is just a little boy.

How will she protect him out here? The boat lights are heading away. Water is everywhere. Then the boat starts to come around. It is coming back.

Joey is coughing and sputtering.

What is she going to do?

Dupont is coming back.

The water is bone-chilling cold.

Joey is going into shock. She has no choice. She must get back on the boat with that lunatic. It is that or die out here in the Pacific.

A wave catches her square in the face as the boat comes closer and closer. She can see Dupont's eyes glistening as he leans over the helm. There is pure evil in them, like nothing she has ever seen.

Lightning above.

She is shaking now too. Her jaw clenches as she tries to control the cold that has gripped her to her core. There is no controlling it.

Another twenty minutes of cold and she will be dead.

And he will have won.

Suddenly something comes flying at her. Her mind does not register what it is. Then she knows.

Life jackets tied to a rope.

He wants them alive.

"Arghh!" she screams, struggles to hold Joey up with one hand and grab for the life jackets with the other. His face is white, his lips purple. Joey's eyes have started to roll back into his head.

He is hypothermic.

Getting worse.

She has no choice.

She puts the life vest over Joey's head and tells him, "Hold on to it, baby." He manages a groan in response. It is all he can muster. She takes his arms and puts them through the sides and ties the jacket around him as best she can.

Joey groans again. He is hurting. Hurting bad.

A light in her face.

Water is all around.

The hull of the boat is about five feet away. She can smell gas fumes from the engines.

He has the grappling hook out. The same one he used to shred her hand.

"Grab hold!" Dupont shouts.

She has no choice.

It is him or drown.

She glances at Joey. He is losing consciousness.

"Grab hold!" The shout comes again. She does as she is told.

"The boy first."

She has no choice.

She must turn over her only child to him or watch Joey die. She takes the hook end of the grapple and puts it around the waist of the life vest.

Cat says a silent prayer. *Please, God, protect him.*

It is all she can do not to scream as she watches Joey move away from her. Toward the monster. He hauls the boy out by the jacket. Joey says nothing. He is limp. Lifeless.

"Now you."

She looks up. Dupont's eyes are all hope and terror, all in one. He smiles a sly smile, white teeth showing. She must get out of the water.

God, forgive me.

"Grab hold of the hook."

By now, her shredded hand is almost useless. She uses the other one to do as she is told.

She is being pulled to the boat.

She is face-to-face with him again. He is grinning. He thinks he has won.

"Welcome back. So good you decided to join me." His tone is chilling, even more chilling than the cold night air.

She looks him straight in the eyes. "Screw you" is the best she can manage.

Exhaustion overtakes her and her legs meet the deck. She crumples into a ball, grabbing hold of her son, pulling him onto her lap.

She cradles him; his lips are white and blue. There is no color in his face. "Come on, baby." She waits. "Open your eyes for mommy."

Joey's lids flutter open momentarily. He says something she cannot make out. His pupils are dilated and wide. She screams over the waves, engines, and thunder, "Do you have somewhere that I can get him warm?"

Dupont's voice is low behind her. "Down below in the galley there is a first aid kit and blankets."

She scoops up her limp child in her arms. As cold as she is, he is much colder. He doesn't react to her touch. Her instincts take over as she rushes him below.

He shivers. His eyes open and close again.

She lays him down on the galley table and starts stripping off his wet clothes. His face is still ashen. Lips a blue shade she has seen before. She opens cabinets, searching for a first aid kit, finding a silver hypothermia blanket. Cat wraps Joey in it.

He does not seem the register the change around him.

Eyes flutter and close.

"Come on, baby, you're okay."

No response. She holds him tighter, rubbing his body, trying to warm him. His body feels like ice.

He is her all now.

He fills her mind and soul.

"Come on, baby. Be all right." She has never meant anything more in her life.

"Please, God," is all she can think to say. "Don't let him die."

Suddenly, something is around her throat, choking her. She hears him practically sneer the words. "So how is *our* little man? Going to make it, is he, *doctor*?"

Whatever is on her throat is bearing down harder. Tighter.

Enough of this.

She wants to scream "How dare you?" But her words are inaudible. No words come out. She cannot find her breathe.

"What? I didn't hear you."

As he clenches down harder, she struggles against him. But with her blood loss, he is stronger.

There is hissing in her ear.

The room is turning black. Black-and-white spots appear. She is sucking air. She is losing consciousness.

No!

Whatever he has around her neck is tightening.

She fights it, trying to get her fingers under whatever it is.

He will have none of it.

"Now be a *good doctor*," he snarls against her left ear, "and go to sleep."

No. She fights him with every ounce of her being.

But she can't help it.

She is blacking out, leaving Joey helpless.

No. No. No. No. No.

Her good hand and her shredded hand have no strength.

Being in the water has taken it out of her. Buzzing in her ears increases. Black-and-white dots are bigger and bigger. A strange metallic taste in her mouth. Her legs cannot hold her weight. Suddenly she goes down. Her last thought and vision is Joey. Lying there surrounded by silver, only his wet hair and eyes visible. Eyes filled with fear.

Then there is blackness.

Deep blackness.

And silence.

THIRTY-SEVEN

Until the day of his death, no man can be sure of his courage.
—Jean Anouilh

Joey says nothing. But sees all.

Dupont is standing over his mother, his face twisted in rage and hatred. Eyes burn into Joey with one quick glance. Then back to his mother, motionless on the floor.

What am I going to do? he thinks. *I have to do something.*

Joey's eyes dart to the fire extinguisher just to his right, mounted on the galley wall. His right hand under the blanket quietly unhooks it from the mount.

Dupont is still transfixed by his mother.

She does not move.

Is she dead? he wonders.

Then rage overtakes Joey's mind. He unwraps the blanket and throws it off, his hand up to the fire extinguisher. He is almost naked, only in his underwear, but it does not matter. The only thing he cares about is hurting this man who has hurt his mom.

Dupont turns, startled.

The extinguisher is up in front of Joey's face. He blasts it down square in Dupont's face. The white chemical covers him—his face, hair, eyes.

Dupont screams as the chemicals react with his eyes. He rips at his mouth and his eyes. With each attempt at a breath, the chemical crawls deeper and deeper into his nose, his eyes, his throat.

Choking him.

He is blind and mute. Choking.

In his mind, he is cursing the boy. But no words will come out.

The white stuff is all over the floor. In his desperation to breathe, Dupont loses his footing, goes down.

The boy is over him, knees straddling his chest.

Little brat, he thinks, trying to say it. But what comes out is something inaudible. He opens his eyes but can see nothing, yet he can feel the boy on him.

And smell the chemicals.

"Arrgh." Some sound finally comes.

Joey does something unexpected. He takes the fire extinguisher up and over his head. He brings it down, right to left, in a strong swing that grazes Dupont's left temple. The child's strength must be fueled by adrenaline, Dupont thinks.

Dupont feels the pain, is staggered by it. *What?*

Astonished by this boy.

Astonished by the child's arrogance. He is *just* like his mother.

Dupont is trying to find air, breathe, to express his shock.

How dare you? is all he can think.

Another blow comes left to right.

His brain reels with pain and lack of oxygen. Chemicals crawl deeper into his lungs, increasing their burn. He can't see or hear anything that makes any sense.

Damn child is his last thought as he descends into blackness.

THIRTY-EIGHT

Courage is resistance to fear, mastery of fear—not absence of fear.
—**Mark Twain**, *Pudd'nhead Wilson*

Cat startles from her own darkness. She is covered in white stuff on her chest and her legs. What is it? It smells like chemicals. Joey is above her. His face is flush and tears well up.

To her right, Dupont is lying motionless, his face contorted into a strange mask. Even though he is out, his face is still twisted in hatred. The fire extinguisher lies next to Joey, also covered in white chemicals.

Joey whimpers, "Mom, I hurt him."

Outside, thunder and lightning. Cat is stunned by her son's bravery; she can find no words.

Tears come as she opens her arms.

He falls into them, his full body weight against her, face buried.

He is sobbing, low and quiet.

He shudders as the tears come harder and faster.

"I hurt him." A tiny voice on her shoulder.

She holds him tighter than she ever has before. *My God*, her mind says over and over.

She starts to cry too. Joey continues to shudder and cry.

"It's okay, baby" is all she can muster. "It's okay now."

Her voice is so low she can barely hear it herself.

Joey looks up; his face tilts to one side.

"Safe?" he whispers.

It is all she can bear not to cry more.

She holds him by his shoulders, looking him straight in the eyes.

She whispers back, "Yes, safe."

THIRTY-NINE

Often the test of courage is not to die but to live.
—Vittorio Alfieri, *Oreste*

he steers his yacht closer into the harbor aiming for an empty dock. With little sailing experience, Cat wonders how she has done it.

Gotten through this.

She had no choice. It was her and Joey. Or Dupont.

It is over.

She smiles as Dana Point Harbor comes closer into view. Moorings stand like glad sentinels around her. The dawn is breaking. The storm is past now. The sky is the color of cantaloupe. A low mist hangs over the water. Joey is asleep, not leaving her side. She wonders what emotional scars this night will leave on him, on them both.

But especially Joey.

His father is gone.

Now he will have to live with this the rest of his life.

Will his scars ever heal?

As the boat nears the dock, she can see McGregor, his face filled with worry.

For her, for Joey.

Charles Dupont, Eric, whatever he wants to call himself, is down below. They managed to tie him up with the netting Dupont used to try to strangle Cat while he was still out. Joey stirs and is immediately at her side. His small arms wrap around her waist as the dock nears.

"I'm scared."

"It's okay, baby. You are okay."

He hugs her tighter. For a moment, she blames herself for what he has been through.

McGregor grabs the rope as they pull up, securing it to a cleat.

Joey clings to her. "It's okay," she says again. But her words seem not to register with her son. He looks up at her, and she realizes he is probably in shock—pupils dilated, breath shallow, skin an odd shade. She shouts to McGregor, "Call an ambulance, he's in shock."

Joey is collapsing at her feet. He is saying something she can't understand.

She takes his face between her hands. "It's okay. We are safe. Stay with me." Her words come at a quick clip.

She realizes she is sucking air, hyperventilating. *Calm down, calm down*, she tells herself. Joey's pupils continue to increase in size. He is now unable to speak.

Her legs turn to jelly.

But she must stay strong.

A bolt of adrenaline kicks in. She lifts Joey in her weary arms. She is sprinting toward McGregor, then passes him.

She can hear the ambulance sirens whine. It is there at the docks.

Her limbs are so tired, one hand is a mess, but none of that matters. All that matters is getting Joey to medical attention, and even though she is a forensic MD, he needs more medical help than she can provide. She feels helpless. This tiny boy she gave birth to, in her arms, looking smaller than ever.

Needing her more than ever. And she can do nothing but run with him.

My God, how did it come to this? How did Dupont do this to Joey, to me?

"No," she says out loud, "I won't let you take my son." She wills her legs to move faster. Her lungs are burning.

She can't feel her injured hand but does not care. She climbs into the ambulance with Joey. Tells the paramedics the basics. They take over as she takes stock of what has happened. She sees nothing but her son.

Suddenly McGregor's arm is around her; he tries to console her.

Fear, grief, and panic fill her. She allows herself to feel them fully for the first time.

The air is thick, unbearable. She watches Joey, who looks small and innocent, as the paramedics work feverishly. The siren is blaring. Lights flash from the siren outside.

She puts her hands up in prayer, bowing her head into her hands. More hot tears.

How did it come to this?

She can't respond. She realizes she is in shock.

She watches as the paramedics work on her mangled hand but feels nothing. Says nothing.

How can she?

It is over.

She is safe and will survive. Joey is safe and will survive.

That is all she ever asked from God.

FORTY

Nothing can be created out of nothing.
—**Lucretius**, *"DeRrerum Natura"*

at wakes in the hospital to a stinging IV drip, the beep-beep-beep of the monitor in her ear for the second time in weeks. She is so tired of hospitals. Her sheets smell like bleach and Bounce. Not a good combination.

Wet hair prickles her neck.

She dreads looking at her bad hand but pulls down the sheets. Some neurosurgeon has been very hard at work reconnecting tendons. Trying to put things back as they were. But how can they be as they were? Her hand is a mass of bandages, but she can feel the pain.

She will never be the same.

Her mind shifts to Joey. How is he?

Bile in her mouth, she is ripping out the IV and pulse monitor, jumping out of bed. The room is cold, cold tile on her feet.

She doesn't care.

Joey.

Where is Joey?

She rams into McGregor as she runs from the room.

"And just where do you think you're going?" he says.

"Where is my son?"

"He's okay. He's in recovery."

Thank God, she thinks. But says nothing.

Her eyes grow wide. "And…?"

McGregor knows what she is asking. He looks at the floor. Looks at her hand. Looks at anything but her eyes. They are boring into him.

"And…?" Her voice is monotone and cold.

"Let me show you" is all he can say. It is not easy for him, she can see. He did not want this. Nor does she.

"No. Tell me the truth."

His eyes meet hers. Then they are away again, darting to the floor, walls, ceiling. She will have none of it. "Tell me." She holds his arm in a vise grip.

His wet eyes meet hers. She does not understand why.

He says two words and she understands. "He's gone."

It is clear he is sucking in oxygen. His eyes refuse to meet hers.

"What? No…" Her body physically refuses to believe it.

Her eyes are stinging. She feels as if every vein in her body is about to burst. Her brain cannot register it.

"What?" she says again, and even that is an effort.

McGregor looks like a small boy for a second.

Good God, Joey has more balls than this is all she can think.

"WHAT?" she says one more time, her voice growing hard and menacing.

"He is gone."

A jolt through her body like an earthquake. She can't believe what she is hearing.

"Let me show you," McGregor says.

Her hand is clutching and releasing in anger. Her blood pressure and heart rate have spiked.

He pulls photos out of a manila envelope, police standard. But there is nothing standard about what has become of her life. Her ex-husband is gone. Joey is forever changed.

Nothing can change that. Nothing can take them back to where they used to be.

Her body is numb, her mind even number. Slowly, McGregor pulls the photos out.

He holds them in front of her, telling her something…she only hears pieces but it is enough. "We went back to the boat. We found the netting he tried to strangle you with. We found the chemicals. He was not there."

"What?" Her brain is numb. She is not aware she is alive now. The world is dead to her. She feels her knees go weak. "What?"

McGregor tries to modulate his tone without success. Beads of sweat are visible on his forehead and upper lip.

"What?" she says again, her voice barely audible.

"He was not there, Cat. Gone. We found his footprints up the steps out of the galley."

Cat is silent.

"Apparently he was watching you, us, as you docked and Joey collapsed…"

With that, her body goes weak. She cannot think. She knows nothing, says nothing. Not even breathing feels normal. "What?" is all she can say.

McGregor is still sweating.

"He was watching you as you brought the boat to the dock. Then, with all the confusion with Joey, he slipped away." McGregor's tone is apologetic, as if any apology could make up for this.

Cat stares at him, utterly silent. What is there to say?

She risked her life. Gave up her hand.

Her child would never be the same, and now this.

GONE. THE MONSTER IS GONE.

ABOUT THE AUTHOR

When trial lawyer and new author Solange Ritchie isn't practicing law, you can usually find her penning her next legal thriller.

Born in the beautiful tropical island of Jamaica of a Jamaican father and a French mother, Solange immigrated to the US at age 11. Since then, she has been a dynamic force for change. Fed up with thrillers that start with a fizzle and longing to see more power women as lead characters, Solange decided to create her own characters. Despite the demands of a busy legal career with her husband, Steve Young, she accomplished her ambitious goal by rising each morning to write before work, dedicating her weekends to writing and even spending her vacation time writing.

Words have always been Solange's passion. Now so, more than ever.

Solange achieved a successful writing career while working hand in hand with her husband doing "last minute trials" mostly in Southern California. Dubbed "the Case Saver," Solange does the "heavy lifting," handling intense paperwork that can either make or break a case, especially in business, labor and employment law areas. With a Bachelor in Telecommunications BA from the University of Florida, and after serving as Editor in Chief of Law Review at Western State College of Law, Solange's passion for writing has always been clear.

When Solange was just 37 years old, her first husband, John Ritchie, died due to gross medical negligence at a Southern California hospital. That life-altering experience shaped her life. She began writing creatively as a way to deal with this stress.

With a passion for philanthropic work (stemming from growing up with an older brother with Down's Syndrome and John's death), Solange serves or has served on numerous charities and legal boards, including The California Women Lawyers Association, The Orange County Bar Association, The Orange County Women Lawyers Association, The Orange County Trial Lawyers Association, The Community Court's Foundation and El Viento. Solange is a proud graduate of the Gerry Spence Trial Lawyer's College in Wyoming.

CPSIA information can be obtained
at www.ICGtesting.com
Printed in the USA
FSOW01n0900170815
10025FS

9 781630 475192